Manchester, Amsterdam, Prague

The Second Edward Church Thrilling Cities Adventure

Ian Jones

Copyright © 2022 Ian Jones

All rights reserved, including the right to reproduce this book, or portions thereof in any form. No part of this text may be reproduced, transmitted, downloaded, decompiled, reverse engineered, or stored, in any form or introduced into any information storage and retrieval system, in any form or by any means, whether electronic or mechanical without the express written permission of the author.

This is a work of fiction. Names and characters are the product of the author's imagination and any resemblance to actual persons, living or dead, is entirely coincidental.

The views expressed in this work are solely those of the author and do not necessarily reflect the views of the publisher, and the publisher hereby disclaims any responsibility for them.

ISBN: 9798412029719

PublishNation
www.publishnation.co.uk

Prologue

Kidnapping was meant to be so easy. But there he was, held face down on the sticky beer-stained carpet of a rundown Manchester pub with a heavy shoe held down on his hand. The pain from the shoe was nothing compared to the agony that pulsed through his head and to make things worse, no one was coming to offer assistance. The pain in the head came from the blow of an almost full pint glass being rammed into the side of his skull. Right now the smell and the scent of a casino in Monte Carlo at 3am would be infinitely better than this predicament. At this moment in time, even the sweat of a Monégasque would be preferable to the stale, sour, musty smell permeating from the carpet into his nostrils.

Kidnapping was meant to be so easy....

Chapter One

Claverton Hall

The smell from the carpet tickled the tiny fine hairs that lined the left nostril of Edward Church. He could not place the perfume but was definitely getting the fruity scent of citrus lemon as well as the bitter orange of Neroli. The expensive rich aroma of vanilla rounded off the fragrance from the carpet but there were other notes of the perfume that Church could only guess at.

'Have you quite finished, sir?'

The stern voice of the housekeeper of Claverton Hall had long since lost the veneer of politeness and patience. Church had been searching this room for almost an hour and was now reduced to pressing his face sideways onto the carpet to look under a bed. He flashed his best, winning smile, but in reality, he was feeling very awkward. Searching through the bedroom of a young woman might frequently feature in the adolescent fantasies of teenage boys, but Edward Church had found the whole episode acutely embarrassing. Even more so because he had failed to find anything in the least bit useful or helpful.

There was nothing enjoyable about the assignment he had been tasked with. A young woman had gone missing, presumed to have run away. But there was nothing to confirm or deny this assumption. The room was, in many ways, typical of a woman in her early twenties. It was an amalgamation of her life from mid to late teens and then early adulthood. A pinboard featured old faded photographs of her and her friends as well as more recent, less faded, ones. Festival ticket stubs and plastic security bands, as well as a couple of well-loved soft toys, littered the windowsill. The top of a dressing table was scattered with bottles and tubes of various colours and sizes, filled with various creams and lotions and make-up containers in almost every shade imaginable. The wardrobes and drawers were literally crammed with items of clothing. This woman obviously liked to shop. Each time he opened a drawer Church could sense the housekeeper bristling with indignation. 'It's not actually my favourite thing to be doing either,' thought Church to himself and he would have much preferred it if this search was being done by police officers. Missing persons are not usually exciting or thrilling investigations. They are rather dull, dismal, often rather pedestrian inquiries into another person's life. Thankfully, in the UK, most missing persons are found alive and well. It is not such a positive outlook in the US where almost half of the people reported missing are later found dead. With that thought running through his head, Church lifted his head from the carpet, brushing away a fine blond hair that had attached itself to his cheek.

'Have you finished now?' the housekeeper asked again.

'I think so, Mrs Dixon. It's very kind of you to wait so patiently,' he replied as brightly as he could manage given the circumstances.

'It is Ms if you please. And I prefer to be called just Dixon.'

Church resisted the temptation to call her *'Just Dixon'* and simply said, 'Well thank you again for your time, Dixon. I think that we can call it a day here.'

'Yes, well it is getting rather late,' she added with just the right amount of acerbity, just a hint, that was hidden behind the veneer of courtesy that staff often develop to let you know when they have been inconvenienced.

Three hours earlier Church had reluctantly stepped off of the train at the tiny station of Stonebridge in Kent. The station building was a scaled-down, Gothic-style mansion a popular design in the mid-1850s. Not that he was reluctant to be here. The county was beautiful, even in the winter. Often referred to as the Garden of England, the county of Kent might have lost many of its apple orchards and hop gardens but it did have an impressive collection of polytunnels that seemed to cover the hills with arches of plastic snaking around the countryside. The train ride down from London had been uneventful apart from the fact that train times and timetables seemed to have been completely forgotten in a cold and wintery December. He was almost thirty minutes late and regretted being talked into taking the train. *'It is the best use of taxpayers' money,'* he had been told. *'The use of pool cars is strictly limited to two or more senior Civil Servants'* and despite his best attempts at persuasion his request for the use of a car had been refused.

Church smiled to himself as he exited the little country railway station because outside stood a beautifully polished *Range Rover*, its two concealed exhaust pipes creating a gentle cloud of steam that flowed majestically from behind. Just the sort of car he would have chosen from the pool of elite vehicles available for senior Government personnel to use on official business. The paintwork looked immaculate and Church noticed how the colour subtly changed from a warm plum to a cool grey across the length of the bonnet, an optical effect of the paint technology used on this range. He considered that it was a shame that yet another British marque had been passed into foreign ownership, but Church had to admit that the investment from abroad had certainly paid off.

A large hand was waving to him through the driver's window that had just been wound down.

'Mr Church? Mr Edward Church?' a voice was calling.

He hurried over to the car, already feeling the chill of the air outside after the warmth of the railway carriage. It transpired that the man in the car, who introduced himself as Mick, had been sent to collect Church from the train station. On hearing the squeal of steel wheels on train tracks approaching he had started the engine and turned on the heaters in anticipation of the hiss of the airbrakes as the train slid to a halt on rolled steel rails. The interior of the car was warm and inviting.

'It was not too difficult to pick you out from the other passengers. There were only three of you who got off the train down from London. And I know the other two.'

Mick, it turned out, was the groundkeeper at Claverton Hall. He also offered to collect and drop off any visitors who might call because it interrupted his day and made it more interesting.

'Gardening is not really my thing and I'm getting too old for it anyway. I'll sit on the ride on mower any day, but the digging and pruning...' he let the sentence trail off but carried on with a long story of his life as a chauffeur in London and some of the celebrities and Royals who he drove around the city. 'My old dad was a Thames Lighterman ferrying goods up and down the river. His dad, my granddad, was supposed to have been one of the last Watermen. They used to take passengers across or up and down the Thames. Me dad wanted me to join him on the water but it was wheels that interested me, not boats. Started off doing the knowledge, passed that when I was still a teenager. Did a bit of cab driving for a while and even had me own *Fairway ninety-five*. It was a good living, but long hours and not much fun for me missus. So I moved into chauffeuring. The money was still good but the cars were something else. *Jaguar, Mercedes Benz, Bentley*. But do you know Edward, do you mind if I call you Edward,' but he did not pause for Church to answer, ' it never mattered how posh the people were who got into the back of my car, they all got up to some right old high-jinks.'

Mick the chauffeur continued with his stories without seeming to draw breath. He recalled stories of minor Royals, film and television stars as well as musicians, politicians, bankers, and businessmen, but never referred to any of the individuals by name. It was 'the chubby Prince who smiled a lot probably because of all of the cocaine he took in the back of my car' or the pop singer who 'looked like an angel but swore like a trouper'. Business executives, bankers and politicians seemed to feature in most of Mick's stories. They were either falling out of his limousine blind drunk or falling into it with a young man or a pretty woman who was not his wife or girlfriend.

'But do you know the biggest hypocrite I ever had in the back of my car, Edward?'

'No, who was that?'

'Oh. We're here already.' Mick added with a knowing smile, 'Welcome to Claverton Hall.'

Edward Church never found out who the biggest hypocrite was. He suspected that it was all a well-rehearsed speech that Mick had made to previous passengers that he had picked up from the railway station. But he did discover that Claverton Hall was a magnificent two-storey Edwardian red brick, red-tiled manor house. And he also discovered that 'Just Dixon' ruled the place with a rod of iron. Mick the chauffeur made his escape after depositing Church partway down the long gravel drive that led from the road and imposing entrance gates down towards the building itself. Dixon was standing on the front step impervious to the cold weather, or perhaps even contributing towards the chill herself.

'Welcome to Claverton,' she said in a flat, unwelcoming tone of voice.

She certainly was the coldest person Church had encountered for a long while. He even began to wonder if she had any teeth because she never seemed to smile.

Dixon showed Church into the lobby of the building, offered to take his coat but tossed it rather casually onto an occasional chair just inside the front door. She turned on her heels and began to walk down a short corridor, but as Church began to follow she turned and said, 'Wait here, please. I will inform the Right Honourable Anthony Fairfax that you have arrived.'

It was an unnecessary use of the honorific title. Anthony Fairfax was indeed a member of parliament and was tipped to be a future Secretary of State for Defence. But at the moment he was a junior minister and MP representing a small safe parliamentary seat in the middle of Kent and also a member of a Defence sub-committee. Parliamentary committees are appointed by the House of Commons to examine the expenditure, administration, and policy of the relevant Ministry they represent. The committee may decide to appoint a sub-committee to scrutinise a particular event or topic. These Parliamentary committees are televised and often make an intriguing or entertaining spectacle when they question someone giving evidence. Many an MP or business executive has been left squirming with embarrassment after a session in front of one of these committees.

The Right Honourable Anthony Fairfax was described, in the dossier that Church had read before his visit, as aged fifty-five once divorced and once widowed. The account read much like an obituary before the person named has actually died. According to the record, his second wife had died quite recently. As a child, he was educated at Eton, then Harrow; then enrolled at the Military Academy at Sandhurst. As a young adult, he was commissioned as an officer in the Household Cavalry, serving with the Blues and Royals undertaking ceremonial duties involving guarding the Monarchy and active duties using a series of armoured vehicles. Tours of active duty in the Middle East and conflict in both Iraq and

Afghanistan led to awards for gallantry and bravery including the Military Medal and the Distinguished Conduct Medal. Unfortunately, it also led to the breakdown of his first marriage. The first Mrs Fairfax cited her husband's unreasonable behaviour as the reason behind the separation. The end of his marriage also seemed to spell the end of his military service and Anthony Fairfax left his Regiment just a few months after the decree nisi was announced. The decree absolute came through shortly after because he did not contest the grounds listed in the divorce papers. Almost immediately, he was selected to be the Tory candidate for the by-election in a strongly Labour seaside town. He lost but made a good show of narrowing the majority of the opposition candidate. A marginal seat became available shortly afterwards and he won by a landslide. A second marriage to his much younger assistant seemed to usher in a happy, tranquil period. A beautiful period property in Kent. A safe Conservative parliamentary seat with a good majority at the last General Election. Membership of a series of Government committees and commissions. A junior ministerial appointment as a parliamentary under-secretary with responsibility for public mental health followed. His ministerial career then stalled. His second wife became ill and died shortly after her diagnosis. The dossier included a brief note that there was a stepdaughter named Amber.

And so Church waited in the hallway of the Claverton Hall taking in his surroundings while he waited for an audience with Anthony Fairfax MP for East Kent.

Chapter Two

An Audience with Anthony Fairfax

The hallway of Claverton Hall was eerily silent apart from the slow tick-tock from a grandfather clock situated in the far corner of the lobby. An occasional chair sat in another corner, with Church's coat tossed untidily over the arm. A small formal sideboard with a mirror above it occupied the only bit of free space left. A staircase led off up to one side of the space and two other doors completed the room. The mirror was a nice touch, a lady could check her hair and make-up before leaving the house, or check her appearance before welcoming visitors at the door. Unfortunately, a large display of silk flowers had been placed on the table, obscuring almost all of the vertical reflective surface. Perhaps the flowers were positioned by 'Just Dixon' the severe housekeeper because like a vampiric ghoul, she cast no reflection.

On a small space of empty wall between the grandfather clock and the staircase was the stuffed head of a Bengal tiger. The beautiful orange black and white striped fur looked dull; the vibrant colour had long since faded. The yellow and black eyes stared lifelessly back at Church as he gazed upwards. He recalled visits made to a local Museum as a child many years ago. The grandly named *Delhi Durbar gallery* was an Indian themed room with intricately carved wood panels, very dark in colour. Hammered brass light fittings illuminated the gallery and the Bengal tiger's head adorned the wall space between two windows which glowed a warm amber shade of illumination. As a child, he was frightened of the stuffed animal head. He had been convinced that the animals' eyes followed him around the room. A fanciful story told to Church by his older brother. As he got older, Church considered that the fate of the poor unfortunate animal was rather tragic. There were no Indian Tigers where he lived in the middle of Sussex and there was no real reason to have this animal head mounted on the wall of a museum gallery. It was not captioned or justified; it was just nailed to the wall to give a sense of the exotic.

He stepped closer to the tiger taxidermy and looked closely at the pale cream teeth set in gums that had blackened with age. At least the wood panelling to which the head was nailed was more cheerful. The lustrous pale timber panels were outlined with frames of sharply carved moulding. There were no knots, splits or flaws and it looked to be as good as new despite the age of the building.

'Perhaps maple?' said Church to himself, 'or ash?'

'Or hemlock, or beech?' a voice beside him made Church jump, 'although I have been told that it is probably ayous wood or African whitewood.'

Anthony Fairfax appeared beside Church, his hand extended in welcome. Definitely hemlock, considered Church, as the housekeeper hovered in the background.

'Welcome to Claverton,' Fairfax said and Church reflected that this was now the third time he had been welcomed to the house. 'It is a handsome property don't you think?' the man added awkwardly.

Beautiful, handsome, attractive might all be synonyms levelled at the house. But none could be used to describe the current appearance of MP, Anthony Fairfax. The former public schoolboy, privately educated, privileged childhood, military hero, decorated war veteran, Member of Parliament and family man was not the man who stood in front of Edward Church. Instead of the swashbuckling, trailblazing, reformist, champion of the centre-right government, a much older, broken man appeared. Slightly stooped and looking as if he had lost a lot of weight over a short period. His straw-coloured hair, which used to be an untidy mop, now looked to be a messy grey topping to a face that had also been drained of colour. The phrase '*a shadow of his former self*' flashed into Church's mind. The other man looked to be way on his way to ending up in the same situation as the stuffed tiger's head. As Church shook the outstretched hand he noticed the yellow sclera surrounding the pale blue iris of the other man's eyes. His face was heavily lined and he looked to have forgotten to shave that morning, or even the morning before. He swayed gently, almost but not perfectly keeping rhythm with the slow tick-tock of the Grandfather clock in the hall.

'Why am I talking like a damn tour guide?' Fairfax said out loud, although he seemed to be talking to himself. 'You are here because Sir Bernard Trueman said that you would be able to help. My daughter, well, my stepdaughter has gone missing you see. Don't know where she is, where she might have gone. Local police up there aren't really interested. Amber, that's her name by the way. But you would know that already, sorry. My head is all over the place. Not really making much sense at the moment. Come through to the drawing-room, there's a nice fire going inside.'

The room was a large comfortably furnished lounge, sitting room, living room or drawing room depending on your age and background. The furniture was sparse but oversized. A display cabinet contained a jumble of ornaments. Two huge sofas faced each other in the centre of the room with a fireplace on the wall to one side. Several other chairs were arranged haphazardly throughout the room. The walls were covered with dark oil paintings of various long gone landscape scenes and people who were long since dead. One frame housed a cross-stitch embroidered picture with the motto '*Always*

There to Always Care'. It was a nice sentiment, considered Church. He recalled his own mother doing an embroidered panel that read *'What Cannot Be Cured Must Be Endured'*. At the time he wondered if it was a family motto, but he discovered later that it was something else. Church observed at least four occasional tables, each with a lamp and some photograph frames placed on top. All of the lamps were switched on and gave the room a warm glow which contrasted with the chill outside. Church glanced at the pictures. Fairfax had been photographed with the current Prime Minister and both faces grinned out of the image. In another frame, a photograph showed Fairfax looking rather younger and more handsome with the last Prime Minister. The last picture frame showed Fairfax and another middle-aged white male who Church was unsure of.

Another table housed a collection of framed family photographs. One showed Fairfax, his second wife Mandy and her daughter meeting Royalty in the gardens of Buckingham Palace. The photographer had captured a perfectly timed picture of the wife and daughter curtsying. Another picture was an artistic black and white image of wife and daughter, cropped close to show just both of their heads and shoulders. The daughter looked to be aged around twelve or fourteen, perhaps older it was hard to tell. Both had long blond hair and easy relaxed smiles. Both mother and daughter wore sunglasses. Amber's were a childrens' *Ray-Ban* style, Mandy's were adult *Aviator* style with reflective lenses. The photograph might have been taken on a happy occasion. In one corner of the room, an impressive drinks cabinet took up half of the available wall space. It was already open.

'Where would you like me to start? What is it you need to know?'

'Just start from anywhere near the beginning, sir,' said Church patiently as he sunk into one of the sofas proffered to him. The promise of help from Church that Sir Bernard Trueman had made was stretching things. In reality, Church was not in the least bit interested in a missing girl. But as usual, Trueman had been very persuasive, asking Church just to take a look around, ask a few questions, and get a feel for the situation and report back in a day or so. 'Tell me a little bit about Amber herself. What she likes, what sort of person she is.'

'Can I get you a drink while we talk?'

It was too early in the day for Church to think about drinking, but he agreed out of politeness. 'Thank you, sir, whatever you are having.'

'You can drop the Sir if you please. Anthony will do just fine. So, what can I tell you about Amber? Well, she looks much like her mother.' Fairfax busied himself with fixing two gin and tonics. 'Amanda was a lovely woman. No, not Amanda! She was my first wife. Ha! Amanda Debenham. Not a lovely woman, a right pain in the arse if you'll pardon my French. We married too young and didn't really know what life was all about. When we got older and we realised what life was actually all about we realised that it was not all about spending it with each other. To be fair to her, when I came back from tours of active service in the Middle East, I was a different person.'

'And your second wife, Anthony?' Church lightly nudged Fairfax to get to the point otherwise he would have had a very good understanding of the first marriage to Amanda Debenham and not much else.

'Mandy Garland, some of my military chums teased me about not having to change the tattoo too much, came to work for me around fifteen years ago. She had written a letter to me asking for help with social security benefits or something that she thought she should be receiving but wasn't receiving. Routine Member of Parliament stuff really. She must have exhausted all other avenues of help and so wrote to me. I was having a surgery, you know meet your MP sort of thing, and my current secretary had left my employment. Things were a bit chaotic back then.' He waved his hand dismissively and some of his drink spilt onto the rug in the middle of the floor, 'She must have been desperate because I didn't exactly have the reputation of wanting to help those on benefits. Not exactly a cause that I would champion. So I said that perhaps she should get a job and she told me that she would if she could, but who would give her a chance, single mother, a child just starting school, no help with childminding in the school holidays, couldn't afford daycare, blah, blah, blah.'

Church could just imagine the scene. Anthony Fairfax was the most unlikely person you would turn to for help in this situation. Mandy Garland, with her young daughter, had probably exhausted every other avenue of help and either in desperation or as a last resort had contacted her MP.

'So I offered her a job. Asked her to work for me, there and then. No interview, no recruitment, just let me know the earliest you can start. It was a combination of anger and interest. I was prone to angry outbursts back then. That was why the last secretary left. But I was also interested to see what she would make of the opportunity. I would much rather give someone a job than give them a handout. Employment means more than wages; it is a sense of being needed, of being useful, wanted, worthy or whatever you want to call it. Anyway, she flashed me an angry look right back in my face and accepted the job.'

Fairfax had been rocking gently and swaying his arms as he spoke. His glass was now empty but he seemed more enthusiastic in his reminiscence. Due to the fire crackling in the hearth, the room was warm. Church could imagine that this would have been a cosy family reception room despite its size.

'And what of the daughter?' Church asked, keen to keep him on track.

'Oh, yes of course. Amber. A sweet-natured little thing. Very quiet, rather withdrawn, but that was understandable really. Apart from the first six or seven years of her life, which I did not know anything about and had only been told about by her mother, she had a happy childhood. Mandy Garland lived locally and Amber continued at the local primary school. Her mother and I were an item by the time Amber was old enough to attend senior school. We enrolled her into the nearby Girls public school; she attended as a day pupil rather than a boarder. Her mother and I both felt that sending her away to board and attend school would not be beneficial. My time as a boarder was brutal and I never forgave my parents for sending me away. I think that might be the reason why I was never close to my father, but he was a hard man to read. Utterly devoid of emotion, never saw him smile or heard him laugh. Most definitely a closed book.'

Church suspected that Anthony Fairfax might lapse into another long tangential reminiscence and asked, 'And what happened after the Girl's Senior school?'

'Well, that was the thing of it all!' Fairfax exclaimed, 'one day in the summer holidays, I can't remember the exact date, Amber announced that she had enrolled at university in Manchester to study drama. I mean, a drama student of all things? It was during that summer that my wife, we had married by then I forgot to tell you that, had her diagnosis. Two of the worst words that can be combined are the words '*stage*' and '*four*'. Actually, the worst word in the English language is *'metastatic'*.' He drained what was left in his glass, 'But Amber seemed settled after the first year at university, and it seemed to help her impediment. She came back that summer and learnt to drive, passed the first time as well. Not surprising really because she had been driving on the estate here for several years. We have a little electric buggy thing with a trailer on the back and she took to driving that around from the age of about fourteen or so.'

Fairfax was waving his arm around once more, gesturing out of the window towards what Church imagined was the place on the Claverton Hall estate where an electric garden buggy might be stored. The other man seemed to notice that his glass was empty and abruptly said, 'Another for you Edward? My glass seems to be empty.'

Church looked at his untouched drink perched on a small table by the side of the comfy sofa and held up a hand as if to say, 'thank you but no.'

'It was during the second year at Manchester University that it all started to go wrong.'

Fairfax poured a very generous measure of spirits as if it would dull the memory that had appeared in his mind.

'The first term in year two can be the worst for lots of students,' Church added sympathetically.

'You're telling me,' Fairfax said as he made his way unsteadily back towards his seat. 'The change in the girl was just incredible. Grades suffered, attendance dropped, telephone calls became infrequent and when she did ring the discussions were strained. Now here we are heading up to the end of the winter term and I have heard nothing. She was supposed to have returned...,' his voice trailed off slightly before he choked out the words, 'but nothing.'

'Has she been in touch with friends, anyone she went to school with nearby? What about other students, or her lecturers at the university?'

'Yes, yes. I have tried all of those. Amber has few friends and nobody has heard anything from her. The university has been as helpful as they can, but Amber is an adult now and they treat her as such. If a student chooses not to attend classes the staff do not force them.'

'I noticed the nice collection of photographs on the table over there. Do you have a recent picture of Amber?'

Fairfax paused for some time, Church even wondered if the other man had not heard him, but finally, he said, 'You stop taking photographs at some point. The tables are full, there are no more frames or it just slips your mind. Then it is too late. The moments pass and memories are lost. Now it is too late. Everything has gone. It's all gone.'

Church longed to get back to little Stonebridge railway station and return to London; he did not like to correct Anthony Fairfax. Every*one* had gone rather than every*thing*.

Chapter Three

Manchester

Manchester Piccadilly railway station is geographically over two hundred miles North of *Stonebridge* in Kent. Metaphorically it is a million miles away. The huge steel and glass railway structure has been evolving constantly since its origins as *Manchester London Road* station in Store Street. Where Stonebridge is a grade two listed building, almost unchanged since it opened, Manchester Piccadilly has evolved and changed to accept vagaries of changing railway ownership, including having two competing railway companies share a single station; conversion from steam to electrification, and the never-ending expansion of the city itself. It has accepted and integrated bicycle, pedestrian, car, bus, and tram systems. As such it is an organised, chaotic, hub. Thronging with passengers who are either regular users in a rush to get into or out of the station building, or first-time visitors looking around and getting slightly lost. Although Church had not visited the city of Manchester for many years he certainly felt himself to be in the first category of passenger, in a rush to get out of the station and into a waiting taxi. He jostled through the crowds milling around the rows of small shops and stalls that were packed in the station concourse and made his way to the Taxi rank in Fairfield Street.

Church climbed into the first cab waiting in line. It was a familiar London taxi that had been brightly painted to advertise a financial institution that had its head office in the city. The familiarity pleased Church as he settled into the back of the cab. It was late afternoon and almost completely dark outside now. The city was shifting from daytime to night-time. During the day the city works, shops and lunches. Commuters and city centre employees were now flocking to the train station to start their travel back home. At night the city parties. Bars open, restaurants begin to serve. Shop windows are illuminated with their Christmas displays. Strings of lights had been festooned across the streets and wrapped around lampposts.

The taxi waited at a set of traffic lights in a line of other vehicles. 'Sorry for the wait,' the driver said. 'It is a busy time of the day.'

Church could not place the accent, but it was most certainly not Mancunian. 'It's no problem,' he replied. 'I'm in no rush.'

'No rush, no problem. That is good.'

The driver made no attempt to make any more conversation and Church was happy to gaze out of the taxi window to see how the city had changed. They made their way slowly along the main road. There appeared to have been an upsurge in tower block construction. Every shop, restaurant, café, bar, nightclub or gym they drove past seemed to have a tower block growing out of it. Church wondered if there could possibly be that many offices based in Manchester, then he realised that many of the towers were private housing. City centre accommodation or serviced apartment blocks looked to be everywhere. *Madchester* or *Manctopia* depending on your age or background.

'We are here,' the driver announced after a few minutes. The trip to the budget hotel booked by the penny watching Finance and Procurement department of the Cabinet Office had been short. So short in fact that Church could have walked it in a few minutes if he had bothered to take the time to look at a map. He decided that he would not put the claim onto his expenses.

The sight of the budget hotel nearly made him reconsider his choice of accommodation. The concrete and glass building looked squat and dull. It was at the end of a row of similar buildings and beyond was a glimpse of what part of the original old town of Manchester might have looked like; a row of two-storey red brick buildings. Some were shops, one was a traditional-looking British pub, another was a dry cleaner. A few of the remaining units were empty and boarded up. The space above the commercial premises had been converted into flats. Beyond this row of shops, traditional terraced housing stretched into the distance.

However, the inside of the hotel could not have looked more different. The reception covered about one-third of the floor space. Thickly carpeted and very warm against the chill outside. Large prints covered the walls, showing Manchester's industrial past; mills, warehouses, canals, factories and similar manufacturing and engineering illustrations. Within a few minutes, his automated check-in had allocated him a room, booked breakfast and offered a reservation for tonight's evening meal.

His room was almost silent, thanks to triple glazing and thick curtains that would block out any unwanted morning light. The bed was spotless and king-sized. A large television covered much of the wall space on the opposite wall. The bathroom had a walk-in shower rather than a bath. Church approved. He hung his jacket in a little open-ended wardrobe and checked that the important envelope was still in his pocket.

Church filled the little travel kettle that had been left on the side of a long desk underneath the wall-mounted television. He flicked through the little sachets of coffee, sugar and individually wrapped tea bags, then stretched out on the bed as the kettle boiled. The miniature kettle must have had an even smaller miniaturised element inside because it took quite some time for the water inside to heat to boiling point. As he lay on the bed, Church felt the sensations of travel, the swaying motions of the high-speed train and the stop-start jerking of the taxi, slowly ebb away. The last of the light of day had faded outside and in its place, the twinkling lights shone through dusk, evening and night. Church decided that instant coffee just would not be enough and throwing his jacket back on he made his way downstairs and out of the hotel.

Walking around the block to get his bearings, Church came across a café still open for business. Its large double fronted windows were steamed up but glowed invitingly among a row of dark shopfronts. Unimaginatively named *Café* it was decorated in equally uninspired furnishings. Linoleum floor, wooden seats and Formica tables; none of which seemed to match one another. But it was spotlessly clean and delicious smells of sweetness and coffee enveloped Church as he stepped inside.

'Take a seat. Be with you in a second,' the middle-aged woman behind the counter said as the door tinkled shut behind him.

Church observed his fellow customers as he waited. A pair of young men, perhaps builders, were deep in conversation. Maybe discussing the day's work or an upcoming job? An elderly man sat alone, apart from his small dog which occasionally got fed a piece of the man's dinner. Two elderly ladies were also deep in conversation. They seemed to be talking about grandchildren and illnesses, common themes of conversation for their generation.

Another tinkle from the door made Church look round to see who else had joined this little tableau. The new arrival was another young man, younger than the two builders who had not bothered to turn round. Thin, wearing a baseball cap and jacket with the hood up, the younger arrival had the rangy appearance of poverty. His jacket was shiny at the elbows and cuffs, his jeans were dirty and frayed at the bottoms. His footwear was the universal choice of youth, trainers, but had probably not been used for anything sports-related. He shuffled up to the counter and Church's senses immediately heightened.

The shabby youngster was deep in conversation with the lady behind the counter. Their voices were hushed and low, Church could only make out a few words.

'Come on, I'm only asking for a bit. Not for long. I promise.'

The café owner was shaking her head slowly from side to side, 'I'm sorry. I told you before.'

Church glanced around at the builders, still talking. The two old ladies had stopped comparing tales of grandchildren and were tutting quietly to each other while peeping sideways at the scene being played out up at the counter. Church got up from his seat and the wooden feet dragged across the polished linoleum floor, he was just about to get the attention of the builders as reinforcements when the middle-aged café owner glanced over at him. She raised her hand, palm facing Church in a universal sign to back off. Church paused, the woman handed some money to the rangy youth and he slouched out.

'Is everything okay?' asked Church as he walked to the counter.

'It's fine, love.' She sighed and attempted to change the subject. 'My son just gets a bit short of money every now and then. Now, what can I get you?'

'If you are sure that you are okay. Just a large black coffee, thanks.' He paused and added, 'and I'll buy a suspended one for someone else who needs it.'

'Well, that's very kind I'm sure. I'll put a fresh brew on. You just take a seat and I'll bring it over to you in a minute.'

* * *

Back in his hotel room, Church stepped out of the shower feeling clean and refreshed. The coffee had done the trick, he felt alert and ready for the long evening ahead. The pale blue envelope containing a letter of introduction was laying on the bed. Alongside it was an invitation card, very thick cardboard with a gold embossed edge. It read, '*St Charles Partners Wealth Management Invite you to an evening of presentation and entertainment.*' The invitation and letter of introduction were the reasons for his visit to Manchester. The letter of introduction was addressed to one of the Members of Parliament for a constituency in this city.

Church dressed quickly, slipped on his dinner jacket and adjusted his bow tie. He was, he thought, a little overdressed for the evening. The invitation mentioned a dress code of *Black Tie Optional* which sat somewhere in between Black tie and Business Casual in the list of formal attire. Church suspected that most people would opt for a formal lounge suit, the sort of thing that people would wear to the office if they needed to dress in an official style for work.

He looked at the pale blue envelope and smiled to himself as he tucked it into his inside jacket pocket. Sir Bernard Trueman, his chief at the department in the Cabinet Office, was a traditionalist. Letters of invitation were most definitely out of fashion nowadays. But they were used in centuries gone by when a person would not interact socially with another without a proper introduction. Although this envelope was sealed, Church knew that the actual letter itself would be handwritten on foolscap sized paper. Slightly larger than normal paper, it would be similarly coloured pale blue and have a crest of the Royal Coat of Arms of the United Kingdom printed in dark blue. The Office of the Prime Minister favoured cream paper and red crest but elsewhere blue was most definitely the colour. Church recalled a conversation with

Sir Bernard from several years ago where the old man drifted into a long tangential dialogue about imperial paper sizes as he ranted against the introduction of a small A5 sized office memorandum. 'Everything is A4 this and A5 that these days. When I started working we wrote on nothing smaller than Quarto or Monarch sheet. Maps would be printed using Emperor or even Double Elephant paper. The names they gave sheet sizes had history, meanings long lost now. Grand Eagle, Quad Demy, Columbier, or Super Royal. Foolscap was given the name because of the watermark on the paper. Broadsheet was a paper size rather than a newspaper size.' Church would chip in with the occasional 'Yes, sir,' but otherwise, he would remain silent until the one-sided speech had ended.

Church picked up his heavy woollen overcoat and tucked it over his arm as he left his hotel room and made his way downstairs. The air was freezing outside, it was pitch black and any heat from the day had long since cooled. He quickly slipped on his coat and buttoned it from bottom to top. The short walk to the Manchester Guildhall would be brisk. Traditionally used as meeting places for artisan or merchant guilds such as stonemasons, weavers, joiners or blacksmiths. The origins of this Guildhall were lost on Edward Church, but the honey-coloured stonework and Greek revival design were impressive. A large triangular cornice and four towering pillars dominated the front of the building. It formed a huge portico or porch large enough to welcome visiting dignitaries who might arrive by coach and horses. The building itself was perfectly symmetrical. Two ramps gently sloped down either side of the imposing entrance. Originally for horses but now used for disabled access, reassuring that something so old can have a use that is so up-to-date. Two wings stretched either side of the grand entrance but modern office blocks or apartment buildings now joined the structure. The lights inside the Guildhall twinkled invitingly. Hundreds of bulbs glowed in cut-glass chandeliers, they radiated a warmth that generously spread to the outside.

A small flight of steps led to the open doors of the Hall. As Church ascended, he saw a trolley of drinks being wheeled up a ramp to his left-hand side. Church fished out his invitation card and nodded to the door staff waiting just inside.

'Evening, sir,' one of the men said. Clearly enjoying the task of supervising this evening's event.

'Good evening,' Church replied. Friendliness costs nothing he thought to himself.

The door staff were dressed identically in black trousers and black polo tee-shirts. They both wore Security Industry Authority, SIA Door Supervisors Licences on lanyards around their necks. One of the men gestured towards a reception area. A long table covered in a white tablecloth staffed by eager young women handing out gift bags and pointing delegates in the direction of the dining hall. Church presented his invitation card to the nearest eager helper.

'Good evening, Mr Church, and welcome to the St Charles Partners Wealth Management event. You are seated at table number thirty-two which is to the left as you go through the dining room doors.'

'Thank you very much,' he smiled in return thinking that the women must have been chosen for their uniform height, size, hair colour and age.

Table thirty-two was indeed to the left as he walked through the set of double doors and, he considered, a rather appropriate option for the politician seated at the table. A large middle-aged man stood with his hand outstretched in welcome as Church made his way to the dining table.

Chapter Four

Meeting Tony Brownstone

Tony Brownstone stood with his hand outstretched. He wore a crumpled dark grey lounge suit matched with a lilac and purple tie in a bold stripe pattern. Brownstone was aged somewhere in his late fifties guessed Church, he was overweight with thinning black hair. But his smile was warm and generous. And his handshake was firm and dry. Church took to the man immediately.

'You must be Edward Church,' Brownstone said in greeting. 'I'm Tony Brownstone.'

'Pleased to meet you, sir,' said Church.

'Please call me Tony. And may I call you Edward? Let me introduce the other guests at our table. To our left are Irene and Reginald and to our right are Giselle and Calvin. These good people are investors with St Charles Partners, I, unfortunately, am an imposter. Invited because of who I am rather than what I invest.'

Introductions were completed, hands were shaken and small talk was made while they waited for their meal to be served. Giselle and Calvin were late-middle-aged, she wore brightly coloured clothes and had equally bright hair and make-up. Her husband was tall and slim, immaculately dressed in a dinner suit that looked similar to Church's. Irene and Reginald were well into retirement age and Church wondered why they had come to a wealth management evening. If he were at their stage in life Church would be out spending any money he might have rather than attending a savings and investment soiree. However, it soon became clear that Reginald was cannier than he appeared.

'I have only got a small amount invested with St Charles',' he admitted. 'Just being a member means that you are in with a good chance of being invited to these evenings. They usually have an interesting guest speaker, have fantastic entertainment and, of course, an open bar!'

Church handed Tony Brownstone the letter of introduction in its pale blue envelope. The other man slit open the letter using his table knife. Not particularly hygienic considered Church, but very neat. As Brownstone read the contents, Church looked around the dining hall taking in his surroundings. Each table in the Manchester Guildhall had a large number on a brass stand in the middle. An arrangement of poinsettia filled the base of the stand. Each table seated at least eight guests and Church counted at least forty tables. The bar filled one side of the room, a low stage filled the far end of the room and a clever arrangement of tables allowed a private, secluded, top table. For the very important investors, thought Church to himself. The table next to his had the number thirty-one on the brass stand. The guests seated around it were young, perhaps early twenties and male. They all wore black tie and seemed to be up for a raucous evening.

The lights dimmed slightly but table thirty-one continued to laugh and joke. However, as the first act of the evening's entertainment took the stage they hushed slightly. It took just one rope and two silk ribbons to calm the room.

The aerial trapeze artist ascended the rope gracefully. She twisted, contorted and wrapped herself around the ribbons for the next ten minutes. Her finale was to hold a perfect T shape with arms outstretched and ribbons billowing either side to form butterfly wings. Polite applause followed from some tables. Enthusiastic applause from others and whistles of approval from table thirty-one.

A comedian followed onstage. He made a crass joke about the trapeze artists and continued his act by making jokes, or insulting, just about every sector of society. The comedian then persisted in his misdemeanours by making some jokes at the expense of the company hosting the evening.

'I would like to thank our hosts for this evening,' he wheezed into a microphone. 'St Charles Partners Wealth management. Do you know the definition of a Stockbroker? Someone who invests your money until it's all gone. Haha. There are two types of Wealth Managers. Those that don't know anything, and those that don't know they don't know anything. Haha.'

He had a humorous quip for each race, creed, gender, religion and non-religion. The jokes were not for Church and, it seemed, not for Irene and Reginald because they left the table with Reginald shaking his head. Church watched them walk over to the free bar and settle themselves onto two stools.

Giselle took the opportunity to strike up a conversation. She used the safe subject of holidays and travel to distract from the offensive comedian.

'Do you live near Manchester, Edward?' she asked.

Church did not explain his reason for visiting but did say that the city had changed very much in recent years.

'Yes,' she said, 'there is little of the old town left now. But that is not particularly a bad thing. There were some very dodgy areas a few years ago and I am pleased to see them go! My husband Calvin used to work abroad and commented that it seemed like a different city each time he came back. I love Manchester. It's got everything you might find in London, shopping, theatres and restaurants. But you might be surprised to know that it is still a small place and people do get to know each other.'

The conversation flowed easily and Giselle told hilarious stories about her life in Africa. Church was interested because of his recent visits to Botswana, although he told none of his own tales.

'I can honestly say that the worst time in my life, apart from listening to this bloody awful comedian, was cradling my youngest child as we raced through the African savannah after she had been bitten by a puff adder. She had been playing in the gardens at the side of our farm and had not noticed the snake. By the time I found her she was drifting in and out of consciousness and because she was so young I knew that we needed to get anti-venomous medicine quickly. After splinting her leg we literally threw ourselves into the four by four. The thirty-minute drive to the hospital took me just over fifteen minutes.'

'Do you know,' added Calvin, 'she still checks her shoes for scorpions. Even here in the UK.'

As if to make the point, Giselle lifted her foot into the air and waved it around with a shriek of laughter. Calvin explained that he once lived and worked in various countries throughout the Middle East but was vague about the detail. Church assumed that they were military contracts and respected the other man's elusiveness. Although, never having visited Saudi Arabia or any other Middle-Eastern country, Church would have been interested to hear more about the nations, people and culture.

'People used to pay me for my knowledge, skills and experience,' Calvin explained, 'and now I do the same to St Charles Partners. I don't mind paying my wealth management fees, even though they might seem expensive. I don't know a hedge fund from a derivative, or futures from unit trusts and it would be hypocritical of me to begrudge paying for their advice.'

Church's financial knowledge was probably pretty sketchy but he did know the difference between a Bond and a Gilt thanks to some antique certificates in his grandfather's study. *'The bonds,'* explained his grandfather, *'are IOUs from companies promising to pay back the money with interest that I have lent to them. The gilts are the same thing but the money is borrowed by the Government. It is a safer investment and to show that it is more secure, they edge the certificate with gold.'* Church suddenly remembered the gilt-edge to his invitation this evening. A tradition carried over from those Government bonds to show that the event is somehow more special.

As much as he was enjoying the evening and the company Church was aware of the purpose of his meeting with Tony Brownstone this evening. Several times he tried to start a conversation with the other man and several times he had been surreptitiously rebuffed. Making the most of the situation, Church continued to take in his surroundings. A string quartet had taken to the stage and were now playing light chamber music, a rather incongruous switch from the offensive comedian. The meal was served and each course swiftly cleared away by barely seen waiting staff. Barely seen by everyone except Church. He noticed that they were without exception female and the uniform that the staff appeared to have been obliged to wear was rather shorter and tighter than they would have chosen for themselves. The waitress for their table, table thirty-two, was also serving the rowdy table thirty-one. Church noticed how she skillfully dodged outstretched arms and wandering hands of the raucous group on the adjoining table. She swerved and danced between the guests. Missing a delegate with an outstretched arm and serving an unsuspecting colleague sat nearby. She would dart in and retrieve a plate or deposit another bottle of alcohol to the cries of 'Champers' or 'Shampoo' or even 'Bolly' even though the Champagne on offer was Taittinger rather than Bollinger, a lighter Champagne that Church considered went better with the food on offer. He also considered that almost any Champagne would be wasted on table thirty-one.

The plates of starters came and went; most of the table had opted for the chicken-based main course saying the sticky BBQ ribs were too rich. Church recalled eating them cold and remembered them being as just as nice. Desserts were devoured as if they were the best part of a meal, which was indeed the case for many people. The guests at Church's table drank little of their Champagne. Giselle preferred cocktails, the other two men preferred beer and there was a limit to how much Irene could drink by herself. It turned out that Tony Brownstone was teetotal. A rarity amongst MPs and yet another contrast between him and Anthony Fairfax with his frequently refreshed gin and tonic. Church considered that he was working and sipped his one glass of drink very slowly. After three hours at the evening's event, it had gone flat and warm and now sat, half-full, to one side of his place setting waiting to be cleared away.

At length, the other guests on their table made their excuses and drifted away leaving just Church and Tony Brownstone alone at table thirty-two.

'A great evening, Edward, thank you for your company.'

'You're very welcome, it was an entertaining evening and I'm pleased that we sat here rather than at another table. Two other nice couples as well, good company.'

'But, as they say, it is time to get down to business. You have met Anthony Fairfax. How did he seem to you?'

'Like a broken man, to be honest. Understandable given that his wife died recently and now he can't make contact with his daughter.'

'It may surprise you, given the opposite political views we hold, but I really like Anthony. We were *'paired'* several years ago. You know, the system whereby members of parliament of opposite sides pair up to agree to oppose each other's votes? It saves a lot of time being wasted on Parliamentary votes in which we vote on party political lines. I think that our respective whips thought that it would be funny to pair Tony with Anthony because apart from sharing the same name we would oppose each other on almost everything. But they were wrong.'

'Oh?'

'Yes. You see, Edward, we actually both want the same thing but just see that it can be achieved in different ways. Anthony wants to improve society by giving opportunities and prospects. I believe that it is not always possible to achieve and that there should be a welfare safety net. He would argue that having a generous benefits system stifles the desire and need to get a job....and so it goes on. We have opposing opinions of solving the same issue.'

'I can understand that people form unlikely friendships. It's something that makes them all the more special.'

'So, when his stepdaughter Amber announced that she wanted to enrol at university and study performing arts and drama, I suggested Manchester. It's a great institution and I could keep an eye out for her while she studied.'

'So what happened?' asked Church.

'Well, year one was good. Manchester is a great city if you are young and even better if you are a student. But year two was not so good.'

'Surely a missing person is a matter for the police?'

'Well, Edward, we are not sure if she is missing. Anthony has the notion that she might have been kidnapped.'

'In that case, it is a job for the security services.'

'That is the problem. And that is why you are here. The police are not overly concerned about a young woman who has not contacted her stepfather. And, quite honestly, MI5 is not going to be involved until there is an actual threat or ransom.'

Church knew when he was being fed false information and he sensed that feeling now. A missing person is a job for the police. If a ransom were to be demanded at some point at a later date, it would be passed to the security services.

'There is another possibility,' said Church solemnly.

'Oh, what might that be?'

'Amber Garland might have run away of her own free will.'

'All we need to do is ask around and do a little digging. I'm too old and well known to go asking questions on behalf of Anthony Fairfax. But you are younger, not too different in age to some of the students. They might open up to you, they certainly would not open up to me!'

'And if she has been kidnapped,' continued Church ignoring the attempt at a compliment, 'the British authorities would never publicly sanction the payment of a ransom.'

Tony Brownstone paused. He looked directly at Church, perhaps sensing that his bluff had been called. A few awkward moments passed before he eventually spoke again.

'That is why a representative is needed. An intermediary just in case.'

'A little bit like an unofficial envoy,' said Church.

'A little bit like a special envoy,' replied Brownstone.

'I like the sound of that,' replied Church.

Chapter Five

Late-night Manchester

The evening of entertainment laid on by St Charles Partners at the Manchester Guildhall was coming to an end. People had begun to drift away from their tables. Church guessed that around half of the delegates had left already. Some guests had left their seats and made their way to the free bar but now most of them were drifting away.

'Come and see me in my constituency office tomorrow morning, Edward,' said Tony Brownstone.

Church took this as an indication that their meeting tonight was over and said with genuine warmth, 'Thank you, Tony. I have thoroughly enjoyed this evening.'

'Me too, Edward. Me too. These letters of introduction are all well and good,' he added, waving the pale blue envelope in front of him, 'but I like to actually meet someone to find out how trustworthy they are.' He stood up and added, 'Don't feel you have to rush away on my count. Stay as long as you like. But do come and see me tomorrow. There is something I need to explain to you about Anthony Fairfax.'

Church felt obliged to wait a little before making his way back to the budget hotel, but the other guests at his table had left and he did not feel inclined to introduce himself to other people this late in the evening. Certainly not anyone from table thirty-one, who were now crowded around the open bar making the most of the offer.

The waitress appeared, clearing away the last of the coffee cups and drinks glasses. Church turned to her. 'Busy night?' he said.

'You're telling me. I can't wait to get home and out of this ridiculous outfit.'

'It is a bit small isn't it,' smiled Church.

'I'm Lucy by the way.'

'I'm Edward.'

'I know. I picked up your name from the conversations going around the table. I don't eavesdrop you know, just that some people are more memorable than others.' She glanced over to the bar.

Church smiled, 'I know exactly what you mean, Lucy. It's been a long day and I've got to get going. Hope you manage to finish soon.'

'Oh well. Thanks, see you.'

The dining room was virtually empty now. Church could see over to the top table, obscured for most of the evening by so many other guests. In the middle of the table, evidently the most important VIP, was a man dressed so differently from the others that he clearly stood out. Dressed in a black thobe and wearing a blue and white check keffiyeh with a black rope agal the man was clearly a visitor from somewhere in the Middle East. Church thought it a shame that the guest on his table, Calvin, had missed seeing the man. But as he walked by the table, Church noticed that the Arabian-looking man was drinking wine.

It was freezing cold outside the Guildhall. Church walked briskly down the stone steps and buttoned his coat, folding the collar as high as it would go. He walked away from the glow of the hall lights and past a modern building next door. It looked to be an office block past its best or doctors surgery built in the 1970s but now closed down, empty and dark.

A voice from the doorway said, 'Spare some change for a cup of tea. Or a glass of champagne, mate?'

Church had taken a pace or two past the doorway, before he stopped and turned around, saying, 'I can't help with the tea, but if you're serious about the Champagne....'

A minute later Church was stepping back inside the Guildhall. The security guards had gone for the evening and Church walked briskly into the restaurant, scanning the room for Lucy the waitress. Eventually, he spotted her and gave her a wave as he walked in her direction. She smiled and, after a moments pause, waved back.

'Lucy, just the person,' Church smiled.

'Yes?' she replied. Stretching out the word slightly.

'Got any of that Champagne left? And I don't suppose you could put a few of those sticky barbecue ribs in a box, could you?'

Lucy looked confused for a second or two, but she nodded her head and Church took off his coat and plonked himself down at the nearest seat. A few minutes later she returned with the bottle and a foil takeaway container with the food inside. It was piping hot and Church felt the warmth on his hands as he took it from her.

'Thanks, Lucy. You're a star.'

As Church threw his coat back on and rushed out of the hall she stood there shaking her head in confusion.

Two minutes later, Church was back in the doorway of the empty building. As he handed over the foil container and bottle of Champagne he said to the man lying in the doorway, 'Careful with the Taittinger. You don't want to wake up with a hangover like table thirty-one.'

* * *

The constituency headquarters for the Labour party in Manchester is an impressive late Victorian building made out of Portland stone. At some point over the years it had been painted, perhaps as a protection against air pollution at the time. Part of the building had been sandblasted clean again, but half was still painted a pale cream, off white, colour. The double front door was painted red, of course. Half of the front door stood open, a welcome to constituents who had booked a meeting with Tony Brownstone. He was running a surgery for anyone living in the community he represented. Open surgeries had now been stopped and as an unexpected result, MPs could actually keep to some sort of timetable. Long waits to see your member for parliament no longer had to be endured.

Edward Church strode into the building, grateful to get out of the foul weather outside. Heavy winter clouds hung over the city. They might have threatened to drop a thick layer of snow across Manchester, but at the moment they simply promised heavy mist and light rain. Church suspected that the city would look dull until late in the day when lights would cheer up the gloom.

At his appointed time, Edward was ushered into Tony Brownstone's office. The man was on the telephone but waved Church to an empty chair. Church sat and waited patiently, wondering who else had sat in this seat during the morning and what problems they had discussed. Eventually, the telephone call ended and Brownstone cradled the receiver in its holder.

'Sorry about that, Edward, just a few last-minute issues to address.'

'No problem, Tony, I expect that you are a busy man.' The two of them were now firmly on first name terms.

'Let's get straight down to it, shall we?' And without waiting for a reply he continued, 'Have you read today's newspaper headlines? Anthony Fairfax will announce his resignation from his ministerial role later this week.'

'I must admit I've not read them, or switched on the news, sorry.'

'The gutter press have photographs of Anthony visiting prostitutes. The headlines in the newspapers make lurid reading.'

'Oh,' was all Church could think to say.

'It's not a crime, of course, but he really has no option apart from resignation.'

Church always thought that it was rather odd how an MP could resign from the Government but stay on as an MP in his constituency. It seemed like having your cake and eating it too. He kept his opinions to himself, but Tony Brownstone answered his thoughts.

'It is only the voters who can sack an MP, not the party he or she represents. Perhaps his constituents will be kind come the next election or by-election. But at the moment he's out of Government. The papers are having a field day of course. *MP in Vice Scandal, Tower of Filth*, that refers to the building he was caught visiting, and *Orgy Secrets of the MP.*'

'How can two people be called an orgy?' asked Church.

'Exactly!' Exclaimed Brownstone with a loud guffaw. 'Here's a photograph of him arriving at Maxwell House in central London, the tower of filth referred to by one newspaper. And another of him leaving.'

'I know that building. It's just along the road from where I live. Always thought that it was a funny name for a building, or named after somebody in poor taste. But these are photographs, not the front pages of a newspaper. Where did you get them from?'

'The Security Services have been keeping an eye on this building for quite some time. Several call-girls operate from here and MI5 have been recording the comings and goings for years.'

'I've eaten in the restaurant that occupies the ground floor, it's Michelin star. And shopped in one of the Men's Outfitters next door, one of the best places in London for tweed. But I didn't have a clue as to what was going on above. Amazing.'

'Here is a list of names that MI5 have managed to match the photos of faces that they've recorded. It's quite extensive. There are other MPs, some judges, business leaders and several foreign nationals.'

'I recognise this name as well,' said Church, 'he's the editor of one of the newspapers running the story about Fairfax. What a hypocrite.'

'Somebody was clearly tipped off about this,' said Tony Brownstone

'And somebody in the Security Services is passing classified photographs to the press. Does Anthony Fairfax know? When I saw him just a few days ago he seemed broken. Utterly broken. I assumed that it was to do with the situation with his step-daughter.'

'Yes, he's been told. And he has known for quite some time. I've spoken to him about it on several occasions.'

'What did he say?' asked Church.

'He knows that it is all over. His career, his prospects, everything. Everything has gone.'

'He said that exact phrase when we parted a couple of days ago. I thought that he meant to say everyone has gone. I thought it odd and I guessed that he had got muddled, but he was thinking of this as well as his missing step-daughter.'

'To his credit, he did not try to deny anything. He explained that he has been feeling lonely and isolated for quite some time. I can sympathise with him there. Being an MP can be a solitary career sometimes. There are long evenings in the House of Commons that the public does not see. You can get back to your London flat at past midnight and obviously, no one is there. But you're not tired. Quite often I am still buzzing from the day's events and it takes a while to wind down. There's no dinner waiting for you, every room is empty, the bed is empty. There is nobody to ask how your day went, and no one telling you their news. Affairs are common. Fairfax told me that quite often he was simply seeking company.'

'That's one word for it,' said Church.

'Oh no, I believe him. He said that on several occasions he would simply sit and watch television with one of these prostitutes. They might cook dinner together, or go out to the theatre or opera for the evening. He is as you said a broken man, Edward. I really want to help him find his stepdaughter. We really need to do this.'

'Okay,' replied Church suddenly softening his opinion to this assignment. 'I think that we can look at this in two ways. Either Amber Garland is missing or has been kidnapped and a ransom demand will be made at some future point. Nothing can be done until the kidnappers choose to get in touch. If she has run away, I can ask around her friends and university colleagues. In the absence of any demand, we can assume it's that scenario. Even if the police cannot help at the moment; we can treat this as the police would treat it. Do you want me to start at the university?'

'Even better than that, Edward, I can take you there myself. I have an afternoon appointment at St Mungo's homeless shelter which is close by. I'll drop you off on the way.'

Chapter Six

University

Edward Church explained the outline of the police procedure on a missing person as they made their way out of the city centre in the car belonging to Tony Brownstone.

'You can make a report of a missing person straight away, it's a misconception that you have to wait a day or so. The police will search the surrounding area where the person was last seen, interview any eyewitnesses. They will interview friends, neighbours and colleagues. Nowadays they will check mobile phone records and other digital footprints.'

'Sadly that won't be possible for us,' replied Brownstone.

'Once a trail of their last movements has been established the police will check CCTV.'

'Well, that won't happen either.'

'They will put a trace on bank cards and credit cards or other electronic payment methods just in case the missing person uses their bank account or another person uses a bank card.'

'I don't mean to sound negative, but that won't be possible either.'

'I'll ask around, Tony, and then make a missing person report to the police. Obviously, they are not going to spare much manpower on a 'misper', but it is the procedure. In the meantime, we will act as the police would act.'

At the university building, Church was passed from one person to another. He began with the vice-chancellor, a friend of Tony Brownstone. Each time he went from one member of staff to another it involved a long walk through the university building. Sometimes he went from one building to another. Each time he was met with someone less interested in actually helping him out. But eventually, he met with the program leader on the Contemporary Performance course that Amber was enrolled on. He was finally passed onto a principal lecturer who reluctantly agreed to speak to Church off the record.

'Students are adults,' she said unhelpfully. 'We cannot be behind them all of the time.'

'No, but you must have some sort of duty of care when a concern has been raised?'

'Well, yes of course, when a concern has been raised.'

'Well, that's okay then. I am raising that concern and I have the approval of her guardian. I just need to see her room in halls of residence and talk to her flatmates.'

'Hmm,' the lecturer replied doubtfully.

'Or,' continued Church. 'When Amber Garland's body is discovered, I can explain to the police how unhelpful you were.'

The room in the halls of residence revealed nothing. Normal student detritus of books, clothes, toiletries, were strewn around the compact bedroom with a tiny en-suite. It was much like his own hotel room but on a smaller scale. Church noticed that there was no laptop computer or mobile telephone which was unhelpful for his search. Two flatmates were in university classes but one was traced to the college refectory, a bleak-looking concrete bunker in the basement of the accommodation block.

The university cafeteria was almost deserted. Bright florescent lights could not lift the gloom of the place. Posters lined the walls offering information for students. Helplines for every type of abuse or discrimination that you could imagine were advertised. Posters that offered help for debt, depression, drug addiction, alcohol dependency. More signs warned that CCTV operated in this area. The refectory stated that it had a zero-tolerance for drugs and would not tolerate any abuse on its staff and would prosecute each incident.

Church was not surprised that the cafeteria was nearly empty.

The monosyllabic replies to his questions to Amber's flatmate were of little help. She pouted and sulked her way through their brief conversation. And Church was relieved to exit the cafeteria in the concrete bunker and step back into daylight, even if the daylight was fast fading. The late afternoon temperature outside had dropped to just above freezing. It seemed that Amber had few friends in her halls of residence, kept herself to herself, had one close friendship with another student named Tomas Kar.

Tomas had not been seen around the university this term, the flatmate mumbled something about, 'Student visa expired'. The housemate seemed thrown when Church asked her what cafes students liked to use in the city centre and what was the best student nightclub in town. It was the only time the girl almost smiled, which was a shame. If she was going to be an actress, thought Church, she would have to learn to smile at some point.

A quick check with the reluctant course lecturer and Church had a photograph of Tomas Kar in his possession. The image showed a young clean-shaven, dark-haired man with a smart haircut. He was back outside and making his way to the Bridgewater Wharf Café, the most popular student coffee shop in the city. Church got lost at one point on his walk to the Café and found himself walking along the towpath of the Bridgewater Canal, the much smaller and original canal system that runs right into the city centre. The more famous Manchester Ship Canal runs up to Salford quays where it morphs into the River Irwell to meander North, out of the city centre. Bridgewater, Britain's first canal, was built over one hundred years before the well-known ship canal. Church almost walked past the Bridgewater Wharf Café, expecting a small low-cost establishment serving students who would be living on a modest budget. The coffee shop was enormous. A converted warehouse whose origins were long-lost now. Exposed brick walls had been varnished to a glossy shine, smooth concrete floors had been similarly polished. Aluminium tables and chairs covered three floors of eating areas and each floor was served by a small army of waiting staff.

Church scanned each floor in turn until he had walked the entire building. No one matched the photograph that he had of Tomas Kar. Of course, there was no sign of Amber Garland either. That would have been just too easy. He made his way back down to the ground floor of the building, ordered a meal, picked up a coffee and found a seat near the entrance of the building. The position allowed Church to observe everyone who entered and left the café which, due to its size, was quite sizable. His food arrived quickly and Church ate enthusiastically, realising how hungry he was. He managed to stretch drinking his coffee for more than thirty minutes, ordered another and let it go cold while he patiently sat and waited. There were plenty of students who looked similar to the young man in the photograph. There were one or two women who looked similar to Amber Garland. As he sat, Church observed a shabbily dressed man walking around each of the tables. He had an annoying cough that sounded like he was constantly trying to clear his throat. Long hair and an untidy beard. Dirty jeans and a coat on top of another coat that hung on his frame. The man would pause by a set of diners, say something and then move on. Church suspected that he was a homeless beggar, asking for some loose change. But the man did not approach Church's table which surprised him. Eventually, the man traipsed off. He decided to walk the entire building, floor by floor, and show the photograph of Tomas Kar to each of the customers in the hope that someone would recognise him. One or two people paused, but most just shook their heads and impatiently brushed away his enquiries. Finally, he ordered a third coffee and drank it quickly before giving up and heading back to his hotel.

He was back outside and making his way past St Mungo's homeless shelter when Church spotted Tony Brownstone's car parked outside the ugly 1970s office block next door to the impressive Guildhall building. All of the ground floor lights were on and the disused Doctors' surgery building glowed invitingly in the chill of the freezing night-time temperature. Not feeling in the least bit tired due to the cups of coffee he had recently drunk, on a whim that would prove significant Church decided to go inside.

He was struck by the warmth and smell of cooking food as he pushed his way through the swing doors and into a small reception vestibule. Another set of doors led to a large waiting area that was now laid up with a smattering of tables and chairs. Many of the tables had just one or two seats and Church wondered if homeless people might not be that sociable. He spotted Tony Brownstone at the far side of the room, shirtsleeves rolled up and arms elbow deep in washing up water. But as he began to walk over to him a voice called out to Church.

'Hey, Champagne man! You okay?'

Church stopped walking and turned to see who was talking. He vaguely recognised the man.

'Champagne man,' the voice said again. 'Don't you recognise me? Wanna cup of tea or something?'

It turned out that St Mungo's was not a shelter as Church had assumed, but a day centre where homeless people could eat a meal and collect new clothes. They could also wash, get a haircut and receive advice from well-meaning charities. And they served tea.

'Hello,' said Church as he moved a chair opposite the homeless man. 'Did you enjoy the Champagne and the sticky barbecue ribs?'

'Did I? They were great. And no hangover from the booze. What you doing here?'

'I was just passing and saw Tony Brownstone had parked his car outside. I thought I'd come in and say hello.'

'Well, that's very nice of you,' the man grinned. 'Hello to you too.'

'I'm sorry, I didn't mean you. I was going to say hello to Tony.'

'I know, I know. I'm homeless, not daft. Just joking with you. Don't have many people to talk to.'

Church settled into his plastic chair and tried to think of something to talk to the man about. When Church handed the homeless man the foil container of food he had barely taken in anything of the other man's appearance. Now Church realised that they were probably of similar age, although the rough sleeper looked older in many ways. The man's face was dark with dirt, not sunlight; his hair was recently clipped short and a pale scabby scalp showed through the haircut. He had black lines under his nails and more dirt engrained into his fingers. There was a tangy smell about him, a sort of stale body smell.

'I'm called Freddo by the way,' the man said by way of opening a conversation.

'Good to meet you, Freddo, I'm Edward. Interesting name.'

'My dad was Italian,' he said as if it fully explained his name. 'So, what have you been doing today, Edward? I've been sitting in the doorway of a department store. Five hours I was sat there and my begging box was still empty, not a single person came by. It turns out that the shop closed down last week.' Freddo let out a loud laugh at his own joke. 'You've got to have done something more interesting than that?'

'Well, I sat in a coffee shop for three hours looking for someone who wasn't there,' said Church, but instantly felt guilty. It was likely that he would happily have changed places with Edward. But it did not seem to bother the other man. Yesterday Church was drinking champagne with the city's great and good, now he was sitting drinking tea with, whatever the opposite of great and good was. But everyone deserves respect. And but for the luck of birth and family it could have been Anthony Fairfax sat here instead of the man who called himself Freddo.

'Who were you looking for, Edward?' Freddo asked seriously.

'Well, a young woman has gone missing and I was looking for a man who might know something about her disappearance. He is, or was, a student at the university here in Manchester.'

'What's his name then, Edward?'

'He is called Tomas Kar, aged twenty-three, six-foot-tall, dark hair and originally from South Kurdistan.'

'You mean Southern Kurdistan, not South Kurdistan. An autonomous region in the northern part of Iraq. Got a photo of Tomas Kar?'

Church indulged the man and showed him the photograph that he had shown the students in the Bridgewater Café.

'I know Tomas Kar, but his name is Snow and he looks nothing like this photograph. Got a pen, Edward?'

Church reached into his jacket pocket and handed the man a pen.

'Hmm, nice pen, Edward. Not many people use a fountain pen these days. Can't get the ink anymore.' He started to scribble on the photograph and Church was just about to grasp it back when Freddo added. 'Tomas Kar, known to everyone as Snow, has lost a lot of weight and grown his hair since this image was created. Got quite a long beard too.'

The photograph was handed back to Church a minute or so later. Covered in sketch lines, perfectly hatched shaded parts and fine lines. The face on the image looked older, thanks to lines around the eyes; thinner, due to the hatched shading that made the cheekbones more prominent and completely different, thanks to the addition of the long hair and beard. It took Church a second or two to realise that he had seen this man before. In fact, he had watched him for several minutes as this man in the photograph walked around each table in the Bridgewater Wharf Café, begging for loose change.

'How do you know this man, Freddo?' asked Church.

'He's well known amongst homeless people. Tries to sell cheap drugs, but they've been cut so much there's nothing left in them. He's always to be found wandering about trying to sell some gear of some sort to somebody.'

'You're a genius,' said Church as he quickly stood up from the table. 'I know just where to find him. Thank you, thank you very much.'

Church turned to rush out of the homeless shelter when the man called after him again. 'Don't forget your pen, Edward. Hard to find the ink these days. Hard to find the ink.'

Chapter Seven

Back to the Bridgewater Canal thence to the *Drift-In*

Church ran out of St Mungo's homeless shelter and sprinted back towards the Bridgewater Wharf Café. He jogged along pavements, swerving around the few people who were still out at this time of night. At some point, it had begun to rain and a glossy sheen covered the roads, reflecting streetlights and shop window displays. A few cars drove by making a swishing sound on the damp tarmac, the noise building gently, then peaking as the vehicle passed by only to quickly fade again as it drove off into the distance. Church did not get lost on his way to the café this time. However, as he turned the corner near the canal basin he stopped short.

The Bridgewater Wharf Café was in darkness. Church was still breathing deeply and clouds of vapour swirled around him. He slowly walked to the double glass front doors and looked at the display board listing opening and closing times. It had shut around fifteen minutes ago.

'Well,' said Church to himself, 'if it was easy, it wouldn't be an achievement.'

Slowly making his way back, Church realised that all was not lost. He searched through his memory to recall the name of the nightclub that Amber's pouty, sullen, flatmate had suggested was the most popular with students. Scanning the almost deserted streets for a likely person, he asked for and received directions to the club.

Thirty minutes later Church stood outside the *Drift-In* nightclub. Situated above an arcade of shops a few minutes walk away from one of the city's shopping centres, the entrance was between a tattoo parlour and a barber's shop. Church reflected that there are a lot of barbers in Manchester. Door security gave him a strange look as he walked up to the entrance of the nightspot but he paid his entrance money and was allowed in. A wide flight of stairs led up to an open landing with a cloakroom cubicle to one side. Double doors opened up to the first level of the nightclub. The stairs reversed round on themselves and presumedly headed up to a second floor. Church shrugged off his overcoat and left it with the cloakroom attendant. He seemed to be grinning at Church as the numbered ticket was handed over.

The music inside was loud. It throbbed through the body and seemed to make the organs inside vibrate in time with the sounds coming through the loudspeakers. The area was reasonably busy, but Church could easily make his way between and around groups of clubbers. The actual nightclub dancefloor was lower than the rest of the room and Church could look over a sea of bodies with heads rising and falling in time with the beat. It was hot, very hot, inside the nightspot. Church could feel beads of sweat forming on his forehead. He slowly made his way to the bar, still scanning the room for any sign of Tomas Kar, with his street name of Snow. Just as he was being served, Church noticed the shabbily dressed man. Long black hair and an untidy beard, just as he appeared in the edited photo and just as Church had seen in the Bridgewater Wharf Café a few hours ago. Tomas had taken off one of his coats but had kept the other one on, despite the heat in the club. The young woman behind the bar was waving Church's drink in one hand and his change in the other, but Church was oblivious.

Tomas wandered out of the double doors and headed upstairs. Church followed behind him. The second floor of the *Drift-In* was much quieter. A more relaxed, chilled, room full of tables and chairs for people to actually hold a conversation and drink a glass of something without it being knocked or jostled. Church's drink was still on the bar counter downstairs, along with his change, but he didn't mind. Tomas Kar approached a group of clubgoers who were sitting around one of the tables and a conversation started. Money was exchanged and a small plastic bag was retrieved from deep inside one of the coat pockets.

'Well,' said Church to himself again, 'that was easy.'

He made his way over to Tomas Kar and said, 'Hi.'

'Alright, mate?' said Kar calmly but Church sensed the other man's nervousness. He coughed more frequently. 'Looking for something?'

'Actually, I'm looking for someone.'

'Candy? Angel? Aunt Mary? I ain't got no Charlie. Just soft stuff.'

Church was momentarily confused but said, 'I'm looking for Amber Garland and I've been told that you were her friend.'

'Got to be worth a drink hasn't it?' Kar coughed.

'Of course,' replied Church.

They made their way back downstairs to the bar where Church was pleasantly surprised to see that his drink and change were still waiting where the bar staff left it. Tomas had lagged behind a little as they approached the bar.

'What would you like?' Church asked the dishevelled dealer of soft drugs over his shoulder.

'To get the hell out of here, mate,' Tomas replied and sprinted towards the exit doors, weaving in and out of the clubgoers as he left Church standing.

Church took a large swig from his drink and set off after him. Not stopping at the cloakroom, he ran down the stairs two at a time and brushed past the doormen and then onto the street. He looked left and right and spied Tomas Kar running full pelt down the main street, then darting into a side road. The other man was rummaging in his pockets and running clumsily. Church followed at a steady pace, careful not to lose the other man if he doubled back or dived down a narrow alley.

They ran the length of the side road, past shops that were closed and late-night takeaways that were still open. The narrow road opened up onto a wide street. A low metal barrier separated the two lanes of the main road and Tomas tripped as he jumped the barrier partitioning the lanes. He picked himself up and carried on running, but now with a slight limp. Church easily vaulted the metal divider and slowed his pace slightly to match the other man. They ran on, eventually reaching a wide intersection where two main roads merged with each other. A yellow-painted hatched grid filled the space in the middle of the junction. Tomas swerved right and carried on running, but his head was beginning to drop now and Church could sense that the other man was losing the strength in his legs. Every now and then his hands would furiously delve into his coat pockets. Another swerve to the right and they were running down a narrow alley. Tall, old, redbrick and concrete buildings lined each side. Every now and then there was a doorway that broke up the continuous line of the walls. Church wondered if the man would try and find a door that was unlocked and then try to lose him inside a warren of rooms and corridors but instead Tomas jogged on.

They ran into a busy road intersection that Church later found out was where Great Bridgewater Street passed by the massive Manchester Conference Centre complex. A late-night metro tram clattered by above them and Tomas turned back to see if Church was still behind him. Somehow finding an extra burst of energy, he sprinted across the road intersection with arms flailing wildly, then swerved down a footpath towards the canal path. This section, named the Rochdale Canal towpath, had no safety barrier between footway and canal. Tomas staggered slightly as they ran under a bridge and Church momentarily paused, concerned that the other man would fall into the water. He did not relish the idea of a late-night swim in some freezing canal water. Church was breathing heavily now, he could taste the tangy industrial smell that still seemed to suffuse the surrounding buildings. Perhaps it was heavy industry, perhaps it was car exhaust fumes, but either way, he was getting out of breath. Tomas Kar must be really suffering now, thought Church.

'Keep going, Tomas Kar, I can run like this all night if necessary,' shouted Church. He didn't hear a reply.

They ran up a gentle incline and past a modern block of waterside apartments. Railings one side, open water the other. Nowhere to run except straight ahead. They ran a little farther alongside an old section of wall, now heavily decorated with graffiti. As they approached another housing development Tomas seemed to stumble. As he staggered past the grey building, each with its own patio opening up to the canal, Church was just a few metres behind. The other man veered to the left just before another building and began to run down a slope. He stumbled on the wet surface, fell awkwardly and skidded along the pavement for a metre or so.

'Okay. Okay, I give up,' he panted.

'Nothing to give, Tomas, and no need to run,' said Church as he squatted down beside him. 'I just wanted your help.'

'You're police right?' he gasped, coughing loudly. 'Plainclothes, undercover, but police all the same? Who the hell operates undercover dressed in a three-piece suit?'

'Like I said. I just wanted your help. I'm not a policeman, undercover or otherwise.'

Tomas looked at Church for a few minutes. 'Running away was not a good idea then, mate?' he coughed.

'And throwing away all of your drugs and pills was an even worse idea,' replied Church sympathetically. 'Somebody will have a lucky discovery.'

Tomas Kar swore and Church helped the man to his feet. They walked slowly back, trying to retrace their route. Tomas found some of his supply of drugs but others had been lost in the race to escape. He was limping badly, still breathing heavily and muttering to himself under his breath. Church kept quiet for a while, deciding not to speak until they were back in the vicinity of the nightclub.

'Do you fancy that drink now?' he asked.

Tomas shook his head. Church offered to collect their coats from the *Drift-In* club cloakroom but the other man shook his head again and said he would collect it some other time.

'Well, my overcoat cost a small fortune so we'll pop up and retrieve it if it's all the same.'

Tomas sulkily followed and reluctantly handed over his numbered ticket as well. They made their way back out onto the street and headed into the first all-night café they came across. The other man guzzled his first coffee down in a few gulps. Church ordered some more and asked about Tomas' friendship with Amber Garland.

'I like her,' he answered slightly more brightly now that they were sitting down. 'We get on well. But I have not seen her for a few days now.'

'Well, tell me a bit about yourself, Tomas,' Church asked to try and keep a conversation going.

'What do you want to know?' he replied guardedly, his coughing had subsided briefly but now returned with a vengeance.

'Anything. How did you meet Amber, what sort of things do you like to do in your spare time? Apart from selling drugs to other students. I understand that you come from Southern Kurdistan.' Church emphasised the word *Southern*.

'I came to the UK on a student visa and have enjoyed studying in Manchester greatly.'

'And?' encouraged Church.

'I met Amber during the freshers week. It is a time before serious studies meant for parties, joining clubs or societies. Things like that. There is lots of drinking but I did not really like alcohol then. Amber is very quiet, timid and perhaps a little shy. She does not enjoy speaking and finds socialising difficult. It might sound silly but we enjoy music concerts, art galleries things like that.'

'Sounds okay,' said Church, although he suspected that Tomas enjoyed alcohol a bit more now.

'Yes, it was okay, mate. It was nice. And then it all went wrong. The town that I was born in, called *Karbala*, was in Syria, right on the border with Iraq. The area was annexed by military invasion and the border re-drawn. Immediately I am not a student on a visa. I am an immigrant from a country that I was not actually born in. Now I have no income for my studies, no status, there is confusion over my student visa. The area is in a civil war, there is no administration now. People are homeless, hospitals empty and looted, schools shut.'

Church felt slightly uneasy as Tomas continued with his story. 'Were the university helpful?' he asked.

'They directed me towards a Wellbeing Officer, who could offer pastoral support. But they soon lost interest and directed me towards the Foreign Office. They directed me to the Immigration Service and then things got much worse....,' his voice trailed off.

'When did you start dealing in drugs?' asked Church.

'Not long ago,' replied Tomas.

'Do you take them?'

'Oh, no. Never take drugs, mate.'

That figures thought Church. His face is not well known by door staff outside nightclubs, but once he gets caught a few times, he will have been identified as trouble.

His picture will be circulated and doors will close to Tomas Kar. Church wondered what would be next for this lost soul.

Chapter Eight

A chat with Tomas Kar

Edward Church sat drinking coffee with the student drug dealer, Tomas Kar, in an all-night café somewhere in central Manchester. He had gone into great detail about how he dropped out of his studies and how his student support had stopped when the village he came from in Syria was annexed by neighbouring Iraq. Now Tomas was explaining to Church how Amber Garland had suggested a way of helping him out.

'So it was Amber who came up with the idea of faking her own kidnapping?' Church asked, not hiding his surprise.

'I did not think that it was a very good idea. And I did not agree to begin with. But as time went on I became more desperate and the suggestion from Amber played on my mind.'

'Faking her own kidnapping? Frankly, it seems ludicrous,' continued Church. 'Her stepfather is wealthy, could she not have simply asked him for money?'

'She said that her stepfather would not give her money for a cause like mine. The more we talked about it the more it became a realistic proposition.'

Church could imagine the reaction from Anthony Fairfax to his stepdaughter asking for money to fund a student who was now to all intents and purposes an illegal immigrant. A student whose visa had been revoked. A young man who was now on an Immigration Service list, likely to be fast-tracked back to his home town or kept in a detention centre while his court case is progressed through the system at a snail's pace.

'So what happened? What went wrong with your daft plan? Amber's stepfather has never received a ransom demand. And you have obviously not got any money.'

'I think that I may have told somebody about our scheme,' continued Tomas. 'When I am depressed, sometimes I say too much. I do not take drugs, but my supplier gives me alcoholic drinks. I have not seen Amber for some time. She has not been round to my flat, she has not been to her classes. No one has seen her.'

'In the case of a missing person,' explained Church, 'the first twenty-four to forty-eight hours are the most important. When did you last hear from Amber?'

'Four days ago.'

* * *

When he eventually made it back to his Hotel, Church slept badly that night. It may have been the amount of coffee he had drunk, but he could not shake an uneasy sensation that was growing somewhere in the back of his mind. He felt groggy in the morning and it took a little while longer than he had planned to get himself organised and out of the budget hotel.

It seemed likely that Tomas Kar had spoken of his plan to fake the kidnapping of Amber and to get some ransom money. Someone else had thought that they would try the same thing. Only this time for real. Church had insisted on walking Tomas Kar back to his flat last night. It turned out to be a squat in a tower block earmarked for redevelopment. The plywood hoarding around the ground floor of the block of flats was covered in illustrations for high-end open plan living apartments. The existing building was to be gutted, completely cleared out, and new living accommodation constructed. Somehow by using the existing skeleton of the tower block, new apartments could be created with greater cost efficiency.

Church considered that the only difference between calling somewhere a flat or an apartment was the price that it would cost someone to buy it.

Last night, Church had squeezed through the narrow opening in the advertising hoarding wrapped around the derelict tower block and walked up to the seventh floor with Tomas limping beside him. A spiders web of electric cables had been added to the block's emergency lighting so that there was some sort of electrical supply inside some of the squats. At night, the lights had dimmed and flickered constantly as they attempted to cope with the demands for volts, watts and ohms.

Now, during the day, the building's decay could be seen for all of its glory. As Church approached the building, he surveyed the decrepit structure. The tower block had probably been a perfectly good building in its day. *Pankhurst House*, as it had been named, would have provided decent accommodation for its residents when it was constructed. If only enough care had gone into repairs and maintenance it would still have been a nice place to live. Another tower block next door was named *Corkling House*. Church did not recognise the famous person after whom it had been named. But like its sister block, it too had seen better days. Almost every window up to the fourth floor had been broken. Smashed by stones thrown by disaffected youths, or even by their angry parents, at having to live in a building that was literally falling down around them. A fire had started in one of the flats and black soot clung to the outside cladding, snaking up several more floors.

Rubbish was strewn around the site. Random pieces of junk that did not match one another but somehow made up the whole picture of life in these tower blocks. A red toaster, a black bedside cabinet. The outside shell of some sort of kitchen white goods, not quite recognizable for what it had been. A smashed television and a cardboard box for a new one. A scattering of carrier bags over the grounds outside the tower block gave the area a dusting of fake, man-made, confetti.

Church had dressed carefully that morning and now made his way slowly up to the seventh floor of Pankhurst House. He was surprised to see that Tomas Kar was already dressed as well, although it may well have been the case that the other man had not changed his clothes from the night before. As Church took in the accommodation, he found it hard to imagine how these homes would have looked when someone who cared for them lived here. The lounge had a small chair, a mattress and a television. There were no pictures on the walls, no photographs on a windowsill, no blinds at the windows. At some point, someone had considered decorating and patches of the wall had been painted with tester pots of different colours. Other walls had been covered in graffiti. The floor of the lounge was carpeted, but its colour was hard to decern. Perhaps beige, perhaps coffee, or perhaps just brown. Now it was stained in various patches, worn and frayed in the doorway. A large patch was missing where the living area opened into a kitchen. That room was equally filthy. Worktops were full of empty food cartons and a cooker that was encrusted with a thick layer of cooking fat. There was a collection of bottles of spirits, it confirmed Church's suspicion that Tomas drunk quite often now. He was pleased to be wearing gloves. Put on to combat the freezing cold but useful not to have to actually touch anything in the squat. Church concentrated on his breathing. Quickly in through the nose and slowly out through the mouth, to try and minimize the odour.

As they walked slowly down the stairs and back down to street level, Tomas was limping badly. He had obviously hurt himself quite seriously when he ran into the central reservation during their late-night chase through the streets.

'Do you need to get that looked at?' asked Church.

'I will be okay. Thank you, mate. Where have you parked your car?'

'No car, Tomas, sorry. I don't suppose you have one?'

Tomas Kar pulled his hands out of his pockets and gave a wide, exaggerated, shrug. 'We can catch a bus,' he said.

The last time Church had been on a bus, outside of central London, must have been fifteen years ago. A trip along the seafront of a seaside holiday town now long since forgotten. But he stood patiently with Tomas at the bus stop waiting for a coach to take them back into the city centre.

'You seem bigger than I remember last night,' said Tomas by way of conversation.

'And you seem just the same,' replied Church as the bus pulled up beside them.

The driver did a double-take when Church boarded and frowned when Tomas limped on after him. Perhaps he had never seen a passenger in a three-piece worsted wool suit with a cashmere wool overcoat alongside another passenger who looked to be one step away from living on the streets. But he paid the fare and they found a seat at the back of the bus. Church was always interested in how a city grows and changes over time. The bus had listed *Sunny Bank* and *Hilton Park* on the route. Nice sounding names thought Church. Although, now that they travelled closer to the city centre, the suburbs were not so appealing. Leafy suburbs merged into high-density housing. Low level, two or three-storey buildings that stretched on for miles. Abruptly, a block of houses had been cleared and a tower block built on the parcel of land. An arcade of shops stretched along the main road. An assortment of retail outlets, many of which were now empty, with flats built above. Some selling fast food, others offering low-cost beauty treatments. A convenience store selling newspapers, magazines, snacks and alcohol. A barber's shop would appear randomly every now and then. Church glanced over to Tomas and wondered when was the last time the man had a haircut.

Eventually, they alighted along with most of the other passengers they had collected on the bus on the route. Church had persuaded a reluctant Tomas Kar to introduce him to his drug supplier. And Tomas promised that the friend would be in a cafeteria near the once imposing Manchester Art Gallery. The gallery building is beautiful, designed by Sir Charles Barry who was also responsible for the rebuilding of the Houses of Parliament in Westminster. Built in the popular Greek Ionic style, the original two-storey structure is now overshadowed by several nearby office blocks which tower above the pale cream finely-dressed smooth stone Art Gallery. The huge portico is supported by six columns and the porch thronged with visitors hurrying inside to get away from the chill.

The cafeteria was not so imposing. However, the warmth and coffee smells were a welcome treat after the drizzle that had begun to start outside. Church ordered beverages and watched Tomas devour thirstily as they sat and waited. Church sipped at his tea, even though the drink was good. He knew that the meeting with Tomas Kar's drug supplying friend would be a waste of time. The other man would hardly admit to kidnapping Amber Garland unless, of course, he was as inept as Tomas. Eventually, Church tired of waiting and suggested they look elsewhere.

'I think that my friend will be at the Indian restaurant down the road,' explained Tomas with a cough.

Church was doubtful but they walked the short walk three doors down. Church strolling slowly, Tomas Kar limping badly. Once again Church ordered food and drinks and watched Tomas devour hungrily as they sat and waited again. At the Curry shop, Church played it safe with a Korma and requested no cumin, his least favourite spice. Tomas opted for a Jalfrazi, washed down with several bottles of Kingfisher lager. Church was suspicious of the other man turning up and doubtful that he was actually a friend of Tomas. After another hour Church was getting restless.

'Sorry, mate, I do not think he is turning up. Perhaps he will be at the Tatoo shop off Princess Street,' said Tomas trying to sound helpful.

'Well, I'm not buying you a bloody tattoo,' said Church. 'And I'm not getting one myself while we wait.'

They walked past the parlour which was imaginatively called *Monsters Ink*, but unsurprisingly it was empty apart from two young women getting inkings to match. It was getting dark now. Lights were on in shopfronts, flashing displays of goods for sale. Twinkling rows of Christmas lights framed a festive window display. A clothes shop mannequin wearing warm attire and standing on fake snow.

'Let us try the pub that my friend drinks in.'

They made their way slowly out of town until Church and Tomas stood outside a large public house named *The Wonky Donkey*. Church's heart sank as they entered. Tomas, dressed in tattered jeans and two coats, looked like any of the other locals. Church, dressed in a suit and overcoat, did not.

As was becoming all too routine, Church bought drinks and they found an empty table. The bar was manned by two people. Church assumed father and daughter, but it could have been landlord and barmaid. He was late middle-aged, very overweight, with a big pot belly and severe crew cut. She was very late teens or early twenties, thin, with long black hair tied back in a ponytail. The landlord eyed Church suspiciously as he paid for drinks for himself and his companion. On the whole, Church enjoyed meeting new people. He was a good listener and would chip in every now and then with a question to keep a conversation flowing. But Tomas Kar was beginning to annoy him now. The other man was getting louder and louder, making more and more outlandish statements backed up with no fact or detail. Church was relieved when Tomas suddenly went quiet and nodded towards two people who had just entered the pub.

'It is them, mate' he said quietly. 'My friend and his associate.'

Church glanced over to the two people who had just walked into *The Wonky Donkey* public house. One was short, had a thin, pinched, weasel-like face and wore a badly fitting suit. The other man was much larger, perhaps as tall as Church, but was dressed in a brightly patterned tracksuit. Large panels of block colours clashed together in a kaleidoscope of fluorescent tones as the man walked up to the bar counter. Tomas Kar went to stand up, but Church placed his hand on his arm.

'Wait just a few minutes.'

'Okay, not a problem, mate. But my drink is nearly finished.'

'That's good, Tomas. Because it's time for you to leave.'

'But?' Tomas protested.

'Just make your way back to your home. I'll get in touch if I need to.'

'It is a long walk back and my leg is hurting,' Tomas whined.

'Best to get a move on then,' said Church absently. He was speaking to Tomas but looking at the weasel-faced man. 'By the way, what is his name?'

'I don't actually know,' Tomas answered. 'We call him Hookman. But I've never found out his real name. Why do you want to know?'

'Because I think that I will go over and introduce myself.'

Chapter Nine

Hookman and Malcolm X

The *Wonky Donkey* public house was reasonably busy for a weekday December evening. Small groups of regular drinkers were gathered either around the bar or clustered around tables. The bar itself was a large half-circle, extending out from the longest wall of the pub. It faced the entrance doors and either side of it were doors that led off to lavatories. The landlord had accepted that Christmas was looming by wrapping some tinsel around a pelmet that ran on the ceiling above the bar and adding some fairy lights. The lights were on a continuous cycle of flashing patterns that Church found annoying after five minutes. A compilation album of Christmas songs was playing in the background. Church suspected that he might get fed up with those as well after a couple of hours.

The weasel-faced drug dealer, identified as Hookman, was sat at a corner table, near to a pool table which nobody in the pub seemed interested in using. He did seem to spend a great deal of his time looking at his phone. Occasionally a younger person would come into the bar, spend a few minutes talking to Hookman and then leave. His companion in the brightly coloured tracksuit did not say or do anything. He just sat.

Church was just thinking that it might be a good time to go over and introduce himself when the pub doors opened and three well-built men walked in. They were dressed in similar, dark, nondescript clothing. They wore jeans or dark canvas trousers and, to Church's instincts, looked like trouble. The landlord clearly thought so too because he pushed the barmaid out from behind the counter and pointed to a far corner of the room away from the weasel-faced Hookman and his accomplice. She tried to look busy, collecting a few pint glasses and wiping down a table that was not especially in need of wiping. Church watched as the landlord reached down under the counter and unclipped a baseball bat, clearly kept there for such occasions.

However, the situation never really erupted. Two of the three men stood on either side of the overweight man in the tracksuit. They gripped his arms as he attempted to stand. The third man kicked the chair from underneath the weasel-faced Hookman, who fell to the floor. One foot rested on his head and another squashed his hand. The third man swiftly grabbed a pint glass that was on the table and rammed it into the side of Hookman's head. Somebody said, 'Kidnapping was meant to be so easy.'

Church was impressed. Not by the unnecessary violence, which he abhorred, but by the balance of the third man. Not easy to stand on someone's head while also standing on their hand. It was only luck and weight that stopped him from unsteadiness. Not a professional, thought Church, but a useful street fighter employed by someone to settle an issue with the weasel-faced dealer.

As quickly as they entered, the three men left.

The landlord hardly managed to say, 'We don't want any trouble here.' As he held the baseball bat in the air, the pub doors swung closed, the three figures disappeared into the night and silence descended. Faintly, someone was singing a Christmas song about peace on earth. The barmaid made it over to Church's table and began elaborately wiping it.

'You can take that glass, my friend has gone,' said Church as she smeared the table.

'Not being funny,' she said. 'But I wouldn't have thought Tomas 'Snow' Kar was your friend. He's been barred from here so many times for selling dealing or using drugs. My dad tries to keep things clean in here but he's fighting a losing battle sometimes.'

'Is Tomas a user? He said that he never touches them. Does he take drugs recreationally, socially, occasionally?'

'Tomas takes them Industrially! He doesn't just take drugs, he devours them.'

'I didn't know that there was entertainment laid on this evening.' Church asked, changing the subject.

'What?' she asked blankly.

'Who has Hookman got with him on his table. Not very useful in a fight?'

'Oh, that's Malcolm. Calls himself Malcolm X.'

'Why?' asked Church trying to sound nonchalant.

'Don't know why,' she replied. 'Makes him seem more enigmatic or something.'

'But he's white? And he hangs around with a dealer? Somehow I can't imagine him campaigning for human rights and civil liberties. But I could be wrong.'

'What?' she asked again. But the barmaid was already walking back to the counter before Church could say any more.

Church waited a few minutes until the atmosphere in the pub had calmed. He did not want to walk over to introduce himself to Hookman and Malcolm X until both men had had a chance to simmer down. On the other hand, he did not want to wait too long and risk both men leaving the pub. The sense of anticipation eventually got the better of Edward Church. Hookman, engrossed in his phone and Malcolm X simply sat, staring into the corner of the room. The *Wonky Donkey* had emptied out a little. Drinkers left after the earlier trouble, and it was now late and very dark outside. Church got up and walked slowly over to where the other men were seated. He stood for a few seconds by their table before Hookman looked up from his phone. Malcolm X suddenly awoke from his trance-like state and revived himself to stand.

'Take it easy, big Mal,' said Church. 'You're not much of a bodyguard and I'm sure that you don't want two embarrassing events to lose face over this evening.'

Before waiting for a reply he turned to Hookman. 'You've certainly got a lot of data on that phone, you've been on it all evening.'

'What's it to you? Are you a mobile phone salesman?'

'No. But I've been told you are the man to ask. You can help me with a search that I'm undertaking.'

'Don't know what you're going on about. I don't know nothing.'

'Well, at least that suggests that you know something,' added Church brightly. 'I'm looking into the disappearance of Amber Garland.'

'Listen, five-oh, I don't know what you are talking about. It's getting late.'

But Church sensed that the man knew exactly what he was talking about. Colour drained from Hookman's face. Malcolm X tensed and twisted in his chair, looking over to the pub doors. He was useless as a bodyguard and not very good at keeping secrets. Hookman looked at the watch on his wrist, shook it and cursed under his breath.

'He broke my effing watch.'

'Why are you being so secretive Mr Hookman,' said Church.

Hookman laughed, 'It's Hookman, not Mr Hookman. You're not police, I can tell these things.'

'You see, you're a smart guy. You do know things.'

'I might know things. I might be able to find out things, but information costs.'

'Well, I've been wiped out by Tomas Kar after buying teas and coffees, drinks and meals and nearly paying for a tattoo. But I know it's time for you to tell me what you know.' Church made a show of looking at the time on his wristwatch.

'Get the car.' Hookman said to Malcolm. 'I've remembered something about Amber back at the flat.'

Ten minutes later, Church was sitting in the passenger seat of an aged, Imola yellow, *Audi RS4* being driven somewhere to the North of the city centre by Malcolm X. Hookman was in the back seat looking at his phone as usual. The car was immaculate, if rather worn and old. The leather seats were peeling, and the gear stick was shiny and smooth, likewise the steering wheel. The engine was desperately in need of attention. The exhaust was too throaty and it coughed loudly each time they slowed down. The bodywork, however, was immaculate.

'Nice car,' said Church to Malcolm X as he drove.

'Thanks. Fitted a tuning box myself. Got extra BHP from the ECU. Changed the exhaust, brake disks, and fitted a high torque clutch too.'

It was all beyond Church. He enjoyed driving but had little knowledge or enthusiasm for what was actually under the bonnet. Malcolm drove steadily, occasionally looking into the rearview mirror and keeping his speed steady in the city. The gentle glow inside the car appeared to change slightly. Pulsing brighter and then dimmer. It took Church a few seconds to realise that they were being followed by a police car. As the blue lights lit up on the police car, Malcolm eased over to the side of the road. He was actually a very good driver, considered Church, more useful in handling an automobile than in a fistfight.

Unsurprisingly, as they stopped at the side of the road, the police car pulled up slightly in front of them. Surprisingly, a plainclothes policeman got out of the car along with a constable in uniform. The two police officers walked slowly back to the yellow Audi. Church could see another officer sitting in the driver's seat of the police car. He wound down the passenger window as they drew level.

'What seems to be the problem,' Church asked.

'Just a routine stop, sir,' the uniformed police officer said. She was tall, well built and kitted out in full police constable equipment. The gilet she wore was full of pockets bursting with useful paraphernalia.

The stop was anything but routine thought Church. Plainclothed officers do not routinely drive around city centres late at night. The WPC leant close to the car door. A routine move, to smell if anyone had been drinking heavily or smoking drugs in the vehicle. She walked around the Audi, looking closely at the tyres and the lights. She took note of the car registration number and called it in on her radio. A reply crackled back a few seconds later, but to Church sitting the car, it was inaudible.

The WPC tapped on the driver's window and Malcolm X wound it down. He looked uncomfortable in his brightly coloured tracksuit.

'Is this your vehicle, sir?' she asked.

'Yes.'

'Are your indicators working properly, sir?'

'Yes.'

'Could you put your hazard lights on please, sir?'

'Yes.'

'Could I ask you your full name please?'

'Don't tell her Malcolm,' interrupted Church, before adding with a smile. 'And keep quiet Mr Hookman, she doesn't need to know your name.'

'Malcolm Jackson,' he replied gloomily.

'And your full name, sir?' she asked Hookman.

'Neville Smallbone,' replied Hookman sourly.

Church looked over his shoulder at Hookman and raised an eyebrow. 'And I am Edward Church, constable,' he added.

She walked slowly around the car once again. The plainclothes officer stood back during this little scene, but his notepad was in his hand and he was frantically making notes. Eventually, he walked over to the passenger side and spoke to Church through the window.

'Good evening, sir.'

'Good evening to you, sir,' Church replied. 'Anything we can help you with? Is the vehicle roadworthy, no bald tyes?'

'No, Mr Church.'

'Is it insured?'

'Yes, sir, it appears to be.'

'Well, my friend Malcolm here is guilty of crimes against fashion. Tracksuits on larger men is never a good look. You might think that he's got poor taste in apparel, or clothes, or cars. And Mr Hookman here had poor taste in friends. But of course, that's not a crime.'

'No, sir, they are not.'

'Well, you've got us fair and square then?' replied Church brightly. 'Guilty of wasting police time.'

'On your way and less of the backchat.'

'Yes, certainly, officer...?' Church let the question hang.

'Detective Inspector Ball, sir. And please don't attempt any more jokes, I have probably heard them all before.'

'And your charming colleague...?' Church enquired again.

'WPC Lamb. Goodnight, sir.'

Church waved a hand out of the window and shouted, 'Goodnight, officers.' The car sped off with a crackle of exhaust noises.

* * *

Hookman's flat was marginally larger than the one that Tomas Kar was squatting in. It was marginally tidier. But it was by no means a show flat or something out of a magazine. The décor was shabby, patches of paint had peeled off the walls in places, worn away by people coming and going or by age, damp or condensation. It smelt closed-up, stale and musty. The sour odour of long ago sprayed deodorant, aftershave or similar cologne hung in the air and had seeped into the furniture. The sofa in the lounge was large, too large for the space it occupied. Perhaps it looked good in the catalogue pictures, but in this flat, it looked as if it had been squashed into the corner of the room. An enormous flat-screen television nearly filled the whole of the wall opposite the seating. Cables dangled down from behind it and from the sides, connections ran to various loudspeakers mounted on the walls or to a large black box sitting on the floor. A games console rested on top of the black box. It looked precarious, balanced for now but could topple at any moment. Piles of computer games and other disks littered the floor.

A large window filled another wall in the front room of the flat. To one side was a door that probably led out onto a balcony. Blinds had been fitted to the window at one point, but these now hung, broken, to one side. The opposite wall had the doorway into and out of the flat. The fourth wall led to a small hallway with doors to presumably a kitchen, bathroom and bedrooms. Church never got to explore the layout.

Hookman wandered into the kitchen and Church could hear the sounds of packets being opened and a microwave door being closed. A short time later he heard a ping and Hookman reappeared eating some popcorn.

'So you want to know about Amber?' he said between mouthfuls of snacks.

'Just trying to find out where she is,' replied Church.

Malcolm interrupted. 'Why do you take the mickey out of my clothes?'

'Never mind me, Kaleidoscope,' Church countered.

'They're designer you know?'

'Well, I look like something off of a wedding cake so I can't really comment,' said Church. He was beginning to warm to Malcolm X.

'Your suit looks posh,' Malcolm said.

'It's tailored you see. Not that I'm a weird size or anything,' Church paused a looked over to Hookman who was still eating popcorn, 'but it can get repaired easily. Something of an occupational hazard. This one has had at least two new sleeves and a new front-facing.'

'Whatever that is,' mumbled Hookman.

'Your suit is a bit like Triggers boom then?' smiled Malcolm.

'If you say so, Malcolm. If you say so.' He turned to Hookman who was shaking the bag of popcorn to get the last of the snacks out. 'Why do you live here Mr Hookman? You could probably afford somewhere a bit…' he paused before adding, 'bigger?'

'I like it here. My family and friends live near me. I grew up here. It's my area.'

Church understood that feeling. It was perhaps the only thing he could find in common with Hookman. One of the reasons he still lived in Chelsea was because Church knew the people around him, knew his neighbours, knew the good shops and restaurants. He liked it that the landlady in the *Rose and Crown* public house knew what drink he wanted if he called in during the day. Church would exchange a few words with the newspaper seller in his kiosks near the Underground station. The man remembered what paper Church read and would fold it ready as he saw him approach. It amazed Church that the man could remember so many people and what newspaper they would buy. The vendor stocked an extensive range of papers. All of the UK national newspapers, the Wall Street Journal, New York Times, Jewish Chronicle, La Monde, La Stampa, El Pais, De Zeit and Die Weld. A sense of belonging mused Church. Hookman jolted him out of his thoughts.

'So you said that you want to know about Amber?' Hookman asked again. 'It will cost you.'

Church did not expect it to be easy. He did not really expect to find Amber somewhere in this flat, but part of him was curious. There was a chance, just a slim chance that this man was holding her, hoping for a ransom payout for himself. Too bad that Tomas Kar would miss out. The double-crossing, Tomas Kar was in no place to make any complaints. Two-faced, hypocritical Tomas Kar, who said that he did not drink alcohol but sunk enough lager to fill a bathtub that evening. Tomas 'Snow' Kar, who said that he never touched drugs and yet took them on an industrial scale.

'How much are we talking about Mr Hookman? What information have you got about Amber's whereabouts?'

'How much have you got on you right now?' sneered Hookman.

'Er, just a few pounds. As I said, I'm afraid your friend Tomas wiped me out this evening. I was obviously too hospitable.'

'You got a nice watch though.'

'It probably tells the time better than your's does now.'

There was a pause in the conversation. In the *Wonky Donkey* pub, Church thought that things were about to kick off when the three thugs walked in and set about Hookman and Malcolm. That little scene had dissipated as soon as it had formed. Church now stood in front of Hookman with the other man eyeing his wristwatch. It was obvious that Hookman wanted to steal it. And it would have been an easy lift. And it was at this moment, with Church stood in the flat facing Hookman, that things actually kicked off. Although not in the way that Church had anticipated.

Chapter Ten

Lights out

Church stood in the middle of the cramped flat somewhere in the North of the City of Manchester. Malcolm the bodyguard sat on the L shaped sofa that was too large for the room. Hookman the drug dealer stood in front of Church. The packet of popcorn had gone from his hand and in its place was now a knife. Church could see the whole scene in front of him. He could also see it reflected in the large picture window with the broken blinds hanging at one side. He was looking in on the scene as well as being in the middle of it.

Church unbuttoned his jacket, no need to get an unnecessary hole in it. He held his hands outstretched on either side of him, no need to risk getting an artery severed. Malcolm seemed surprised by Church's reaction to having a knife pulled on him because he had a blank look on his face as he sat on the sofa. It was Hookman who broke the silence.

'Get his watch, Mal.'

Spurred into action, Malcolm eased himself awkwardly off of the seat and grabbed Church's outstretched hand. He fiddled clumsily with the watch strap, eventually figuring out the double butterfly hinge clip. He handed it to Hookman who looked at the chunky metal bracelet strap and the classic oyster case. He looked closely at the serrated bezel enamelled with a band of dark blue to match the watch face. He peered at the makers' mark behind the hands, a chunky hour hand with an offset square and an equally chunky minute hand. The much thinner second hand with smaller offset square swept gently round.

'Tudor? Never heard of them. Is it worth anything?' he asked Church

'Not the most expensive,' Church replied. ' But worth more than you are, you useless piece of....'

And it was at that very moment that things really did kick off. Hookman lunged towards Church with the knife in one hand and Church's watch still in the other. Church turned slightly to deflect the point of the knife. Hookman changed direction and tried to slash sideways. The knife stabbed straight through Church's shirt and stopped. Hookman paused for a second. Then the lights went out.

Church crouched down instinctively and looked at the reflection of the room in the large picture window. Hookman stood in front of him, Malcolm sat on the oversized sofa. The front door of the flat crashed open. It flipped off of its hinges and lay awkwardly on the floor of the hallway.

Malcolm said, 'Shit!'

Hookman started to say, 'What the....?'

Other voices filled the apartment. Most saying either 'armed police,' or 'put down your weapons.' Hookman's body suddenly went rigid. He toppled backwards and fell to the floor. Malcolm's legs buckled and he lay sprawled on the sofa, his body rigid with the electric charge that was shooting through it. Edward Church might have been hit with a taser as well but it did not register.

Four or five police officers in full tactical riot gear had smashed into the room. They spread out in perfect formation, arms raised and ready to fire. Luckily they were carrying non-lethal electronic devices, although at that very moment Hookman and Malcolm might not have seen it that way. Fifteen feet of insulated wire shot out from the front of each device. Two darts lodged somewhere in the body of each of them. A direct hit is not essential for a taser dart to be effective. A shot in the body, arm, leg, hand or even foot would have the same effect. Fish hook barbs would pierce through clothing, stab into the skin and deliver a burst of 50,000 volts through the flesh of an unsuspecting victim. The high voltage electric charge would thump for five seconds at a high rate of nineteen pulses per second, then a slightly longer fifteen-second pounding at twelve pulses per second. The stunned victim would get the briefest reprise of half a second before another nineteen pulses per second and then a lower but still agonizing eight pulses per second pulsated through their body.

Hookman was the first to be struck by the taser darts. His body went rigid as the metal barbs punctured his skin. Neural signals from his brain were interrupted by the electric shock, neuromuscular incapacitation followed and he twitched uncontrollably as every muscle in his body went into a spasm. The taser did not affect his heart. The short bursts of high voltage were absorbed by his skin and muscle before travelling to any vital organs. He dropped to the floor in front of Church who quickly grabbed the mobile phone from Hookman's pocket and retrieved his watch from the rigid fingers of the other man.

Malcolm X made the mistake of trying to fight against the shocks and for his troubles was tasered twice. Church simply knelt on the floor with his hands on his head. He waited for the inevitable push to the floor as two sets of arms roughly twisted his own arms down and behind him as handcuffs were secured on his wrists.

Familiar words were spoken, words that had been said to him once or twice before, and as Church twisted his head sideways he saw a familiar face. Familiar because he had first seen it just a few minutes before now.

'Mr Edward Church,' said Detective Inspector Ball. 'I am arresting you on the suspicion of drug trafficking, the cultivation, manufacture, distribution supply and or sale of substances which are subject to drug prohibition laws. You do not have to say anything, but it may harm your defence if you do not mention when questioned something you later rely on in court. Anything you do say may be given in evidence. Do you understand the charges?'

Inspector Ball did not wait to hear an answer from Church but turned on his heels and walked out of the room. Other police officers swiftly read Hookman and Malcolm their rights when they began to regain consciousness. Church noticed that they were charged with lesser offences but it was a technicality really, the three of them had been arrested.

'Do you expect me to talk? Do you expect me to talk?' Hookman repeated over and over again.

Eventually, a disgruntled Police Officer said, 'No. I expect you to shut up and get in the car.'

Outside, a small group of interested onlookers had crowded around the entrance to the flats. Two police constables were trying and failing, to keep people back. Residents had heard the commotion and wanted to know what was occurring. Several had mobile telephones and were recording the events, but it was dark and the ineffective lights on their cameras would not illuminate very far. One burly police officer supported Hookman, but it took two to try and guide the much larger Malcolm X to a waiting law enforcement vehicle. He would falter every few steps and the two policemen would have to lunge to save him from falling over. Church followed some distance behind, accompanied but not supported by a WPC.

The drive back through the outskirts of Manchester and back into the city centre was probably much slower in the Police issue *Skoda Octavia vRS* than their outward journey a few minutes ago, thought Church as they cruised along the A34. The flashing blue lights were on but it was unnecessary because at this time of night, or early morning, there was very little other traffic on the streets.

Edward Church was processed by a desk Sergeant who had initially looked bored when he was led to the desk, flanked by two police officers but looked slightly more excited when he read the charge sheet against Church.

'Put him in room three,' the Sergeant said.

Church tried to explain that if they could be encouraged to make a telephone call to his office in London, things could be cleared up very quickly.

'If you think that I am going to call some number that you're giving me off the top of your head and 3am in the morning you've got another thing coming.'

'Surely it's another think coming?' enquired Church.

'Don't try and get smart with me. I'm not calling any telephone numbers at this time of night. It will probably be a politician or something and you'll be having a good laugh at my expense.'

They waited in a holding cell for a few minutes before Church was led down a series of corridors to the custody suite. The contents of his pockets had been emptied and logged. His shoes, belt and tie were removed and his jacket taken away. Finally, the handcuffs were removed. He was tired but patient as he settled down into the small room. It was larger than the standard six-foot by eight-foot room he had been expecting. It had grey linoleum floor and a small bench bed covered in a blue thick vinyl cover. The walls were painted off white and a blue line ran around the entire cell. The thin blue line Church thought to himself with a smile. A stainless steel toilet was housed in one corner of the room on the same wall as the door, which might have afforded some privacy from onlookers. He noticed a security camera fixed to the corner of the ceiling behind a protective cover. It appeared that privacy concerns only went so far.

Church expected to be called from his police station cell at any moment, but as time went on his anticipation faded. When the lights in his cell dimmed, so did his expectations. He settled down for an uncomfortable and noisy night. Every few minutes there seemed to be a noise or a shout from one of the other cells in the custody suite. Church was aware of someone looking into his room, checking on him every thirty minutes or so. There were shouts from other prisoners asking who was in the next cell and what they were being charged with. Church did not bother to answer and, after a few expletives, the questions soon dried up.

Early the next morning Church was faced with the amusing prospect of choosing his own breakfast. He selected the full English with tea and was presented with a plastic carton with two sausages in a container of beans. The tea was in a small styrofoam cup. There was an all-in-one fork, spoon, knife implement which was supposed to be used for eating with. However, it was so flimsy that Church did not risk cutting up the sausage, he simply speared each of them and ate them in four small bites. The tea was weak, bitter and diluted with long-life milk. It tasted like a cup of chemicals but Church was so thirsty that he drank the whole lot down quickly.

Several hours later, he was sat in an interview room opposite Detective Inspector Ball with another colleague introduced as Detective Sergeant DeWinter. Church was imagining the comedy combinations of these two surnames when Sergeant DeWinter introduced herself as Elsa.

'I am on secondment from the Dutch city of Rotterdam,' she smiled.

Church gave details of a telephone number he would like called, either by Inspector Ball or Sergeant DeWinter and the interview was promptly ended. Three hours later he was back in the same room. Was it Church's imagination or had the atmosphere towards him changed? Certainly, Inspector Ball was still frosty but not quite as cold and emotionless as before. He was guarded but nonetheless interested to know the answers to his questions.

'Who walks around Manchester at three o'clock in the morning wearing a UK Police issue stab-proof vest? I worked at the Police Scientific Development Branch before it transferred to the Home Office. I recognise that vest. It's top of the range. SP1, spike protection will deflect a pickaxe; KR1 will stop a knife blade. No wonder the tasers just bounced off you!'

'I did try to explain to your desk Sergeant last night,' replied Church calmly.

'You were in the company of known drug dealers. No identification, no wallet, very little money.'

'That was thanks to an expensive evening with Tomas Kar.'

'Another dealer who is known to us, Mr Church. Thank you very much for nothing. God only knows how much paperwork I have wasted on you already and I have got yet more to complete now that you are going to be released. I thought that we were over the threshold for the CPS to prosecute you. Now it seems we are on the same side!'

And with that, Inspector Ball stood up and walked out of the room, leaving Church and a confused DeWinter sitting opposite each other.

* * *

Once again, Edward Church stood in front of the desk Sergeant. Once again, the officer behind the police officer behind the desk looked bored. However, the Sergeant appeared slightly more interested as they explained the misunderstanding surrounding Church's confinement. The officer looked to be aged in his late fifties, slightly overweight, balding and certainly past official retirement age. He had probably seen a great deal of the worst of life pass through the cells that stretched in a long line behind him. Perhaps it was the rare occurrence of someone being released without charge that pricked his interest, or perhaps it was something else. It soon became clear to Church that it was indeed something else.

'Detective Inspector Ball cocked it up again then?' he asked.

Detective Sergeant Elsa DeWinter did not answer and so Church said, 'It looks that way, Sergeant.'

'Let me get your possessions, Mr Church.' The older man retrieved a set of keys from under the desk and made his way over to a row of lockers. He returned several minutes later and meticulously went about the business of returning Church's property. Each item was described in meticulous detail. 'Black leather shoes made by Loake Brothers with soft rubber soles and four eyelet laces, very useful for a stealthy getaway, Mr Church. UK size eight which would be continental size forty-two. Black leather belt with a silver buckle, unbranded, to fit a waist thirty-four to thirty-six inches. Very dark grey suit jacket made by Anderson and Sheppard, chest size forty-two inches, material Merino wool, the lining is silk if I'm not mistaken.'

'Could we speed things up just a little, please,' interrupted Elsa DeWinter impatiently.

'Silk tie, colour dark burgundy,' the desk Sergeant continued unhurriedly, ignoring her. 'Wallet containing ten pounds and seventy-five pence in change. A Tudor Black-Bay watch, navy blue face, silver metal strap, model number fifty-eight. A key pass for a budget Hotel. A Samsung mobile telephone with a slight crack in the screen. My grandson wants one of those for his birthday. And a....' he paused and squinted at the label, '...a

Xiaomi mobile telephone. Never heard of them.' Finally, he heaved a heavy black garment onto the desk and said with a smile that lit up his face, '…stab-proof vest. Government issue. Sign here, Mr Church.'

Chapter Eleven

Released from Custody

Edward Church and Elsa DeWinter sat opposite each other in the police station canteen. Aromas of sweet coffee and toasted bread filled the space. Traces of the smell of cooked meat and boiled vegetables hung permanently in the air. It was painted in the same institutional colour as the rest of the building, something of a mix between cream and pale yellow. The floor of the police refectory was a dark green, almost olive, colour. The plastic seats were red and the tables were an off-white, ivory colour. Nothing matched.

'At least the tea is a nice colour,' said Church as he looked into the mug.

'What?' DeWinter said.

'Nothing, just thinking out loud. Will Detective Inspector Ball be joining us?'

'I think that he will not be joining us, Mr Church. He will be processing Mr Hookman and his associate Malcolm, but he thought that you were the person worth questioning. He has lost some credibility because of you. Initially, he was sure that you were a person of interest much higher up the drug supply chain. He referred to you as a 'top plug' and that he was fed up with chasing 'hoppers and jugglers'. I do not understand the terminology he uses but I do know that arresting street dealers is not the way to tackle this serious organised crime. Then he assumed that you were undercover police. The lack of identification in your wallet and the stab-proof vest of course. Inspector Ball was furious that he had not been informed of another operation in his region and insisted that you be kept overnight to teach a lesson to those involved. But then I think that he became worried about any repercussions or reprisals from the National Crime Agency. Now I think that he just wants you out of the building so that he can get over his embarrassment.'

'He's proud?' asked Church.

'He is beyond proud. He is conceited, self-centred and he thinks that it is acceptable to make a pass at a colleague from another police force, from another country.'

Church concluded that Ball and DeWinter did not work well together as a team. Her face flushed and she was animated as she spoke angrily. He had not really bothered to pay any attention to her appearance before now. DeWinter looked to be aged around thirty, slim with honey blond hair cut in a severe, short, choppy bob and dark brown eyes. Almost as dark as Church's. She wore silver heavy rimmed glasses that looked slightly dated and old fashioned. The frames needed to be heavy to accommodate the thick lenses contained within. Her face was the shape of a heart, eyes set wide apart, lips full but unpainted and the chin small. The glasses had the effect of magnifying her eyes to make them even larger than they naturally were.

'Go easy on Malcolm X,' said Church. 'He is not too bright, despite his clothes, and I suspect that he just likes to be useful. Hookman is just a street weasel.'

'As I mentioned to you last night, Mr Church, I am on secondment from the Dutch authorities of Interpol. And as such, I have little jurisdiction in these matters. However, it just so happens that I agree with you. You see, in Holland, I am also at the rank of Inspector. When I was transferred to the United Kingdom, I had to take the reduction down to Sergeant on the insistence of Mr Ball. My secondment was to investigate the link in organised crime between the United Kingdom and Holland, not to be involved in the arrest of small-time, low level, street dealers.'

Church decided that he liked DeWinter, he liked her a lot. 'Is there somewhere private we can talk?'

'It is private here, Mr Church,' she answered warily.

'This is Mr Hookman's mobile telephone,' he said reaching into his jacket pocket and pulling out the Samsung mobile phone.

'Are you withholding evidence, Mr Church?' she asked with a grin.

'I'm holding evidence. And I'm giving it to you. Perhaps we could work together. Although I have got a rather different agenda. It would be really helpful to take another look around Hookman's flat.'

Elsa DeWinter paused for a few moments, looked over at some of her police colleagues on another table, then swore to herself under her breath. 'Why not? They do not take me seriously here and I am returning to Holland in one week! Keep possession of it, for now, Mr Church. If I accept this evidence, it will have to be logged here and I would rather that not happen.'

'I need some proper sleep, Elsa. Could we meet up for a chat later on today?'

* * *

Church awoke with a start. He felt momentarily disorientated. Then, as the sensation of consciousness returned, he remembered where he was. Light streamed around the sides of the blackout curtains in his budget Hotel room. He stretched out in the large King-sized bed. An alarm on his telephone was purring gently, the screen lit up the darkened room with a soft glow. He leaned over to switch it off and checked the time display. Two-thirty in the afternoon. He had grabbed a precious few hours of sleep after leaving the police station late that morning. Inspector Ball had not seen him depart, had not apologised or said goodbye. 'Rude!' thought Church to himself with a smile.

He picked up his discarded shirt from the back of the chair in the corner of the room and looked at the four holes in the back panel. His fingers poked through two of the punctures. He examined his suit jacket and found four similar perforations on the back, just above the vent section. 'If only they had Tasered me in from the front, the barbs might have missed my jacket,' he said to himself.

Stopping off at the reception desk on the way downstairs Church asked the young lady on duty for a small box, some packing tape and a sheet of writing paper.

'We don't have anything like that, sir,' she replied apologetically.

However, in the ever-helpful way of hotel reception staff the world over, she returned from the back office with a sheet of paper from the printer/photocopier, a roll of sticky tape and an old padded envelope from the pile of cardboard and paper recycling. Church thought that Sir Bernard Trueman would approve. 'A good use of taxpayers money,' the old man would say. Church wrote Trueman a note with instruction to pass the contents of the envelope to Alexander Drake, the technology specialist at the Cabinet Office. He carefully placed Hookman's mobile phone inside the envelope, wrote the address 70 Whitehall London SW1A, wrapped the package with plenty of sticky tape and asked the hotel receptionist to hold it until a courier collected the envelope late that day.

As he made his way out onto the street an hour later, it was beginning to get dark. At some point during the time he had been asleep, it had rained in Manchester. The streets were slick with a film of dampness. Cars and busses made a swishing noise as they travelled along the road. Even though there had been no heavy industry in the area for many years, the air smelt tangy. A slight atmosphere of pollution hung around the city.

Church spotted Elsa DeWinter in the café that they had arranged to meet in. She was cradling a large cup of what looked like coffee in between her hands, perhaps trying to absorb the heat from the hot drink. The steam rising from the cup momentarily fogged up the thick lenses in her spectacles every time she took a sip. Church ordered toast and coffee and they struck up a conversation that Church felt was stilted and uneasy on her part, but totally at ease on his. The café was warm and the staff were friendly. It was a city centre branch of a worldwide chain of coffee shops and as such the percolated brews on offer were standard but reliable. The table in their booth was immaculately clean and Church and Elsa were left quietly alone for the whole time that it took to drink their coffees.

It took Church a little while to realise that Elsa DeWinter was not drinking a standard brew of coffee as he had ordered. The aroma of something very different was drifting across the table. The cinnamon flavour reminded Church of long ago Christmases spent with an aunt somewhere in Hampshire. The aunt, who was, in fact, a great aunt, used to brew her own herbal drinks and had concocted a winter infusion of cinnamon, cloves, hibiscus, rosehip, apple, ginger and plum. It looked a strange brown colour and so she had added a little beetroot juice to turn it a rich deep red hue. Strange how smells can transport you back in time to another place altogether.

'What made you put in for a transfer to the UK?' Church asked by way of an opening sentence.

'There was an incident in Rotterdam,' she said circumspectly. 'And the best way to follow it up was to apply for a temporary posting to England.'

'Have you been in the police force for long?'

'A short number of years compared to many of my colleagues.'

An answer that anyone could say of any profession thought Church to himself. Trying to change tack, he asked, 'Do you think that we might work together temporarily? It does seem that our paths have crossed in this case. A drugs investigation for you and a possible missing person for me.'

'I can see no problem with us cooperating for a short while, Mr Church.'

'Look here, Miss DeWinter, it is Miss I take it?' added Church. 'Why don't we just take a look at young Mr Hookamn's flat together? I will send his mobile phone to London to see if anything useful can be lifted from it and promise to share whatever I find with you. Does that sound like a start?'

'Yes, that would be helpful, thank you,' she seemed to relax a little, taking a long sip of her coffee before adding. 'I have not enjoyed my time in Manchester very much. I miss my home and my family in Amsterdam. I have difficulty understanding what is being said to me here.'

'I thought that you said you worked in Rotterdam?' asked Church.

'My family live near Amsterdam in a city called Haarlem. Your colleagues in England seem to find the name funny.'

'Not my colleagues, I'm afraid. But carry on.'

'The drive to Rotterdam is less than one hour, the roads are very good, very flat, very fast. The centre of this city is level but the suburbs are all hills.'

Church had fleetingly visited Amsterdam on a few occasions but knew little of the rest of the country. They talked for a few more minutes before their hot drinks and Church's toast had been consumed.

'Shall we go?' asked Church.

'I would like to show you around Holland if you are ever in the country in the future, Mr Church,' she said hastily.

It was the sort of offer that is made in a thousand conversations between people but never acted upon. In many cases, it is an insincere offer. Even if made genuinely, life, events and any other of a hundred issues get in the way. Church suspected that in this instance it might actually happen at some point.

'Do you mind if we stop off at a clothes shop on the way to Hookman's flat, Elsa? I seem to require a new suit.' She hesitated for a moment but smiled when Church stuck his fingers through the back of his jacket. 'Criminal damage.'

Apart from its vibrant contemporary music scene, Manchester is the ideal place to shop and eat. Someone wrote a guide entitled *'Around the World in 80 Days and 80 Meals'*. It listed all of the different world cuisines that could be found in a small three-mile radius of the city centre. Manchester is also the ideal place for those who love to shop. A Mecca for consumerism.

Elsa DeWinter waited patiently for thirty minutes in one department store while Church tried on a selection of suits. None of them appealed to Church, they seemed too fitted, the cut of the trousers too narrow and the material too thin to withstand much use. After thirty minutes in another, she lost patience and wandered off to another floor of the vast shop. She returned once her boredom had waned, carrying a large branded bag of purchases. Church was not sure what was inside but the container looked reasonably heavy.

Chapter Twelve

Shopping

The Northern Quarter of Manchester City centre is almost entirely given over to shops, cafes and restaurants. The enormous glass-fronted main shopping centre occupies a huge area bordered by the wide and straight Market Street, High Street and Corporation Street; and the gentle curve of Shudehill. The old town centre, where the rivers Irwell and Irk confluence, is long lost underneath Manchester Victoria railway station, but some of the original street patterns from the middle ages remain. The sweeping bends of Shudehill confirm its medieval history amongst the wide mid-Victorian roads nearby.

The main thoroughfare inside the shopping complex is wide enough for two lanes of traffic. However, it is entirely lined with pale cream marble tiles worn smooth by the feet of countless pedestrian shoppers. Church liked shopping but even he was relieved to step outside the busy conglomeration of shops. A short walk to the West brings you into the tangle of lanes and narrow roads such as Tib Street, Warwick Street or Spear Street. Many of these medieval streets end abruptly when they meet the fringe of the main ring road to the North-West which cut through most of these narrow alleys when it was constructed.

Hidden amongst an assortment of retail and food outlets is the quaintly named *Apps & Sons Gentlemans' outfitters and hatters*. The shop may have been amongst the last of the independent, family-run clothing businesses, in the city. The gold lettering on a glossy black background must have been overpainted numerous times over the years. The typeface font was a very traditional

Times New Roman. The windows were still wooden frames, with curved corners and intricate leaded light panels which ran across the whole shop front, underneath the sign. It sits on the corner of the road, at the end of a small row of shops. A beacon of fashion with six plate glass windows displaying suits, jackets and trousers that many younger Mancunians would not even pause to glance at if they walked past. They might look into the shoe shop next door that is owned by the same family. That establishment has some of the most sought after footwear concessions in the city, brands not found in the high street shopping centre. They would carry on walking past and perhaps pay more attention to the fish and chip shop, hairdressers, tattoo parlour, speciality butchers shop or the open all hours convenience store. But few would enter the clothes shop.

As Church walked in, a bell tinkled above the door to welcome them inside. He could sense Elsa DeWinter sighing beside him as they stepped inside. The elderly owner, presumedly Mr Apps himself, bade them a 'good afternoon' and rang a bell on the counter. Church returned the greeting, but Elsa remained silent. A dog lifted its head from where he had been asleep on the floor beside the shop counter, the chocolate brown Labrador eyed the new customers suspiciously for a few seconds then settled back down to sleep. Boxes of all shapes and sizes and in an assortment of colours lined the back of the counter. Church could make out the labels on a few of them and it confirmed his suspicion that this was indeed a very traditional outfitter. Cartons and containers spilt over themselves containing cummerbunds, cravats, braces, bow ties and even replacement starched collars. A huge run of hanging rails stretched either side of the worktop behind which the old man sat. One side contained jackets, trousers, waistcoats, evening jackets, dinner jackets and tuxedos. The other housed less formal lounge suits.

Church gravitated towards them. A small section was devoted to sale items. Odd sized suits that would not fit a man of standard proportions. Church thought that the very short Hookman might have picked up something that fitted him better in this shop. Hookman's jacket had been much too long for the short stature of his body size.

Eventually, a very young male assistant wandered over. The younger man was dressed in a tight-fitting fashionable suit, similar to the ones Church himself had tried on in the previous shops. He wondered if the shop could have been renamed Apps & Grandson, but decided that it was best not to presume. Elsa found a comfortable looking chair and settled in for what she might have thought was a long wait.

However, fifteen minutes later Church was standing by the till and the elderly Mr Apps tilled up Church's purchase. A brief verbal tussle had added an extra five minutes to his time in the shop when the younger sales assistant had insisted that Church try on a forty-inch, long, suit jacket. Church had insisted on a forty-two, regular, but had acquiesced simply to appease the younger man's assertion. The other choice was a low price sale rail item, a size that was probably hard to shift in a shop with few customers. Unfortunately, the sales assistant had taken a shine to the slim longer fit of the suit and as much as Church protested the more the assistant contended that the style was much better suited to Church physique. He even looked over to Elsa pleading, imploring her to back him up, but she just sat in the chair looking at the screen of her phone. Her blank eyes magnified by the lenses in her glasses gave nothing away.

'This suit is so much less expensive than the full-priced forty-two inch one,' he pleaded to Church. 'I could even ask if a little more could be taken off of the price of this one?'

'No. Thanks all the same.'

'But it fits you very well.'
'I'll take the full-priced suit.'
Whatever happened to the phrase, 'the customer is always right', thought Church to himself.

As Church and Elsa stepped back onto the narrow streets, they were both clutching bags full of clothing. Her's was unknown to Church. His was an expensive, full-priced, mid grey, old stock, Austin Reed single-breasted suit with twin rear vents in a heavy 100% wool. Not a good use of taxpayers money. Their route led them to briefly rejoin the Rochdale Canal towpath. They could have been any young couple walking home after an afternoon at the shops. Loaded with shopping bags and looking forward to getting indoors out of the late afternoon chill.

The towpath was wide and they could easily walk side-by-side until they came to a tunnel underneath a road bridge. There the path narrowed and they had to walk single file. Street lights were coming on as they strolled farther out of town. Church was pleased to be walking because it kept the chill away, he wondered if Elsa was feeling cold. She was certainly frosty enough at the best of times but Church had recently detected a thaw. They marched on along the walkway.

Canals, by their very nature, run more or less level. Any gradient has to be overcome by a cutting, an embankment, a series of lock gates or even a viaduct. The water in a canal does not flow like a river but lays still until a lock is opened. Then the water flows out quickly and is replenished from farther upstream. The lock closes and the water is still again. Rubbish does not flow downstream but collects in small piles. Groups of plastic bottles, bags and other detritus floated in the waterway. Locks were few and far between on this stretch of the Rochdale Canal. The ones that they passed on their journey out of town looked to be poorly maintained, at odds with the beautifully refurbished gates in the city centre. Many of the centrally located ones had been completely replaced. Here the pavement was a mix of potholed tarmac, original cobbles, paving slabs and patches of concrete. Some bridges over the canal were low and they had to detour back up a slope to cross the road. Low-level housing estates stretched either side. A high red brick wall stretched for great sections of the length of the waterway. Sections had been covered in graffiti. How had they managed to get across the water to spray the wall, thought Church? The letters spelt out gang names or initials, some had been overpainted to show where one gang had taken over the area of another. Endless letters had been repeated at length across a section of the wall, only to be almost entirely obliterated by another set of initials. Eventually, the gang members would grow older, they would either spend time in prison or end up being killed by a rival group. Many would ultimately grow up, meet someone and perhaps start a family. They might get a house in one of the estates on the other side of the green space that lined the canal. Other youngsters would come along and paint letters on this stretch of brickwork.

'No similarity to the canals in Amsterdam, Elsa?' asked Church.

'None at all,' she replied flatly.

The block of flats that Hookman lived in came into view. Church glanced down at a bench set into blocks of concrete framed by a low metal fence. Two bunches of flowers had been tied to the corners with little pieces of ribbon. One bunch was long dead. They had transformed into an arrangement of dried flowers. The other bunch, although fresher, had begun to wilt in its little cellophane bag. Just beyond the bench, a burnt-out car sat at an awkward angle on a patch of grass. Two tyres had deflated as the vehicle burnt and the only intact window was on the rear passenger side.

Elsa DeWinter fished around in her bag and retrieved a set of keys. They walked up the flight of steps to Hookman's flat and let themselves in through the recently repaired front door. A hole in the plastic door panel had been temporarily fixed with a panel of plywood. The repair reminded Church of the badly maintained block of flats he visited with Tomas Kar. He hoped that the door would eventually be replaced, but he doubted it. The police assault and subsequent patch-up would probably remain for quite some time, adding to the general decay of a once appealing estate gone to ruin.

'Where shall we start? What exactly are you looking for?' asked Elsa.

Somebody once told Church that fear makes a mockery of memory. But as he stood in the large front room of the flat, every detail of the events of the previous night came back to him. Hookman stuffing his face with a bag of popcorn. Malcolm sitting in his brightly coloured tracksuit on the oversized sofa. The large picture window with the broken blind. Now, it was late afternoon and his reflection in the window was less clear than it was the previous night; when he had watched the scene played out in the reflection in the glass.

'We'll start in here and work through each of the rooms in turn. I'm not really sure what we are looking for. Perhaps a trace of the missing girl I'm searching for, perhaps something that will lead us to where she might be?'

'Do you have latex gloves with you, Mr Church?'

'Not as a rule.'

'Here, put these on.' She tossed a pair of pale blue thin rubber gloves towards Church. He struggled to get them onto his hands. 'Unfortunately, they are my size,' she added with a smile.

They picked through Hookman's collection of computer games. The console that had been precariously balanced, fell off of its perch. Church carefully rebalanced it. Elsa wandered off into another room but he carried on working his way methodically around the lounge. He looked at the pictures on the wall. 'Artistic Glamour' might best describe them. But the sunlight had faded them and the women were ghostly apparitions with yellow faces. A reproduction cinema poster advertising the latest spy thriller was tacked to another wall. Church moved his attention to the oversized sofa, gingerly he lifted each of the seat cushions of the large seats. Under the fourth one, he discovered a roll of banknotes neatly kept together by a rubber band. Carefully rooting around under the seat he found other notes bundled together. Instead of leaving them in situ, he piled them up on a small table and continued to work his way around the room.

Church made his way to the bathroom. A collection of bottles, tubs and tubes filled a small shelf. Some of which might eventually end up floating in the canal outside. The small shelf had six bottles of shampoo, four bottles of shower gel and two of bubble bath. Why, thought Church to himself, does someone not use up a bottle of shampoo before opening another one? Empty cardboard toilet roll tubes were neatly stacked along a glass bathroom shelf. Church casually picked one up. It was heavy, too heavy. He held it up to his eye and looked through the hollow tube. Except that it was not hollow. The cardboard roll had been stuffed with banknotes rolled up in a similar way to those under the sofa cushion.

As he peered at the toilet roll tube, Elsa DeWinter appeared in the bathroom doorway.

'What do you make of these?' she asked, holding up a pair of women's knickers, a tiny lace triangle held together by some elasticated silk ribbon.

'I don't think that style suits our friend Hookman and they certainly don't fit Malcolm,' replied Church.

'Or this,' she added, holding up a matching bra, material as fine as gossamer. 'In fact, there is a collection of female clothing in amongst a pile of dirty laundry in a bedroom. Let me show you.'

Church followed her to the doorway of a large bedroom. The curtains were drawn but a soft glow of light was coming from table lamps dotted around the room. A large mirrored wardrobe ran along one side of a wall, the kingsized bed was sited along another and the third wall housed a large window with roller blind pulled down and a row of three chests of drawers.

The room was strangely gender-neutral. At odds with the rest of the flat. Church would have expected a gaudy, tacky, silk duvet cover. Masculine furniture and male choice accessories. But it was obviously the only bedroom in the flat and it was surprisingly well furnished.

Church looked into the only other doorway and observed a collected jumble of domestic detritus. An exercise bike and running machine, an old stereo HiFi with huge loudspeakers, another television screen, an old PC computer and bags and bags of old clothes. Hookman has never heard of Charity shops observed Church.

He stepped into the bedroom and made his way around to the left side of the large bed. Why is it, thought Church to himself, that men almost always sleep on the right-hand side of a bed? A collection of clothing had been laid out on the bedspread. Small t-shirts, short skirts, jeans so tight that looked as if Malcolm would have struggled to fit one leg in the material used to make the pair. He reached around and opened the top drawer of a bedside cabinet. It was crammed full of more rolled-up banknotes, designer watches, gold chains and other expensive trinkets. DeWinter let out a whistle.

'Whoooo. I would like to find that stuff in my bedside drawer.'

'It certainly beats a Gideon bible,' said Church.

DeWinter reached round to the other side of the bed and opened the top drawer of that cabinet. She pulled out a bottle of women's perfume and squirted a fine mist into the air.

'This stuff is expensive too,' she added.

The fruity perfume of citrus lemon as well as the bitter orange of Neroli filled the air. The expensive rich aroma of vanilla rounded off the fragrance from the bedside cabinet but there were other notes of the perfume that Church recognised immediately. Aromas are powerful memory aids. He was instantly taken back to the bedroom in Claverton Hall. To the search through the private belongings of Amber Garland.

Chapter Thirteen

Dinner

'Could these be her belongings?' asked DeWinter as she showed Church the clothes laid out on the bedcovers in Hookman's flat.
'Maybe?' said Church. 'I don't know her dress size or fashion sense. Although I recognise the perfume.'
'It is expensive but quite popular.'
'I think that we need to ask Mr Hookman a few more questions.'
'We?' asked DeWinter archly as she tidied away the clothes back to where they came from.
'Perhaps just you then, Elsa.'
'Let me finish up and then let's get out of here.'
Church left her in the bedroom, replacing items and rearranging things as best as she could to make it seem like they had not been in the room. He did the same in the bathroom except that every other roll of money was pocketed by Church. By the time he had finished in the front room; replacing rolls of cash in a similar one for you-one for me manner, his pockets were bulging. He found his large bag containing his new suit and quickly stuffed several thousand pounds worth of notes underneath it. 'Waste not, want not' as someone might say.
As they left the flat and walked down the concrete stairs out onto street level, the bag bumped with a reassuring solid weight against Church's leg. It was dark as they made their way back towards the city centre. The working day had long since ended and evening had turned into night-time. A group of ten or so youngsters had

congregated on a grass space next to the canal. Elsa DeWinter took Church's arm as they approached. The sweet, grassy smell of smoked cannabis wafted in the air as they got closer. Some of the youths were occupied with the burnt-out car, others were sat on the bench. Church remembered the half-dead bunches of flowers tied to the side of the seat.

One of the teenagers looked over to Church and DeWinter as they walked past.

'Nice car,' said Church. 'But it will need a couple of new tyres, a windscreen and a paint job tomorrow.'

The teenager sniggered. It set off his friends sitting on the bench laughing as well.

Elsa clutched his arm tighter as they walked on. But even though he had a carrier bag full of banknotes, Church appeared as calm as a millpond. As calm as the stagnant water that drifted slowly down the canal that now flowed beside them.

'Are you hungry, Edward?'

'Now that you mention it. I'm famished,' he replied. 'Do you know somewhere nice to eat?'

'My hotel has a good restaurant, we could eat there.'

'It's probably better than the eatery in my hotel.'

'Come quickly, step it out,' said Elsa and she squeezed his arm tightly. 'I am freezing.'

The Manchester Metropole hotel is one of the original grand late eighteenth century hotels in the city centre. Extended and re-modelled in Victorian times, it fell into disrepair but was saved from demolition by local pressure groups and the city's preservation society. The preservationists had plans for a community space and artisan workshops but at the last minute, the whole site was purchased by a foreign sovereign investment fund. The hotel was boarded up for a decade but when it was uncovered, like a butterfly emerging from a chrysalis, a beautifully restored and state of the art late Regency masterpiece was re-introduced to the city.

As they stepped into the lobby, Church immediately fell in love with the place. The high ceiling was dominated by a large chandelier that twinkled invitingly above them. The walls were painted in panels of cream and duck-egg blue. Row upon row of sconce wall lights added even more illumination to the interior space. As they walked past the reception desk, Church realised that the building was laid out as a wide four-storey frontage with wings that stretched back, down each side of the building. The centre was a single storey area that had been split into bars, restaurants, a tea lounge and a wide spacious palm court. This palm court was built as a huge Orangery, with a vaulted glass panel ceiling.

'Would you wait here a few moments while I freshen up?' she asked.

The previously frosty DeWinter appeared to have thawed a little more. Church looked around for an empty table and settled himself in for a long wait. His past experience suggested that a wait of a few minutes would be considerably longer. A member of the waiting staff appeared and he ordered drinks which swiftly appeared. Church slowly scanned the room, languorously observing his fellow diners. His gaze fell from one table to the next, pausing for a moment before moving on to the next group of guests.

A family group caught his attention for a moment. The wife was rather loud, rather tall and barely paused for breath as she spoke at length to her husband and a younger man, who Church presumed was their son. The husband never spoke but was dressed in a brightly-patterned festive shirt. The son nodded every now and then and chipped in a few words when he could. The younger man's clothes seemed at odds with the formal surroundings of the dining room. Torn jeans and a baggy out of shape tee-shirt. He had shaved all of the hair from his head but had a wispy beard that he stroked every now and then. His face reminded Church of old portrait photographs of Victorian Doctors or Professors that lined the walls of the Library at his university. Church doubted very much that a younger version of the bald, bearded Professors was the look the young man was hoping to achieve. More likely he was aiming for the image of a rock star, or a guitar player in a heavy metal band.

His attention swiftly moved on to another table of guests. A much bigger group of around twelve or so seated around a large circular table in the middle of the palm court. They seemed to be equal numbers of young men and women. Church thought that he recognised one or two of the people. Were they football players, actors, musicians? He could not be sure. It can be odd to see people outside of their normal surroundings, disconcerting to see people who you might be used to seeing on the television but that are actually sitting at a table opposite you eating dinner. One of the women constantly fiddled with her dress. It fitted badly and she seemed acutely aware that it gaped open each time she leant forward to eat. Her companion, a young man dressed in a shirt too tight for his frame, pushed her hand away each time she adjusted a strap of the fabric. The woman was clearly annoyed by this, but the man seemed oblivious. Presently, the man's attention was distracted by something and she could finally fit herself back into her dress.

It was then that Church felt disconcerted for the second time. The man had been distracted by the sight of Elsa DeWinter walking through the middle of the palm court dressed in the outfit she must have bought early that afternoon. The thick glasses were held in her hand, her hair glowed in choppy waves of honey blond and she was dressed in an amazing figure-hugging burgundy dress. It fitted her beautifully, draped low to the floor, but with a deep slash high up her leg.

'That's quite a transformation, Elsa,' Church said as he got to his feet. A waiter appeared from nowhere and pulled out her chair before Church had a chance to step around the table. 'You look stunning.'

'Thank you, Edward. I wanted to show that you are not the only one who can dress well.'

'You've certainly made your point. And it seems to me that quite a few of the men in here agree. They can hardly take their eyes off of you.'

'It is just as well that I am not interested in them. Shall we order? What do you think looks good,' she paused and added, 'from the menu.'

They both examined their menus and Church was pleased to see on offer a wide range of food influences from around the world. They settled on ordering Italian food. Elsa chose to start with *Caponata*, an aubergine based dish that also contains pine nuts and raisins as well as celery, red onions tomatoes olives and capers. The chef had decided to add mussels and shrimps to his version of the recipe. Church was not particularly keen on seafood and decided to play it safe with a *pasta alla norma*. Another aubergine based dish. This meal adds lashings of tomatoes, basil and salted ricotta. Elsa said that she would choose the wine and spent a long time studying the list before announcing that they would drink *Chianti* with their meal.

'I think that Chianti red wine will go nicely with our food,' she said.

Church might have searched for a *Novella* on the wine list to keep in with the Sicilian theme of the meal, but he was certainly not going to be a food or wine snob tonight. When it arrived, the dinner was delicious. The wine was drinkable, the surroundings exquisite and his dinner companion was beautiful. Elsa had transformed from a serious work colleague into something altogether different. She still wore her glasses when they ate and her eyes looked even bigger than they had earlier on that day. The dress showed off a previously hidden figure that was slim, rounded and firm. Her make-up looked natural and her hair, freshly brushed, glowed in the light of the dining room. For Church, the most amazing thing about the whole transformation in her appearance was that it took less than thirty minutes. They chatted easily, moving from the topic of the missing girl to other related issues before going off on conversational tangents as is wont on a long evening in each other's company.

'So do you think that your missing girl might have been at the flat, Edward?' she asked again.

'The facts are flimsy. Some women's clothing and the same perfume that she wears. But as a hunch or a feeling, I would say that it's worth finding out about a little more. And to be perfectly honest, it is the only thing that gets even close to a lead on finding her that I've come across in the past few days of asking around. I can't stay here looking for Amber Garland indefinitely, I would be told that it is not a good use of taxpayers money.'

'Do you like it in Manchester? I am looking forward to getting home in a few days.'

'It's nice enough. The people are friendly and the city has a life of its own,' replied Church honestly.

'I do not like the people. Apart from you, Edward. My colleagues are not kind. I think that it has put me off enjoying the city.'

'You might be right. I remember being taken here as a child. We were to meet some distant cousins in one of the big houses nearby, Hopwood Hall. But they were not particularly friendly and I was pleased to get home.'

'Oh, I have not visited there. A shame because I have spent most of my spare time going to see the local attractions. We could have gone, but I have no more time off before I leave.'

Church did not explain that he had stayed in a private capacity and that his family were related to the then owners. He briefly recalled running along a long ditch with a slope on one side and a retaining wall on the other. It snaked along a great length of the grounds. An aunt explained that it was called a *Ha-Ha* and was meant to keep sheep and livestock out of the pleasure garden without spoiling the view with fences, walls or other barriers. Apparently, her second husband had wandered off one day after several drinks, and fallen into the ditch. Not noticing the long drop from the top of the wall he had died of his injuries. As a child, Church did not think that it was funny at all and could not fathom where the name *ha-ha* came from.

A commotion at another table in the palm court restaurant interrupted his train of thought. The woman in the poorly fitting dress had jumped up and was shouting at her dinner companion, in the ensuing hullabaloo a bottle of wine was toppled and fell to the floor with a crash. The woman turned and with one last adjustment of her outfit, stormed out of the dining room. Church could not be sure, but he suspected that Elsa was more interested in the footballer's wife than in the football player.

'What do you miss most about your home town in Rotterdam?'

'My home is in Amsterdam. My work is in Rotterdam, Edward.'

'Sorry, Elsa, I forgot. What do you miss most about Amsterdam?'

'I miss my home, my friends, my cats. I have two cats, but we are trying to start a family as well. Children love pets. And I miss my wife. Does that shock you ?'

'Starting a family does not shock me at all, Elsa,' replied Church.

It would have taken something a great deal more surprising than her statement to shock Edward Church, although he felt slightly foolish for misreading her friendly signals as flirtation. Even if he had been surprised by something she had said, he certainly would not have shown it.

Chapter Fourteen

A good use of taxpayers money

In the palm court restaurant of the Manchester Metropole, food was consumed by Church and Elsa DeWinter and cleared away swiftly by the ever-attentive waiting staff. Church was disappointed with the desert that she insisted on ordering. The Gelato was actually Ice Cream. Much colder, much lighter and more whipped than traditional Italian ice cream, it also tasted fattier and coated the inside of Church's mouth with an unpleasant film. He was pleased to receive a complimentary shot glass of Lemoncello because it stripped away the layer of creamy film that coated the inside of his mouth.

At her insistence, once again, they had moved on to the crystal bar for after-dinner coffee and drinks. Unlike the rest of the hotel, the crystal bar had been refurbished in a 1920s style. Mirrors covered much of the available surface area, furniture was chrome and leather and the tables were topped by high-gloss black reflective glass. Elsa DeWinter sashayed through the room, expertly swerving between tables and chairs. She clearly looked to be comfortable in her surroundings and Church considered that evidently, the Dutch taxpayer is far more generous than those in the United Kingdom. As they sat, Elsa leant a hand on the tabletop leaving a clear hand-print. She must have hot hands considered Church, but his thought was interrupted by her asking if he liked drinking gin.

'I'd prefer a nice whisky if that's okay. They seem to have quite a selection.'

'Nonsense,' she shot back. 'They have a choice of eighty different gins here, one for every day around the world. There are only seventeen choices of whisky.'

'More than enough for me, but I'm fine with gin,' replied Church politely.

The drinks came and they were pleasantly, refreshingly, welcome. Her first choice of gin was bright and zesty. She raised her glass and Church took a sip, classic flavours of juniper, coriander and citrus complex leapt out and hit his taste buds. The good quality tonic had just the right level of bittersweetness, slightly acidic lemon and a hint of a herb that he could not quite place. The drink was served in a glass that was thick and heavy, it had been chilled and the copious amount of ice hardly melted as they sipped their drinks. A droplet of condensed water dripped from the outside of Elsa's glass and fell onto the table as she lifted her glass to drain it. It splashed onto the highly polished surface leaving the shape of a perfectly formed corona.

Elsa drank her gin and tonic as if she had a serious thirst to quench. After five or six glasses had been drained, Church struggled to keep pace with her. He gave up trying to match her pace of drinking when they reached double figures. At some point in the evening, the larger group from the circular table in the Palm court dining room came into the bar. Their language was getting even more colourful as the number of drinks they drank increased. Suddenly Elsa stood up.

'I need to go to bed,' she said.

Church stood out of politeness and the room swayed a little. She took a step towards him and hugged Church in a tight clinch. It was an embrace rather than a kiss. She held him for a moment and said, 'Thank you.' Then she walked expertly and skillfully between the tables and chairs, stepping past groups of people in the crystal bar. Church watched her meticulous progress until she disappeared through the wide double doors leading to and from the room, and then up a flight of stairs until she turned a corner and then she was gone.

* * *

Church sat on the end of his bed in his budget hotel close to the railway station in the middle of Manchester. He had decided to try and clear his head a little by walking back from Elsa's hotel, the Manchester Metropole. It was now very late at night, or early hours of the morning, depending on how time was viewed. While he waited for the little electric kettle to boil, Church tore open a small sachet of instant coffee. While he waited for the coffee to cool down, he took a shower. By the time he had finished the shower and the drink, he was ready for bed. Casually, he glanced over at his phone and saw that there were two messages.

A brief flicker of excitement was swiftly replaced by the dull ache of disappointment. He replayed the first message.

'Hello, Edward, it is Bernard Trueman here,' the distinctive voice of his chief was unmistakable. 'I am not sure how much progress you have made up there. Yet to receive an update. Unfortunately, there has been a development and you are required to return to London tomorrow morning.'

This was typical Sir Bernard Trueman, thought Church to himself. A message late at night telling him, Church, to return back to London without even so much as an explanation. The subtle disapproval in the old man's voice was easily recognised by Church. The man was unhappy that there had been no headway made in finding the missing girl.

Church was just about to play the next message when Sir Bernard Trueman continued to speak. 'I am sorry to say that Anthony Fairfax has been admitted to hospital having suffered an ischaemic stroke.'

He was not surprised. Fairfax looked to have been in a bad way when they met a few days ago at Claverton Hall in Stonebridge. You did not have to be a medical professional to see that the other man looked to have high blood pressure and raised cholesterol.

Church listened to the other message. The voice of Alexander Drake, the technical wizard at the Home Office, drifted out of the earpiece. Even though the other man was in his mid-thirties, his voice seemed to be stuck at that of a nineteen-year-old. It was as if he had breathed in a little helium so that his voice was pitched too high. Drake was obsessive-compulsive. Half maniac, half genius but totally driven and obsessive about any task he was given.

'Hello, Mr Church,' he said, formally and awkwardly which only added to the impression of a much younger person. 'Thank you for the package that you sent me the other day. It arrived safely and I have had a quick look over it. It is a nice mobile phone but the security passcode took me seconds to crack. Why is it that people are so predictable? I did not even get on to birth date, month, day combinations or local area landline codes. The password was a date of birth. Entered backwards. Stunning security!'

Church smiled to himself as he listened. He could imagine Drake being disappointed that the code was not harder to crack. The man certainly liked a challenge. He continued listening to the message.

'I will have more information in a day or so if you would like to give me a ring. Or you can always find me in the usual place at lunchtime.'

Church quickly checked the times for the first train down from Manchester to London, Euston. He set an alarm for two hours time and tried to get some sleep. As his head hit the pillow, Church replayed events of the evening back over in his mind. The shopping trip, the search of Hookman's flat, the discovery of a large amount of money and the meal with Esa DeWinter in her hotel. As the image of Elsa sashaying out of the crystal bar flashed into his head, the alarm went off.

Bleary-eyed and slightly hungover, he packed his few belongings and made a quick exit from the hotel. He made the short walk to the station in less time than it would have taken to hail, ride and pay off a taxi. Not that any were around at this early hour. It was a crisp, chilly start to the day. Clear skies overnight had permitted a ground frost to settle across the city. Clouds of hot breath streamed from his nostrils as he stepped smartly up to the railway station. There is something very eerie about a busy metropolis that is virtually empty. Church hardly saw another soul as he walked along pavements that had once been bustling with people. No cars passed by and it was too early for the city's tram system to start to run.

The stillness and the peace ended as he entered the train station. Brightly lit, busy with early morning commuters catching the first trains to Liverpool, Sheffield or Leeds. Or in Church's case, the first train to London. He grabbed a paper and was offered a free paperback novel as a seasonal promotion by the newspaper publishers when he went to pay. He hurriedly chose a John Buchan novel, partly because it involved a train journey but also because he had read all of the other novels on offer.

The book was swiftly forgotten as he settled into his seat. He skimmed the newspaper headlines but almost immediately his eyes felt heavy and his head soon began to droop downwards. Church was asleep before the locomotive passed through Stockport.

* * *

It was just after 7am when the train pulled into London Euston. Church stretched his legs and stiffly walked down the platform, through the ticket barriers and out into the capital. He crossed over an unusually quiet Euston Road, then dog legged his way through Fitzrovia and Mayfair. By the time he skirted Wellington Arch and the back of Buckingham Palace gardens, he was feeling brighter. In Belgravia, he walked briskly past the Embassies of several countries. Flags fluttered gently above doorways in the early morning breeze. The flag of the Kingdom of Norway looked a little tattered, but the marble panels on either side of the doorway had been freshly washed. The Embassy of Bahrain looked immaculate as usual. The wrought iron security gates over the doors were still firmly in place at this time of the morning. He made it back to his apartment in an hour, unpacked his bags and settled down to finish the newspaper just as the sun rose above the city. He considered that it was good to be home. He also considered that the walk back had saved a taxi fare and was most definitely a good use of taxpayers money.

Somebody had told Church that they had watched every film in a long-running series of blockbuster movies and never once saw the lead character do a load of washing or clean his kitchen. The depiction of domestic chores in books, on television or at the cinema is nearly always overlooked. Probably, remarked Church to his friend who recounted the story, because they are incredibly dull, boring and monotonous. Church was still thinking about this as he queued up at the checkout till in Waitrose supermarket in The Kings Road. His basket was half full of only essential items. There was no point in buying too much food and then having to throw it away when it goes out of date or mouldy.

More thoughts of being thrifty went through Church's mind as he dropped off his suit to be cleaned and repaired.

The elderly man behind the counter smiled in greeting as Church walked into the shop. The aroma of chemicals wafted around the shop. It was mixed with a steamy warmth and the sound of presses hissing or machines being operated somewhere in the back rooms.

'Oh dear, Mr Church,' the old man exclaimed politely as he poked his fingers through the holes left by the police taser. 'Some repairs to your jacket are needed from my wife.'

'Yes, sorry about that,' replied Church.

'There is no need to apologise, sir. We will return it to you as soon as possible. Shall we say three weeks next Tuesday?'

Church considered that returning it on that day would be unlikely as it would be Christmas Eve, but he thanked the man and left the shop with one less bag than he had entered it. On a whim, he decided to hail a taxi to the Old Admiralty Building to purloin a lunch in the canteen. Still one of the best meals you can find in a London staff canteen outside of a military regimental headquarters. As he had expected, Church spied Alexander Drake sitting alone at one of the tables in front of a tall window overlooking Horse Guards.

'Hi Edward,' said Alexander Drake as he lifted a hand and waved towards Church.

'Hello Alex, same lunch as usual?' asked Church. 'Can you tell me anything about that mobile phone I passed to you?'

'I certainly can, Edward. The security PIN was a joke, took me a few minutes to work my way through the hundred or so obvious options that it could have been. But then it got a little bit interesting.'

Chapter Fifteen

Things get a little more interesting

Edward Church sat in the staff canteen of the Old Admiralty Building listening to Alexander Drake, the technical specialist from the Home Office. Drake explained how he had tried a few dozen variations of a passcode to guess the security PIN protecting the mobile phone that belonged to Hookman. Church explained how he had grabbed the phone just before being tasered and arrested by the police in Manchester. Drake found that highly amusing, his high-pitched voice going even higher when he laughed.

'Why did you not hand the phone to the police when you were arrested?' he asked.

'It's a long story, Alex. What can you tell me about the phone?'

'Well, I had a good look through the image files, video files and even his music files. Are these photographs of your missing girl?'

He passed some printed images to Church who quickly flicked through them.

'I'm not entirely sure about some of these. They don't really show her face very clearly,' replied Church.

'No, but the fellow obviously knew her quite well. Strange taste in music too. I looked through all of his social media apps, recent messages, chat, et cetera, et cetera. His recent telephone calls were rather interesting,' Alexander Drake said.

Drake paused as if he was expecting Edward to say something, but Church just raised his eyebrows a little to try and encourage the other man to continue.

'So, he appears to send a lot of phone messages. Rather short, none more than a few characters, and to a lot of different numbers. Which is rather strange don't you think? I mean, I make a lot of telephone calls but they are to a few people. Actually, they are usually to only one person, but that might just be me.'

'Hookman did not strike me as the sort of person to have a wide circle of friends. But he is dealing in drugs which might explain the telephone calls?'

'No, no, no. Nobody would actually speak to someone about a drug deal. Messages would be sent via an encrypted messaging system. Interestingly, there was none of these installed on the phone.'

'Is that your interesting point?' asked Church impatiently. He was beginning to feel exasperated.

'Well, there are two interesting points really. One is that the performance is very poor for a top of the range smartphone. There is hardly any memory left, even though there should be and the processor is overworked, even though there are not many apps and programs running.'

'And the other interesting point?'

'All of those phone messages to different numbers were actually sent to one other device. And that device was always in the same location.'

Drake paused again but Church did not quite understand what the other man actually meant.

'So do you mean he made a lot of phone calls to people at the same location? Like a football stadium or something?'

'Even better than that, Edward. The phone calls were made to the same domestic address. I used Global Positioning Systems to precisely locate the destination of the calls being made. The GPS system is a bunch of navigation satellites orbiting the earth. Did you know the satellites were launched by the United States Government in the 1980s and 1990s? And due to the historic special relationship between our two countries, we have access to the data they receive.'

Church did know that a great deal of information was shared between the United States and the United Kingdom, but he did not like to interrupt Drake.

'Can you pinpoint the address?' he asked instead.

'Of course, I can.' Drake replied, sounding a little hurt by the question of any doubt in his abilities. 'Number twenty-seven Withinlee Drive, Wilmsbury. Which is located approximately thirty miles South-West of Manchester. It is the home of Godfrey and Maureen Timson.'

* * *

Church left Alexander Drake to finish his lunch in peace and made his way back to his apartment in Chelsea. Looking around the place, and having little to do before he travelled to the Hospital to visit Anthony Fairfax later that evening, he decided to carry on the domestic chores and vacuum the flat. Ever since his time at university, Church had been happy undertaking housekeeping tasks.

He dragged out his ancient vacuum cleaner from the press in the hall. The large cupboard just next to the kitchen door, where all useful items are stored, had always been referred to as the press by his mother. Access to it was via a set of double doors, floor to ceiling, cupboard space within was crammed with boxes on shelves, essential household items, suitcases, sports equipment. It was also the hiding place of a great many items that, if Church was honest with himself, should really have been disposed of.

The smallest bedroom in Church's apartment had been given over to a study come library arrangement. Not being one to have lots of guests to stay overnight, several years ago he had fitted the room out with sets of shelves, a medium-sized office desk and a chair. The room had a small window with not much of a view and by this opening, he had placed a comfy but worn-out armchair. At some point in its history, it had been a recliner chair with a button that opened up a footrest and tilted back the seat using a concealed mechanism. He thought that the mechanism had stopped working years ago. As Church started to vacuum the item of furniture with the cleaner, the chair opened up with a muffled snap.

The vacuum cleaner immediately stopped working. Blocked up with some unknown item that had been sucked partway up the flexible tube. As Church fished out the offending article from the cleaner, he spied an old mobile telephone wedged down between the armrest and seat of the chair. His attention now turned to the phone. He dropped the vacuum cleaner and picked up the old telephone. It was a dated model from quite a few years ago. Church was not even sure when he had lost it, or if it was even one of his telephones. The charge had long since run out and he squinted at the small screen which stared blankly back at him.

Much later that day, with all thoughts of housework and old technology lost down the side of a chair put to the back of his mind, Church made his way to the enormous hospital complex that is Guys and St Thomas'. There is something quiet, peaceful and almost otherworldly about a hospital late in the day when many of the staff have gone home and there is just a skeleton staff keeping patients comfortable during the night. Church walked down empty corridors and past reception desks that had been closed for the night. He knew the location of the private ward he was looking for. Church had visited several relatives in this hospital over the past few years. Hospitals throughout the world have the same clinical, sterile, smell. An aroma of antiseptic cleanliness that gently stings the nostrils as you inhale. His shoes squeaked on the highly polished linoleum floor as Church walked along the corridor. The lighting was harsh, bright and equally clinical. Rows of Light Emitting Diode lamps illuminated the space. Large windows were now canvases of black, the glow of a thousand other buildings at night-time could not compete against the ceiling lights in this hospital.

Eventually, Church navigated his way to the Cardiac Care Unit. Within that unit, he looked at the list of names on the large wipe-clean board behind an empty reception desk and found the correct ward. Once inside that ward, he made his way to the suite of private rooms and, checking the names written on panels outside each door, he found the hospital bed containing Anthony Fairfax.

The room was spacious and contained one bed and two chairs. But an array of equipment filled all of the available space. Screens showed readouts of various signals, wires were connected to other pieces of equipment. Tubes feeding oxygen, fluids and other medication ran from yet more apparatus into the body of Anthony Fairfax. One or more of these pieces of equipment emitted the sound of a beep every few seconds. A pump somewhere in the background would whir and hiss at the correct moment, humming and purring in reassuring contentment.

In the chair next to the bed at the far side of the room, sat Sir Bernard Trueman. His chief, superior, and director of the department at the Cabinet Office that employed Church. The older man was wearing full, white-tie, evening dress. The evening tailcoat jacket had a slightly harsh line that cut back towards the body. The waistcoat was white, of course, and cut low to show off the pleated shirt. The shirt itself, with single cuffs and wing collar, was fastened at the wrist by simple mother of pearl cufflinks. The trousers were high-waisted with double braid stripes and seemed to Church, to be rather too tight for Trueman's expanding girth. The bowtie, white once again, of course, was immaculately hand-tied. Although

Church could not see from around his side of the bed, he knew that the old man would be wearing a pair of black patent leather shoes.

'If I had known that this was such a formal occasion, sir,' said Church in a greeting to the old man.

'No need for any of your impudence, young man,' replied Trueman. ' I just so happen to be on my way to an important function later tonight.'

'I thought that it was a bit overdressed for a hospital visit, sir.'

'If you must know, Edward, I am on my way to the opera. *La grotta di Trofonio* by Giovanni Paisiello. Lady Trueman suggested it, perhaps because the characters in the story are even more miserable than she is.'

Church was not an opera fan. He knew one or two of the more well-known compositions and had been to the London Coliseum and Royal Opera House in Covent Garden on two or three occasions. He had been more preoccupied with the company he was with than with the story. Instead, he offered an update of his enquiries around Manchester and the contents of the mobile telephone that Church had lifted from Hookman.

'I traced one of her friends, a student who has dropped out of his studies and now tries to deal street drugs to other students. But I suspect that Amber moved on from Tomas Kar. I met up with a slightly more important dealer by the name of Hookman and managed to acquire his mobile telephone. The photographs on the phone are very likely to be Amber Garland.'

'Likely?' interrupted Trueman.

'Well, sir, it is difficult to tell if it is her exactly. The images are rather, err, blurred. And the device was also used to make a series of telephone calls to an address a few miles outside of Manchester. Different mobile telephone numbers but the same location each time.'

'Making lots of phone calls to the same address is not a criminal offence, Edward. If it was then my daughters would have been arrested years ago. Might have saved me a fortune in telephone bills.'

'The property is owned by Godfrey Timson who lives there with his wife and children. I am sure that the mobile can give us some more information. Alexander Drake is using his technological know-how to find its secrets.'

'Try to keep on track with this enquiry,' Trueman sighed. 'The history of this Government department has been to protect cabinet ministers, senior politicians, and members of the Royal Family. I am well aware that young people take drugs and that Amber's disappearance might be drug-related. But Godfrey and Maureen Timson do not sound like kingpins in a drug syndicate, Edward.'

'Yes, sir.'

'For over one hundred years, in one form or another, my department has been looking out for people like Anthony Fairfax. Either protecting them directly or sometimes protecting them from themselves,' Trueman looked down at the supine figure of Fairfax resting in the hospital bed. 'I do feel as though I have let him down.'

'What happened, sir?' asked Church, keen to change the subject.

'He was on his way up to London from Claverton Hall down in Stonebridge. Anthony had been forced to appear before a House of Commons enquiry, a Parliamentary Affairs Committee upholding standards in public office. He had been asked to explain his recent, erm, indiscretions. He had a stroke just as he stepped off of the train at London Bridge station. An intracerebral haemorrhage. The only lucky part of it, if you can use the word lucky, is that he was close to Guys Hospital. The hospital has been running tests all day. An Angiography x-ray and an MRI scan have been done. A Magnetic Resonance Angiography is booked in for later tonight.'

Trueman Paused for a moment before adding, 'Why are you here so late, Edward?'

'I thought that I would leave visiting until the family members had left for the day.'

'Well, that is very thoughtful. But Anthony Fairfax does not have any other family.'

A brief silence passed between Church and Trueman. After a few seconds, it was disturbed by the door to the hospital room opening and a young healthcare assistant walking in. She paused, looking at the two of them.

'I'm sorry to interrupt, gentlemen. I just need to change a piece of equipment.

'Is it not working?' asked Trueman anxiously.

'Oh no, sir. It's working fine, but not sending diagnostic reading through to the hospital server.'

'Sounds complicated,' added Church.

'Not really,' she added, turning to Church, 'technology within technology, lots of the equipment we use in the hospital send information and messages through to a central computer server. You can't see it, but readings are being taken sent and saved all of the time.'

She left with the offending, malfunctioning technology, closely followed by Sir Bernard Trueman, who wished Church a 'good evening' and suggested he stay a little longer.

'I think that you could spend a few more days on this, Edward. It's the least we can do for Anthony Fairfax.'

Church found a vending machine that dispensed hot drinks and made himself comfortable in the hospital chair next to Fairfax.

'You really need to get yourself better, Mr Fairfax,' he said in a one-sided, one-way conversation with the unconscious Anthony Fairfax. 'I have made a good start in locating your step-daughter. It didn't take long to track down the first of her friends and her university have been very helpful.'

Church paused and thought of the shuffling, skinny, emaciated Tomas Kar. And his visit to the university and their lack of co-operation.

'I met some more acquaintances and have a definite lead to more of Amber's circle of friends.'

Church paused once again and a picture of Hookman and Malcolm X popped into his mind. The photographs on the mobile phone flashed into memory and the suggestion from Sir Bernard Trueman that Godfrey and Maureen Timson sound like improbable leads. Leads that were on a tangent and probably associated with pushing drugs than related to his search for Amber.

His thoughts were interrupted by the healthcare assistant returning with the new piece of equipment. She fiddled with some leads, attached something to a sensor attached to Fairfax. Finally, she plugged the contraption into a wall socket, smiled and left. Technology within technology.

Chapter Sixteen

Back up North

Church slept badly that night. He had decided to walk from the hospital in South London to his flat in Chelsea. But the exercise did little to clear his mind. Thoughts of Anthony Fairfax laying in the hospital bed filled his dreams. Church had watched the man on television several times, he thought that he knew something of his politics and beliefs. But it turns out that you can never really know someone. The man had no living family, just a stepdaughter. And she had got mixed up with some interesting characters. Poor choice in company. The man must have been beside himself with worry and then he had to appear in front of a committee to explain his very private life.

As the alarm went off on his phone, Church was still dreaming. He dreamt that the phone was hidden in a chair and that he could not find it. The alarm was ringing and ringing but Church could not find it to switch it off. Eventually, he managed to cancel it, but it took several presses of buttons before the thing would respond. The mobile technology running slowly, like Hookman's phone. More alarms were set off. Triggered by the first mobile telephone. He found one of the alarms and cancelled the ringing but other alarms were still going off, hidden from his view. Church was frantically trying to find them when he suddenly awoke. His arm was already outstretched, reaching to cancel the wake-up call.

He lay in the dark, listening to the silence. Sensing his heartbeat slowing down and his brain functions speeding up, Church was alert now. Wide awake and ready to start the day. It was just a few moments later that the idea struck him.

An hour after that, he was standing on the platform of London's Euston station waiting for an express train to take him back to Manchester. He patted the jacket pocket in his suit and felt the reassuring bulge of his wallet and passport. For some reason Church often carried his passport, in fact, he had three copies of the official identification document. One for the United States, one for elsewhere in the world and one, a clean one, for Europe. Many countries do not allow entry of a passport that has been stamped from another, unfriendly, country. Hence Edward Church owning more than one.

Church idly looked around him as he waited patiently for the London bound commuters to stream from the carriages. Fewer and fewer people wore suits and formal clothes to work these days. It was hard to tell whether the passengers disembarking were office workers, shop workers or early morning tourists. Cleaners or bankers. Managers or Directors. They all looked equally, casually, dressed. The days of bowler hats and briefcases had been replaced with shirts, coats and backpacks.

As Church steeled himself into the railway carriage he reached for his phone. The familiar high-pitched voice of Alexander Drake came through on the other end of the line.

'Morning, Alex,' said Church. 'I hope I haven't woken you up.'

'Not at all, Edward. I have been up for ages playing with that phone you gave me. I knew that there was more to it than some bad music and dubious photographs.'

'I had a thought about that too. I'm wondering if there is something concealed inside the phone. Not physically hidden, but hidden technology.'

'How did you guess? There actually is a phone within a phone on this handset. A complete system software, text, email, browser, call log, et cetera. But only one messaging application is used. Messages exchanged via this app are automatically deleted or burnt, within two weeks. It is called *Enkryptation*. Very cool. I have been in touch with a colleague at the National Crime Agency to see if they can help. If the company is based in the UK they will apply for a warrant to search the computer servers, but I suspect that hardware will be housed offshore somewhere. It may be impossible to trace. But the messages we have been able to retrieve are very interesting. What made you think that there might be something hidden in the phone?'

'A reclining chair and a piece of hospital equipment.'

'Oh,' replied Alexander Drake.

Two hours later, the train approached Manchester Picadilly railway station.

* * *

'Good morning, sir. And welcome to the Manchester Metropole. Do you have a reservation?'

'I made a booking an hour ago under the name Church,' replied Church.

'Ah, yes, good morning, Mr Church. We have arranged a room on the third floor with an early check-in as you requested.'

He collected his pass-key and thanked the lady on the reception desk. Then rode the lift silently to the third floor and deposited his small travel case on the stand just inside the door to his room. A quick check over the appearance of the room told him everything he needed to know. Church carefully placed the John Buchan novel on his bedside table. It was the book he had picked up with his newspaper two days before and he had managed to read most of the slim publication on his way up to Manchester on the train.

Church had booked himself into the Metropole not because of the luxurious surroundings, although they were an added bonus, but because it was the same hotel that Elsa DeWinter had been booked into. He enjoyed her company and he knew no one in the budget hotel he stayed in before. For some reason, he found himself empathising with Elsa, he could relate to her feelings of being treated as an outsider. She was actually rather good company outside of her working environment. As if on cue there was a knock at his door.

'Are you good to go?' asked Elsa DeWinter.

She stood in the doorway of Church's room, casually leaning against the door jamb with the weight of her body resting on one leg and one arm resting on her hip. She was dressed formally, for a day at work. Flat shoes, comfortable cotton mix trousers, a drab coloured jacket with a pale coloured blouse underneath. The only hint of feminine fashion was a small scarf tied loosely around her neck with a side knot. A nod to European style that looked somewhat out of place in England.

They walked the short distance from the Hotel Metropole to Manchester's Central Police station; weaving and jostling between the other pedestrians who were filling the pavements early in the morning. Office workers, students and shop staff as well as elderly residents who were early risers, converge for an hour or so of overcrowded madness before the streets quieten down mid-morning.

The Police station reception was an oasis of calm compared to the pedestrians outside and Church was pleased to be away from the crush.

'Quiet night, Jim?' Elsa asked the desk Sergeant.

'Not too bad, Miss. A couple of stabbings, as usual, when will they ever learn? A few domestic disturbances and one death from a drug overdose.'

'Anyone we know?' she asked casually.

'The death? A student from the university, by the name of Tomas Kar.'

'Never heard of him,' Elsa replied as quick as a flash.

But I have, thought Church to himself and just for a second, his stomach dropped as he thought of the student dropout who tried to make a living selling drugs to other students but ended up taking them himself. According to the young barmaid in the *Wonkey Donkey* public house, taking them on an industrial scale. Which tragically ended his life. Church was snapped out of his thoughts by Elsa speaking to the desk Sergeant

'We need to sign out a car, Sergeant White,' Elsa asked. 'An unmarked police service vehicle.'

'Well now,' the Sergeant sighed, 'most of the little Fiestas have services due and the rest have been booked out already. The Skodas have steering issues and need to have the tracking adjusted. I'm not really sure what PSVs we have got left.'

'What is available?' asked Elsa with a hint of despair creeping into her voice.

'Just this,' the Sergeant answered with a half-smile.

The middle-aged man reached behind him and grabbed a clipboard and a set of keys. Church looked over Elsa DeWinter's shoulder as she signed the paperwork to reserve the vehicle. He could not quite make out the type of car, but Church was not disappointed as they made their way out to the vehicle car park.

Elsa pressed the key fob and the lights of a new black BMW X5M flashed back at her. It was a beast of a car and Elsa looked like a child as she climbed up into the driver's seat.

'Where are you taking me?' she asked, barely able to contain her smile.

'Number twenty-seven Withinlee Drive, Wilmsbury. The home of Godfrey and Maureen Timson, the most unlikely named drug dealers South of Manchester.'

They headed out of the city centre. Making good progress as they drove out against the last of the inward road traffic travelling to whatever workplaces they were headed. The car sped down the dual carriageway that is Princess Road; cruising through Moss Side and the endless suburbs that stretch out from the centre. Her large eyes, magnified by her thick glasses, constantly scanned the surroundings. Flicking between the road ahead, to the rearview mirror and the wing mirrors. Elsa kept the car in the middle lane and they drove over the Outer Ring Road, crossing the River Mersey that is just a narrow river running through Kenworthy Woods this far inland. Much farther downstream it transforms into the much wider waterway as it flows through another Northern powerhouse, the city of Liverpool.

The road seamlessly transformed into the motorway at Wythenshawe and they continued on the motorway until they passed by Manchester Airport. It was only once they had passed the airport turning that Elsa eased the vehicle into the left-hand lane ready to take an exit at junction six. Here, the Wilmslow Road skirts the far end of the airport runway and runs directly underneath the main runway and the emergency approach by way of two long tunnels. Very disconcerting if a car journey coincides with an aircraft approach or take-off, a few hundred metres above.

Elsa DeWinter drove quickly and confidently, but smoothly and safely. Church was impressed. The usual commute from her home in Amsterdam to her workplace in Rotterdam clearly gave her the taste for driving. Large towns eventually gave way to smaller villages with extended periods of green spaces separating them. The names flashed by but Church caught sight of a few of them, Wilmslow itself passed them by unseen, somewhere to the right of the dual carriageway. They turned onto a minor road and drove through endless tree-lined lanes. A signpost welcomed them to a village called Kirkleyditch, another asked them to drive safely through Greendale. Every now and then a clearing in the trees showed a gated drive leading to a large detached house.

Withinlee Drive turned out to be a gated, private road, that led from a long leafy street. Two wide gates made out of polished steel bars prevented their entrance. Either side of the gates were two concrete pillars. Security lights had been built into these squat columns. High walls ran from either side of them before trees and bushes obscured the view. Luck was against them and it took a wait of nearly an hour before a vehicle approached the gates of the private road from within Withinlee Drive. Church and Elsa heard an electronic click and the wide, heavy steel, gates swung gently open. The driver turned onto the main road and drove past their BMW, accelerating fast as it disappeared into the distance, vanishing in a swirl of mid-morning mist.

Church jumped out from the passenger side of the car and waved his hand in front of the electronic sensor at the side of the gate. Just as he had hoped, the gates' sensors detected an obstruction and, as a safety precaution, swung open once again. The manufacturers obviously foresaw a vehicle pausing at the exit of the gates waiting for road traffic and made sure that the heavy metal construction did not automatically close on an expensive motor car.

He climbed back into the passenger seat. They drove slowly along the private road and slowed to a stop one door away from number twenty-seven. Each of the large detached houses had yet more gates outside. Some were wooden field gates that afforded a glimpse of the property beyond. Others were fully enclosed wooden closeboard gates that completely blocked the view. Church waited for another minute or two and was just about to open his door again when he was startled by a screech of van tyres behind them. A white delivery van had pulled up outside the steel barriers. The driver jumped out, pressed a button built into the side of one of the concrete columns and as if by magic the gates swung open for him.

'The houses need to get a delivery at some point,' said Elsa flatly. 'It is probably on a timer and locks people out after eleven o'clock or something.'

'Sorry, Elsa,' said Church.

The white van sped past them and pulled to a stop outside number twenty-seven. Church watched as the driver pressed another button at the side of the wooden gates. Once again they swung open, inviting him inside. Less than a minute later the driver returned and sped off to another delivery. Church and Elsa walked slowly and purposefully towards the large detached house that belonged to Godfrey and Maureen Timson.

Chapter Seventeen

A Phrase Springs to Mind

As Edward Church walked up the gravel driveway leading to the home of Godfrey and Maureen Timson, the phrase *'money can't buy you taste, style or decency'* sprang into his mind. The house itself was nice enough. A large double fronted modern building with rendered walls painted a bright white stucco. The dark coloured window frames and matching roof tiles suggested a clinical, industrial, or factory-like appearance. But it was the additions to the property that jarred Church's sensibilities. Two enormous life-sized, cast-concrete lions stood on either side of the entrance porch. They had been coated with gold paint which had begun to peel on the heads. Two fake topiary trees sat just inside the overhang of the porch.

The long gravel drive had been constructed out of bright, electric blue, marble stone chips. Perhaps they were meant to look like Lapiz lazuli? But to Church, they looked like fake, blue glass, chippings. In fact, to Church's eye, a great deal about the dwelling looked fake. It was a shame because the house next door, which they glimpsed as they crunched up the driveway, looked to be a near-identical dwelling that had been updated, extended and stylishly accessorized.

Number twenty-seven Withinlee Drive seemed to be a hive of activity. Several cars were parked on the blue driveway and the front door was wide open. Church was suddenly aware of Elsa DeWinter standing close by. She looked different and something about her appearance had changed. It took Church a second or two to realise that she had taken off her jacket and scarf.

'Shall we go in?' she whispered.

Before Church could answer a voice from inside offered them a solution to her question.

'Are you with the caterers or the florists?' an unseen voice bellowed.

'Neither,' answered Church. 'We are friends of Mr Hookman looking for Amber Garland.'

'Never heard of him, never heard of her,' came the curt reply from within. And in a flash, a short, overweight figure emerged from the house and brushed past the two of them. He squeezed his portly frame through an open car door, climbed awkwardly inside and drove off.

'He is also known as Neville Smallbone,' said Church to himself as the car silently glided across the stones and out of the grounds of the house. 'But you didn't give me the chance to ask.'

'After you,' said Elsa raising her arm and pointing an arm towards the inside of the house.

'Hello,' called Church as he stepped inside, 'anyone at home?'

If the house looked odd from the outside, nothing could have prepared Church for the appearance of the inside. Black polished marble tiles lined the floor. Pale marble panels had been built into the walls, interspersed with full-length mirrors. The panels of the mirrors had been edged with gilt frames. More gilt adorned the ceiling which had been painted with a mural depicting night from one end and day from the other. The large open space of the hall had been furnished with odds and ends of furniture that were a mix of contemporary and classic. To Church's eye, it did not blend well together, it did not blend together at all.

'Are you with the caterers or the florists?' another voice asked.

It sounded softer, kinder and more polished than the angry bellow from Mr Godfrey Timson. As Church looked down the gaudy corridor at the end of the hallway, a woman approached them. At first glance, she looked to be aged in her late thirties or early forties. Slim built, auburn hair and a natural, easy, smile. As he looked at Maureen Timson another phrase sprang into Church's mind, *don't judge a book by its cover.* She looked nothing like the woman suggested by her rather plain, rather old-fashioned name. And he had to be honest with himself as well, Sir Bernard Trueman was probably right, she did not look like the wife of the boss of a drug-dealing gang.

'Caterers?' she asked a little uncertainly, before adding, 'or florists?'

'Actually, we are looking for Amber Garland,' replied Church not bothering to make any explanation for their visit. 'I'm Edward and this is Elsa. We thought that she might be here today.'

'Amber. Amber?' Maureen said the name and creased her brow a little as if she was willing the answer to come out of her mind. She tapped an immaculately manicured fingernail against her temple. 'Is she a friend of Daniel, or Stuart, or perhaps even Oliver? I'm not sure. But she won't be here yet. It's much too early for the youngsters to have turned up.'

Church looked at Elsa standing beside him. She had not spoken yet and Church was willing her to say something constructive, but she stood and looked at Maureen Timson with a polite half-smile on her face. Church looked back at Maureen.

'Do you cook young man?' she asked Church.

'Not very well, I'm afraid.'

'Good. You can help me choose my outfit for tonight.' She turned to Elsa and said, 'you can help with the food, we are so behind with the preparation any help will be appreciated.'

She guided Elsa down the corridor towards a large open plan kitchen and set her up in front of a huge pile of unprepared food. As Maureen led Church upstairs, Elsa pulled a face at him as if to say, 'what is going on here!'

* * *

'Zip me up, sweetie.'

Church sat uncomfortably on the end of a huge king-sized bed as Maureen Timson changed into her third outfit in as many minutes. The room was a large cavernous space filled with furniture. A row of wardrobes ran along the entire length of the room. It was equally as badly decorated as the rest of the house. How could anyone relax, let alone sleep, in a room like this thought Church?

'What do you think of this one, darling?'

'It looks very formal,' replied Church. He really did not know that much about ladies fashion, in fact, he would probably have been more helpful in the kitchen.

'You're probably right, Edward. It is Edward, isn't it? My children have so many friends that I have trouble remembering all of their names. Perhaps I'm getting old and forgetful.' She paused for a second before adding, 'unzip me, darling.'

Maureen Timson had explained that it was her youngest son's twenty-first birthday today. Church did the maths and estimated that she must be in her late forties or even early fifties, but she certainly did not look it. The pause after her remark about getting old was clearly to fish for a compliment, but Church was too prepared to be taken in by a comment like that.

The waiting game ended after her fifth change of outfit. Church gently lifted the hair at the back of her head and smoothly ran the zip up the full length of a simple fitted black dress. Maureen Timson did not look old and was probably not in the least bit forgetful. In fact, she looked stunning.

It was with a sense of relief and a little disappointment that Church eventually made his way back down the stairs. Maureen led the way, as usual, and they joined a group of people beavering away around a large kitchen island unit. Five or six people were milling around the kitchen weaving around each other, fetching food from bags piled up along a marble worktop or retrieving something from a large double fronted refrigerator. Church spotted Elsa with her sleeves rolled up filling some pastries with a concoction of food that had been mixed together in a bowl. She looked up from her endeavours and pulled a face at Church.

'Nice of you to join us,' she said ironically, making no effort to hide the sarcasm in her voice.

'I am so sorry, Elsie,' replied Maureen. 'Come and sit down with us in the lounge and have a cup of tea.'

'It is Elsa,' said Elsa. But Maureen Timson had already turned and walked out of the kitchen.

The lounge of number twenty-seven Withinlee Drive was enormous. A vast open space that stretched along the whole length of the ground floor. Several massive sofas were dotted around the room, a full-sized bar occupied one corner of the room and a giant television screen hung impressively over the fireplace. It was much bigger than the screen in Hookman's flat and had been installed in such a way so that no cables were visible. The room was larger than the squalid flat that Tomas Kar squatted in. It was larger than the flat occupied by Hookman. In fact, most of Church's apartment could have fitted into this one room.

Church was taking it all in when a screech from one of the elderly ladies perched on the sofas interrupted his thoughts.

'Oh my goodness, it's Edward isn't it!'

For a split second, Church looked blankly at the woman who had spoken. She looked familiar and Church was desperately searching his memory for where they had met before.

'Just the other night we had dinner at the St Charles Partners dinner. I told you that Manchester was a small place and that people know each other!'

Church should have remembered immediately. The brightly coloured clothes, hair and make-up should have stuck in his mind more than they did. Seeing someone completely out of the context you first met them can be strangely disconcerting. Giselle's conversations were exciting, every sentence seemed to start with an 'Oh' and finish with an exclamation mark. Church sat himself down on the sofa opposite her and smiled. She was sitting with another woman, older and much, much fatter. The other woman appeared to be bursting out of her dress, her head and neck seemed to have merged into one. Most disconcertingly, her eyes bulged out of her head and appeared to look in two different directions at the same time. Giselle made the introductions and the woman spoke at once.

'We are new to the area and it is so nice to be invited to meet people,' she said. 'My husband and I travelled a great deal due to his work. He enjoys that staying at home feeling but I just love to travel. It broadens the mind and inspires the senses. Different cultures and histories are fascinating. I am hoping to persuade my husband back to Egypt to do that whole Agatha Christie, Miss Marple, Death on the Nile thing.'

'Poirot,' said Elsa.

'What, dear?'

'It was Poirot who investigated Death on the Nile.'

'Yes. That is what I said, Death on the Nile. I really do believe that travel is vital to life. To travel is to live I ask, what would we be without travel?'

'We might be dead,' replied Church.

'Exactly, dear. But now we are in England. And very much alive.' The woman turned away from Church and continued, 'We recently purchased Hopwood House, it is a total wreck but my husband and I are going to fully restore it. Bringing it completely up-to-date and completely re-landscape the grounds. It comes with nearly thirty acres.'

'I love visiting stately homes,' said Elsa, trying to add to the conversation. 'I am sure that it will look beautiful once it is restored.'

'It's not open to the public, dear. Although we are keen to reintroduce traditional pastimes. We want to do the whole Country Life living thing. I rather fancy riding with the hounds.'

Church was silent. Giselle, out of sight of the woman, rolled her eyes.

'I think that it is rather cruel,' said Maureen Timson.

'I agree,' said Elsa.

'Oh,' said the woman flatly.

'Did you know that Hopwood Hall is haunted,' said Giselle brightly, trying to save the woman's discomfiture. 'And it has got a secret passageway in the downstairs hall.'

'Yes,' the woman replied, 'it was a priest hole or something.'

The woman continued her long rambling, self-centred, conversation. Church realised that he was sitting on the edge of his seat. His body language suggested a classic, ready to leave signal that Elsa DeWinter picked up on. She proposed that they leave the little afternoon tea party and return later when the younger generation would gather for the birthday party. After goodbyes were exchanged and double kisses from both Giselle and Maureen were given to Church and Elsa DeWinter, they made their way silently down the driveway and to their car. Church was still silent as they drove back through the country lanes and onto the main road leading back to Manchester city centre.

When they had been driving for nearly half an hour and Church still had not spoken, Elsa broke the silence.

'You did not much like that woman and the talk of her country house?'

'I didn't much like her at all. You don't ride *with* the hounds if you are hunting, you ride *to* the hounds and I think that the whole fox hunting tradition lost its way a long time ago. Any aspects of land management were lost to the pomp and tradition of fancy dress. To be fair, I'm surprised that she found the priest hole. Although there is another one on the top floor. That was a better hiding place because it was concealed underneath a large wooden toilet seat. And thirty acres isn't that big a deal for a stately home of that size. That's nowhere near enough land to support the house. I knew the people who lived there and visited once in a while. The last time was when the grandfather died. Most of the grounds had been sold off over the years. The family had little wealth by then and money needed to be found to pay death duties and inheritance tax. The last owner tried to raise money by getting involved in a foreign investment scheme. He had family in Persia, but it was at a time when this country was going through a nationalistic phase and it was seen as passing our heritage over to foreigners. His scheme collapsed and he was vilified in the press. In the end, the family had to offer the house to the nation but in a perverse twist of fate, it was decided that the nation could not afford to pay for the upkeep. And so it was left empty.' Church paused for a moment before adding, 'I liked that property and the people who owned it before her. It was a nice home. Grand and impressive, but warm and welcoming at the same time.'

'I thought that it was not open to the public?'

Church lapsed into silence once again.

Chapter Eighteen

Farewell St Mungo

Edward Church wanted company. Good company. People who were genuine, honest and true. As he and Elsa DeWinter drove through the city centre of Manchester, Church asked her if she could drop him off at the St Mungo's homeless shelter.

'I've got a couple of loose ends to make good,' he said, reaching behind him to retrieve a carrier bag he had placed on the back seat earlier.

'I have to return to the Police station to file my last report before I return to Rotterdam. You might have taken a shine to Maureen Timson, it seemed like she could not wait to get her immaculate nails into you. But I want to do a background check on her husband Godfrey. During a conversation in the kitchen, somebody told me that his wealth comes from Nail Bars, Eyelash and Brow Salons, Barbers and Money Transfer shops. '

'He must be pretty successful.'

'They are all perfect cover businesses for laundering money and also for dealing drugs. He could be legitimate but I very much doubt it.'

'Shall we meet at around eight-thirty to return to the Timson's house party?'

'It is a date,' replied Elsa with a sarcastic smile.

The lights were already on at St Mungo's even though it was mid-afternoon. Church pushed his way through the swing doors and the warmth of the building briefly enveloped him, a reminder of how cold it was outside. He glanced around the large room that was being used as a temporary kitchen and dining area. A smattering of homeless people were dotted around, keeping apart from each other as if they did not want to engage in conversation. There was a young mother with a toddler and baby who she was trying to feed as well as amuse the young child. On another table, an elderly woman cradled a stuffed toy for company. The toy was filthy and had come apart at the seams, stuffing spilt out onto her coat sleeve. Next to her was a man who was difficult to age because of the mass of hair on his face and a big bobble hat, minus its pom-pom, pulled down over most of his head. Church spotted Tony Brownstone with his sleeves rolled up and elbows deep in soapy washing up water.

'Hello, Edward,' he smiled between dipping mugs in the hot water. 'What's in the carrier bag, have you been shopping? Grab a tea towel and make yourself useful. How goes the search for the missing girl?'

'Not very well I'm afraid, Tony. If nothing comes of the trail I am following up on tonight then I will have to admit to Anthony Fairfax that I've rather let him down. I really don't want to have to do that.'

'Poor old Sir Bernard Trueman tried to get a D notice issued to keep the story out of the newspapers, but it didn't make any difference. The news of Anthony's, erm, indiscretion has leaked out and the media is full of lurid discussions. Now they are feeding on the news that his step-daughter is missing like a flock of vultures.'

'It's a wake,' replied Church gloomily.

'What?'

'A group of feeding vultures is called a wake. If they are sitting around in a cluster they are called a committee.'

'If you say so, Edward. Whatever it's called it's a messy situation.'

D-notices or DA-notices, as they are sometimes referred to, are advisory notes issued by the government to try and stop the publication of sensitive news stories on the grounds of damaging national security. The system of trying to suppress damaging information began before the First World War and was frequently used in both that conflict and the subsequent Second World War. Initially, a department within the War Office, the current Defence and Security Media Advisory Committee exists as an ad-hoc department within the Ministry of Defence. As well as Civil Servants the committee is made up of representatives from the major television broadcasters, print publications such as newspapers or magazines and internet search engine providers. Current DSMA notices fall into one of five categories. Notice 05 specifically covers personnel and their families who work in sensitive positions.

'Are you in charge here at St Mungo's?' asked Church.

'No, not me. Audrey is the lady who runs things around here. She looks like your favourite aunt or something but don't be fooled by appearances. She is as hard as nails is our Audrey.'

The swing doors opened, announcing the arrival of another patron. Church glanced around inquisitively before continuing his conversation with Tony Brownstone. But something about the brightly coloured clothing that the new visitor was wearing made him look back. The unmistakable sight of Malcolm X, dressed in luminous shades of lime green, scarlet, orange and yellow, strode into the large dining area. He walked straight into the kitchen where Church and Brownstone were stood, looked at Church in surprise before taking off his jacket and gathering some mugs together.

'Alright, Tony,' he said to Brownstone.

'Hello, Malcolm, how are you doing?' Brownstone replied.

'Okay, thanks.'

'Malcolm volunteers here three days each week, Edward.' Brownstone turned to Malcolm and said, 'This is Edward Church, Malcolm. He's in Manchester for a few days looking for someone.'

'I know. We've met.'

Malcolm checked the urn of hot water with the back of his hand. Satisfied that it was hot enough, he poured two mugs and added tea bags and milk before walking one of the beverages over to a table. He returned a moment later and spoke to Church.

'Hookman is not happy with you, you know. The police busted down his front door and made a right old mess. Kept us in the station for questioning for ages. Let me out first but I waited another couple of hours for Hookman. Are you a policeman or something?'

'Something.' Church replied.

'Do you want a tea? I'm not trying to bribe you or anything.'

'Thanks, Malcolm, that would be good.'

'No problem.'

'How come you volunteer here?' Church asked as they settled at a table.

'It's a long story. You probably won't be interested.'

'Try me,' said Church. 'You'll be able to tell if I'm not interested. Your quite a judge of character.'

The compliment seemed to cheer Malcolm and he took a swig of tea from his mug before leaning back in his chair, making himself more comfortable.

'I got friendly with Hookman because we went to the same school and lived in the same children's home. He's a couple of years older than me but I was tall for my age and he didn't mind me hanging around with him and his friends. I wasn't born in Manchester but grew up around here. We came up here, me and my mum that is, after my dad died.'

'Oh, I'm sorry, Malcolm. How old were you?'

'Dunno. About six or seven. I can't remember how old I was but I do remember getting up to go to school one day and my dad was there but the next day he was gone. It was freezing cold and my mum insisted on me wearing a scarf and gloves to walk to school. It seems that my dad was hit by a car early that morning. Accidental death or something. The police thought that the driver might have skidded on some black ice. But someone said that they thought the driver didn't take the time to clear their windscreen properly and was only looking out of a small clear patch of the screen. Whatever happened, he was there one day and gone the next. The school and my teachers were good about it and we had some help for a while. But my mum couldn't cope. She took to drinking in the evenings during the week, something she would have frowned on before. She lost her job, but it didn't matter because we didn't have enough money to live on anyway. We moved up here for a bit of a fresh start. Except that with no family, no job and no friends my mum was less able to cope. She would be drinking during the day, every day, and we really struggled for money. I got behind at school, then in trouble for missing classes, eventually I got expelled. I was placed in a children's residential home and a different school. It was shit. I met Hookman there and we got on okay. But at sixteen they chuck you out and for a year or so I didn't see him. Then at seventeen, the council helped find me a flat with some other people. I think that they call it a house of multiple occupation. It wasn't a house, it was a flat and Hookman lived in the same block. Small world ain't it?'

'What happened to your mother?'

'Oh, that's her over there with the teddy bear. She doesn't recognise me now even though I give her a cup of tea every day. They think that she has got alcoholic dementia or something, but she never goes to the hospital for any appointments.'

Malcolm lapsed into silence and Church was in no rush to break it. After a while, he reached into his jacket pocket and fished out a pair of gloves. Then he reached into the carrier bag that he had been keeping safe and removed three of the rolls of banknotes retrieved from Hookman's flat. Church laid them on the table next to Malcolm's mug of tea.

'I'm not trying to bribe you either. It's only money, you can choose what to do with it. Something good or something not good. Why don't you buy your mother a new teddy bear? And I know that Hookman is your friend, but hanging around with him is not doing you any favours. But it's not my place to judge your taste in friends.'

'Thanks, Mr Church. You're alright, you know? I don't care what Hookman says about you.'

'Thanks, Malcolm. I'll take that as a compliment. Now, do you know where I might find Audrey? I've got something I'd like to give her.'

'She's got a little office just down the corridor. Be careful though. She looks alright, but she's got a temper on her. Frightens the life out of me sometimes.'

The idea that a solitary woman could scare Malcolm amused Church as he made his way down the passageway. Malcolm was a huge guy, well over six feet tall and must weigh around eighteen stone. Hookman obviously liked having Malcolm around because of his size. But even so, as he knocked on the door of Audrey's little office, Church paused and took a deep breath.

Tony Brownstone's description of Audrey as your favourite aunt was pretty spot on. A short woman in her late fifties or early sixties sat behind an old office desk. An equally old computer screen occupied half of the available space and she had to peer around the side of it to see that Church had come into the room.

'Can I help you?' she asked guardedly. 'No offence, but you don't look like the usual visitors we have here? Sit yourself down, take your gloves off and make yourself at home.'

'I wonder if I can make a donation,' said Church.

'Oh?' she asked again. 'Has Tony Brownstone pricked your conscience or something?'

'Not just Tony, but someone else as well.' Church realised that every sentence she had uttered had been a question.

'Well, we don't get too many of those although I regularly canvass around local businesses. Would you like to make a regular payment or a one-off donation?'

Another question thought Church to himself, but he answered, 'A one-off donation this time, I think.'

Audrey reached into a desk drawer and with easy efficiency, pulled out a pre-printed donation form.

'Do you have your bank details…?'

But her voice trailed off as Church lifted a large carrier bag onto the remaining desk space. He neatly stacked rolled-up tubes of banknotes in a long line, then another line and finally a third row.

'I expect cash donations are a bit of a problem, Audrey,' said Church.

'They are if they are that size. Can I ask where you got it from?'

'Best not to. But it is a genuine donation.'

'I can't put that much money in a bank account without being asked some questions.'

'Hypothetically, if I left the carrier bag here and you found it later, you could hand it to the police as lost property. Twenty-eight days later it would be yours to claim back. I won't come back for it. And no one else will. Or you could drip feed it into the bank account for this place after some very successful fundraising weekends, I've heard that the people of Manchester can be very generous.'

Church paused. He could see that Audrey was tempted. Indecisiveness was written on her face.

'Not only Mancunians are generous it would seem,' she said with a smile.

The temptation of the money and all of the good that it could potentially do won over. She hesitated for a moment. Then reached across the table, picked up the carrier bag and placed the rolled-up notes back inside. Church got up, pulled a glove off of one hand and offered a handshake to the woman. He turned and left the little office.

'Thank you,' she said as he left.

Chapter Nineteen

Partyland

As Edward Church was driven through the late-night city streets of Manchester, he looked around and surveyed the centre of the town. To pass the time he told her about the discovery of the hidden application on Hookman's phone. Elsa DeWinter sat in the driver's seat of the BMW X5M skillfully manoeuvring the big car through busy traffic and pedestrians spilling out onto the road. Her passion for cars and driving reminded Church of Malcolm. It was a chilly night but thanks to the car's air conditioning the windows were not steamed up. She had ditched her thick glasses and now wore contact lenses. She looked ill at ease with them in and if Church was honest with himself, he preferred the glasses.

Manchester derived its name from joining the old English name for a hill, Mamm, and the Roman name for a fortified settlement, Chester. A simple connection leads to the portmanteau Manchester. The Latin name for Manchester which is often quoted as Mancunium is very close to the current term for the people of the city, Mancunians. However, history was lost on Church as he stared out of the vehicle passenger window.

He looked around him at the people out on the streets of Manchester this evening. Young men in slim-cut trousers and even tighter teeshirts walked around in groups of four or five. The fashion for showing off a gym-toned physique was popular at the moment. Prowling through the night, the males were looking for female company. Some men carried it off better than others. The overweight struggled to look good in this style. The men who tried to cheat at the gym looked strangely out of balance, too top-heavy. A large torso carried by stick-thin legs. The women looked glamorous, some stunning, some rather too old for the look they hoped to convey. Others fell short of the idealised body shape that was probably achieved through retouching photographs rather than natural beauty. The occasional 'jolly' girlfriend could be found within a gaggle of women. The one who wants a laugh, a good night out and a kebab to end it all off with. Several of the women were pretty enough to be 'faces' on television or models on the catwalk if they were a little taller.

Manchester has more nightclubs per head of population than anywhere else in the United Kingdom. Quite possibly as a result of this, its younger community consumes more soft recreational drugs per head of the population than anywhere else in the world. Hedonism, debauchery and night-time shenanigans are closely associated with the city. Because of the size and scale of late-night entertainment, it even has its own night-time economic advisor.

By contrast, London barely makes it onto the list of the top fifty wildest cities, placing it behind Paris, New York, Los Angeles Rome and Milan. Church rather missed his home comforts. Perhaps he was getting old? Perhaps he was feeling disenchanted because he failed to find Amber Garland? Tonight felt like the end of a trip away. The next day he planned to return to London and Elsa would return to Amsterdam.

The thoughts going through Church's mind were interrupted by a stretch limousine heading towards them in the middle of the road. Elsa gently braked their car and moved its position to the edge of the street. At the last moment, the limo corrected its course and passed by them in a long black streak. It was crammed full of young women and two of them had taken advantage of the open sunroof to stand up and wave a bottle of prosecco and champagne glasses in the air. Another party vehicle passed them by, this time coming up from behind them. It was a converted single-decker bus and had been decorated with neon lights, mirrored panels and a music system that blasted out House, Hip hop, Urban and Grime music inside and, thanks to externally mounted loudspeakers, outside as well.

Another car raced by beside them. This time it was a flash of yellow. And Church recognised the shape and colour of the vehicle. It was an Imola yellow *Audi RS4* and it was being driven at speed by Malcolm X. The back of the speeding vehicle was illuminated by a pulsing blue light. Church registered the panicked face of Malcolm as it rushed by, closely followed by a marked police car with its sirens blaring and its lights flashing. Before Church had a chance to ask, Elsa swiftly increased the speed of their car and followed some distance behind.

He reached furiously for the police radio which had been switched off for their evening journey. Voices crackled through speakers in the big BMW in which they travelled. They followed the pair of speeding cars up Bridge Street and into Deansgate. Modern office blocks flew by either side of them. At the intersection, customers scattered at the *Sawyers Arms* public house as the police vehicle took the corner a little too wide. Malcolm and Elsa both cornered as if their cars were on rails. The yellow Audi took a sharp left just before a large department store a little farther down. Cheery Christmas lights and window decorations did little to dilute the tense atmosphere. At the end of Kings Street West, the trio of cars took a left-hand turn, then immediately left again even though the route was barred to through traffic. They headed down Bridge Street once again but this time continued onto John Dalton Street. The man was credited with discovering atomic theory two centuries earlier. Church wondered what the elderly scientist would have made of the trail of cars speeding down his road following the tram rail tracks in the middle of the street. They veered off to the right, through a No Entry sign at the end of Princess Street and shot past the impressive City Council building. Architectural splendour was wasted on the convoy of speeding automobiles and Church was more concerned about meeting another vehicle and having a head-on collision. They shot through the first intersection and Church had a glimpse once again of the Manchester Art Gallery. He glanced at the speed display inside their car and realised that they were approximately three times over the city centre speed limit. Princess Street narrows to a one-way section of road after the intersection with Portland Street but at least they were headed in the right direction.

Traditional red brick and yellow brick buildings flashed by in the high-speed chase. There were precious few pedestrians around this part of the metropolis. Offices are not the place for late-night revelry. A smattering of pubs and take-away shops indicated that they were close to the canal. Suddenly, Malcolm steered the speeding Audi down Canal Street narrowly missing two automatic bollards that were meant to keep out traffic but luckily for him were lowered to ground level. They raced along the side of the canal, a few feet away from the murky liquid slowly drifting downstream. Buildings raced past on the passenger side, empty water stretched out on the driver's side. For some reason, there were few female clubbers in this part of town. The reason was lost on Church because up ahead the Audi appeared to have come to a total and immediate stop. The police car braked hard but skidded and slid into the back of the yellow RS4. Elsa braked hard but kept control of their vehicle, slowing down to a stop a few metres behind the police car. Church looked over at her and noticed how calm she appeared. However, she was breathing deeply and slowly trying to control the adrenaline and he did notice the flush of excitement running up her neck. A crackle of radio signals broke the silence.

'RTA at the intersection of Canal Street and Minshull Street. One vehicle, one driver no other casualties.'

'Ten-Fifty. Ten-Fifty-One. Ten-Fifty-Two, ambulance in on its way.'

Church was out of the BMW before any more codes were announced. He briefly checked the two uniformed officers who seemed to be in a trance. Two more paces brought him to the side of the wrecked Audi. Malcolm had not been so lucky at this end of Canal Street. Another set of automatic bollards was in the raised position. One of the pillars was at a crazy angle, the other was buried deep inside the engine compartment of the bright yellow Audi.

Church was struck by the silence after the noise of the car chase. The engine of the Audi, crushed beyond repair, ticked slowly as it cooled down after the effort of the chase. Liquid dripped from the shattered radiator, it collected in a small pool around the front of the vehicle. The rainbow film on the surface looked similar to the polluted canal water farther upstream. He made his way around to the driver's side door and pulled it open. Malcolm sat bolt upright, his face partially obscured by an inflated airbag. Church reached inside and ripped the bag to one side. It took him a second to register where the clip of a five-point seatbelt was. Intuition suggests that a seatbelt clip is towards the centre of a vehicle. It took him another second to register that the front of Malcolm's brightly coloured tracksuit was covered in blood, as were his hands. Mercifully the engine block had not crushed Malcolm's legs as a result of the impact and a superficial glance suggested that he was not seriously hurt.

'Try and not to move, Malcolm. Help is on its way. You are going to be okay.' Church tried to reassure the man.

'My car! My bloody car!' Malcolm repeated over and over. 'I'm going to need a mechanic.'

'You're going to need a medic,' said Church.

Church could see the police officers approaching and realised that he would have to back off and let the professionals do their job. He could not help but feel sorry for Malcolm. Sat in his crushed car in his brightly coloured tracksuit, about to be arrested.

'He's dead, Mr Church,' Malcolm said.

'Who is?'

'Hookman. I went round to his flat and he was laying on the floor. Been stabbed loads of times. Blood everywhere. I tried to help but just got myself covered in his blood. He was still breathing but there was nothing I could do apart from cradle him while he passed away. Hookman wasn't religious but he made his peace when he met his maker.'

'I don't understand, Malcolm.'

'He was saying that he will meet God. That he was seeing God. It was kind of sweet but weird at the same time. Then I heard sirens and legged it out of the flat and back into my car. Then these guys were chasing me and I sort of panicked.'

'Did someone break into his flat? Did you notice if anything was missing?'

'I let myself in as usual. I've got a key remember? And I've no idea if anything was stolen because the place was a mess. Everything had been busted up, smashed, broken, the place had been destroyed. Hookman must have put up quite a fight though.'

But before Church could ask any more questions the two policemen had made it to the side of the Audi, one was still on his radio, the other had handcuffs at the ready.

'We'll take it from here, sir,' one of them said.

Church walked slowly back to Elsa, who was sitting patiently in the BMW. She skillfully manoeuvred the large car back down the street and took a side turning to steer them away from the carnage. She cruised back onto the main road and Church glanced over to two buildings on either side of the road. One was Manchester Crown court, the other was the Probation service. Poor Malcolm thought Church to himself, another client would be on the way soon.

As they drove away from the accident and out of the city centre, the roads became quieter and thanks to the street lights being less frequent it got darker and darker. Was this an ominous sign, considered Church? Or just the laws of geography and physics. The accident had undoubtedly upset him. But Church had the nagging misgivings about the death of Hookman, Malcolm's arrival at the flat and the police being called to the scene so quickly.

'Do you think that it is odd that the police were on their way to Hookman's flat before he had even died?' he asked Elsa.

'You should be a detective, Edward.'

'Do you think it odd that two people associated with Amber Garland are now dead?'

'Two people?'

'Hookman died tonight and Tomas Kar, a friend of hers from university, died last night. The desk Sergeant at the police station told you this morning.'

'You really should be a detective, Edward.'

Chapter Twenty

Dreamland

Withinlee Drive was in darkness. But as they approached, Church could hear the rhythmic thud of music coming from behind the gates of number twenty-seven. The wide impressive wooden gates were open and Elsa nudged the car into the drive and turned the car around to face outwards. The fat tyres on the BMW crunched over the ornamental blue stones as she manoeuvred the vehicle, Church assumed, for a quick getaway.

'It is strange that they have door security for a house party,' Elsa said as they approached.

'Suspicious mind, Elsa. Suspicious mind.'

She shivered slightly as they stood in the doorway. The temperature must have been around freezing point and a keen wind blew now that they were out of the city centre.

'Come in you two,' said a woman's voice from within the house. 'It looks like it's going to be a wild night.'

'That's a promise, sweetie,' came the reply.

The voices belonged to Maureen and Godfrey Timson. She was wearing the black dress that she had tried on earlier that afternoon under Church's supervision. Godfrey was wearing trousers from a suit and a brightly patterned floral shirt. They looked like an odd couple observed Church. She was cool, slightly aloof and certainly sophisticated. He was slightly shorter than his wife, overweight, balding and appeared to be much older than her. He was also rather ugly.

Church did not warm to the man and Elsa fairly bristled as Godfrey lingered over a double kiss to welcome her.

'Food is in the kitchen and drinks are too, but there's another bar in the lounge,' Godfrey said.

'She knows that, darling. Elsie helped us out this afternoon, they are friends with the children or something,' replied Maureen

'It is Elsa.'

'Of course it is, darling,' Maureen said absentmindedly. 'The kids will be round the back somewhere. Make yourselves at home.'

Maureen Timson spun around, checked herself in one of the hallway mirrors and led them down the passageway with the black polished marble tiles and into the kitchen. Food covered almost every surface in the kitchen, laid out on plates, trays, platters, dishes and bowls. Any worktop surface not occupied by food was stacked with bottles of drink. A group of partygoers brushed past Church and Elsa.

'Oh my God! Look at all of this food,' one of them said.

'My diet plan has just been broken,' replied one of the others.

'It's alright for you,' said another, who Church would have categorised as the 'jolly' friend in the group of women, 'I've still got four kilos to lose this week.'

Drinks were foisted into the hands of both Church and Elsa, even though she protested that she was driving. Church was scanning the room looking for any sign that the missing girl Amber Garland was attending the party. It was a long shot, but Amber might just have moved on from Hookman to going out with one of the Timson sons. He walked with Elsa into the vast open plan lounge that was now full of people aged between twenty and thirty-five. A very different crowd from the older generation who had gathered for a cup of tea that afternoon.

They circulated round the room, glancing at each of the guests, at a party to which they were not invited. The irony was not lost on Church. Elsa DeWinter swapped her drink at the bar for something without alcohol and continued to scan faces with Church. After an hour they drifted back into the kitchen and continued their search.

'Try one of these? I made them this afternoon,' said Elsa offering Church a plate of filled vol au vents. 'I made them all myself.'

'What's in them? I'm not too keen on raw fish,' asked Church.

'No idea, Edward, but they taste delicious,' she replied taking a big bite out of one of the stuffed puff pastry cases. 'I think this one is mushroom.'

Church hesitated before taking the plunge. It did not taste like mushroom, but he considered that uncooked edible fungi do not have much of a taste. The pastry disappeared quite literally in a waft of air and he quickly swallowed the tangy, gloopy filling, not enjoying the experience.

* * *

Three hours into the party and Church's enthusiasm was beginning to wane. The music seemed too loud, he felt queasy and unsteady on his feet even though he had been pacing his drinks throughout the night. At one point someone had been sick and the 'jolly' young woman had made a joke about 'I'll have what she's had, that's an easy way to lose four kilos' as the unwell woman was helped to an upstairs room. A great deal of food had already been consumed from the plates and dishes laid out on kitchen surfaces. Some of that empty worktop space had been taken up by people chopping up lines of cocaine. Church suspected that cocktails of other drugs were being consumed elsewhere around the house. For the last hour, Elsa had been dancing by herself. Gently swaying along to the music. Church had watched her for a while before his attention was caught by the sight of Godfrey Timson dancing as well.

Church had to admit that his impression of the man had changed somewhat during the evening. He was gregarious, extroverted and outgoing. It frequently spilt over into being overfamiliar to the opposite sex. But when the older man danced, he completely lost himself in the music. Arms flapped around, head bobbed up and down, legs shuffled randomly in a style that was out-of-time with the beat of the music. But the man was clearly enjoying himself. Lost in the moment and with a lopsided half-smile on his face. He waved his phone in the air with the light turned on as if he were at a stadium concert and then flopped into a chair, dropping it on the floor.

Elsa was beside him in a flash. She scooped up the mobile phone and her fingers danced across the screen as she slowly turned in an elaborate and deliberate arc, in order to hand it back to Godfrey Timson. Church watched the whole thing as if in slow motion. Godfrey aimed a drunken kiss towards Elsa, her backing away and then another figure on the scene. Two large hands gripped her arms. The hands belonged to equally powerful arms that hung either side of a well-built man. Clearly, Godfrey had bodyguards and clearly, they were good. Church had not spotted them before now. Elsa was trying to simulate an elaborate mime, but one hand still gripped her tightly. Church began to walk over, scanning the room as he went. He felt sluggish, his feet would not move as quickly as his brain instructed them to. But just as quickly as the scene erupted, it subsided again. Elsa slowly walked over to where Church had halted.

'Nice moves,' he said.

'I saw you watching me dance and went all out,' she replied.

'I meant with the phone.'

'Of course, you did,' she smiled sarcastically and then added. 'The phone that Godfrey Timson was waving around had the *Enkryptation* app. The same application that you told me you found on the phone you took from Mr Hookman. And did you see the size of the hands on that ape who manhandled me?'

'I did. And I saw the bruises and the grazes on his knuckles too. Those hands looked as if they had been in a fight recently. They didn't look too good,' said Church.

'Speaking of which, you do not look so good yourself.'

'Actually, Elsa, I must be honest I don't feel too bright. I would suggest that you don't eat the fish. I think that I might need a bit of fresh.....'

He never got to finish his sentence. The room began to slowly turn. As he spun, Church saw a door open and a couple of newcomers joined the party. One was a young man who looked much the same as any other, his female companion was unmistakable. Slim, blond and older than her photographs at Claverton Hall. However, it was obvious that this was the same person as depicted in the close-cropped, black and white photograph. It was Amber Garland. Then the room went dark.

* * *

Church did not see the floor rising up to meet him, he only sensed it. In reality, it was his head along with the rest of him, that slowly and gently dropped to the floor. He did not see Elsa DeWinter rush off to make a telephone call to the police to arrange a raid on number twenty-seven Withinlee Drive, South Manchester and then make another phone call requesting an ambulance to the same address.

He did not see an immaculately manicured hand carefully reach out and take Church's Champagne glass out of the palm of his hand. He did not see the shock on

Elsa's face or hear the protests from her when she returned from making the telephone calls only to find that Church's body was no longer on the floor. In fact, Church was nowhere to be found. He never heard the denials from Godfrey Timson and see the blank look on his face as, suddenly sober, he denied that Church had ever been at the party and then questioned who had even invited Elsa to the evening's celebration.

'I am sorry, my dear, but we do not know you and you are not friends with any of our children,' protested Godfrey.

'But we have been here for hours. Looking for Amber Garland. We came to your house earlier on today and saw you just as you were leaving,' implored Elsa.

'I don't know you. My family do not know you. This is a private party and I am asking you to leave.'

Godfrey's protestations were cut off by the sound of sirens. Quiet but unmistakeably getting louder. There was a flicker of anxiety on his face which swiftly disappeared when his wife appeared.

Edward Church was unaware of all of this. His first recollection after passing out was of trying to make his legs work when, in reality, he was being supported by two bodyguards on either side of him. He could not understand where he was but could feel the chill of the cold night air on his face. Church was certainly aware of being bound and gagged then manhandled into the back of a car. The boot lid shut and, as the engine started he heard the crunch of tyres across the blue stones driveway. They gathered speed and rushed down twisting country lanes. Church could not see but could clearly hear a collection of sirens shrieking out from emergency vehicles. One ambulance and several police cars passed them at some point on the car ride, going in the opposite direction.

After a period of time that could have been a few minutes but could equally have been an hour or so, the car came to a halt. In reality, unlike in a Hollywood movie, it is nearly impossible to judge distance by time. And it is certainly impossible to trace a route that is being driven without being able to see it. Church heard the boot lid open and tensed his body as arms reached inside to manhandle him once again. This time he was lifted out of the car and unsteady legs carried him forward. He tried to make out the whispered voices on either side of him.

'Are we going to kill him?' one hushed voice asked.

'I don't know yet. Just been told to get rid of him for now,' came the reply.

The little group took a few steps onward until suddenly the ground seemed to disappear from underneath Church's feet. He stumbled for a second in mid-air before crashing down onto a hard surface that rocked gently under the impact. The dull rhythmic slap against the side of whatever he fell into suggested to Church that a journey by small boat ensued.

As a small outboard motor started and a little boat began slowly making its way along the Bridgewater Canal the police raid on Withinlee Drive was being wound up for the night. Apart from a generous selection of class A and B drugs the only item of interest found at number twenty-seven was a powerful state-of-the-art computer. However it was not the computer itself that was of interest, but the mobile telephone SIM farm that it was connected to.

A SIM farm looks like an ordinary black box, with multiple slots on the top. The slots can hold up to a hundred mobile telephone SIM cards. Subscriber Identity Module cards hold a small memory chip that stores information about the mobile telephone in which it is supposed to be installed. On it, there is a seventeen-digit code that designates its country of origin, the mobile phone operator, and a unique user ID. In addition, they also store contact information, telephone numbers and

SMS messages. Short Messaging Service is better known as text messaging, initially limited to one hundred and sixty characters and beloved of people all over the world.

The SIM farm and its contents of SIM cards was the only item of interest that the police removed from the home of Godfrey and Maureen Timson. Elsa DeWinter was left wondering what happened to another item of interest, Edward Church.

Chapter Twenty-One

We Didn't Mean to Go to Sea

Church had done a bit of sailing in his youth. He recalled struggling to keep up with his older brothers as they all rowed tiny skiffs off the shore of Sussex. His skills had improved at university where membership of a rowing club was almost obligatory, but he was nowhere near good enough or dedicated enough to make it onto a team. If he was honest with himself Church preferred the launches, the little powered motor boats that carried the team coach rather than the lightweight racing shells that carried the eight rowers as they sped down the upper reaches of the Thames.

On foreign holidays he would pester his parents to hire a cabin cruiser so that they could navigate around whatever Greek island they had chosen to holiday on. The walk around the shipyard was just as enjoyable as the sailing. They were always a hive of activity. Electric power tools would be either cutting, drilling or grinding. In the boat repairers fight against friction, the paint would be scraped from old surfaces and nails would be hammered into new wooden boards. The cacophony of noise would be accompanied by the ting-ting-ting of a halyard rope slapping against a mast.

From his position in the front cabin, Church could not tell that he was on a little *Sargo 25* cruiser motorboat. The two bodyguards were standing in the other cabin on this vessel, towards the stern of the craft. At some point, as they made their way slowly down the canal, the little boat made a series of turns and began cruising down the River Irwell. Unseen by Church but glimpsed by the two bodyguards, the lights from the famous Old Trafford football stadium drifted by to the port side. A little later on the pleasure craft entered the Salford basin and the lights of the BBC studios reflected on the still water to the starboard.

For the next four hours, the industrial landscape on either side of the boat passed them by in the darkness. Sporadic lights could be seen in the distance as they floated underneath the railway bridge at the small town of Irlam. But the bridge on the disused branch line farther down went by without them noticing it. Just outside of Warrington, the canal intersects with the River Mersey. However, they continued to journey down the straight man-made waterway rather than deviate onto the meandering shallow river. The canal changes name to the Thelwall at some point near here and it continues to skirt the River Mersey through the towns of Runcorn, Stanlow and Ellesmere Port; thereupon the canal name changes once again, this time to the Manchester Ship Canal.

The little boat continued to cruise through the darkness. The sun would not rise until at least 8am at this time of year. Church continued to drift in and out of consciousness. During lucid moments he would try and remove his blindfold, but after a few minutes of exertion, he would lapse into a blackout and drift into oblivion as the boat floated downstream. As the group of two kidnappers and one victim sailed past the disused Hale lighthouse, Church regained his sense of cognition. He was now fully aware of his situation and he had to admit that it did not look good. Carefully, he checked each of his limbs and was somewhat cheered to sense no serious damage. It took an hour to partially wriggle out of the blindfold. He scanned the space around him with one eye. Unlike the lighthouse whose single all-seeing eye scanned the dangerous sandbanks of the Mersey Estuary, Church could only make out parts of the small cabin which held him captive.

Church tried to stand but cracked his skull on the deckhead. The throbbing pain made him sit down again and he decided to try and make himself comfortable while he waited for the journey to end. The tiny cabin in which he found himself was little more than a seating area. Two minuscule portholes showed a view port and starboard. There were extra cushions and plywood panels that could be used to convert this space into a sleeping area. Two small swing doors built into the bulkhead separated him from the wheelhouse where the two thugs now stood. Through one of the swing doors, he could see two figures, one steering and one on his mobile phone. The light from the screen cast an eerie glow. Church shuffled about in his small confined space. He decided to call the two captors *John* and *Roger*. John was clearly the leader, pointing the way and furiously texting on his phone. Roger was less experienced, no doubt bossed about by the other thug and ordered to do any unpleasant tasks.

As nicknames go they were pretty unimaginative and Church wondered why he had thought of those two names above any else? In the darkness, boredom seeped into his mind. He thought about schoolboy nicknames and wondered what had become of the young men with high dreams and great aspirations. There had been a period towards the end of one summer term when there was a popular trend of joining Christian names and surnames together to make a portmanteau sobriquet. Church became *Chudward*, his classmates were *Hoskard*, *Bevin* and *Chark*. Church was none too impressed by his moniker and he was pleased when the summer holidays came. His youthful reminiscences were broken by noises from above.

'Any news on what we are supposed to do with him?' asked the one nicknamed Roger.

'The boss just said get him out of here,' came the reply, presumably from John. 'Now he says take him to the flat.'
'What? All of the way?'
'No, we're gonna do a swap just out to sea. You just concentrate for now. We're coming up to the Eastham Lock.'

Church could not see, but he could feel when the little boat nudged its way past a series of landing pontoons and into one of the three sets of locks at Eastham in the mouth of the River Mersey. The *Sargo 25* motor cruiser navigated to the smallest lock and Roger jumped out to close one gate and open the other. Unseen by Church, he gave a cheery wave to one of the tugboat pilots who observed them from a distance. The level of the water inside the lock lowered to match that of the river and Roger swung the second set of gates open. Church listened as he hopped back onto the boat and after a brief exchange of words, John throttled forward.

The boat picked up speed and the sensations inside the pleasure craft changed immediately. The water in Manchester Ship Canal had been smooth, as still as a millpond. The river water in the Mersey Estuary was tidal, slightly choppy and more exposed. The small cruiser bobbed around in the water as it made its way slowly out of the mouth of the inlet and headed towards the Irish Sea.

The sound of gentle scraping against the side of the hull startled Church. As the tide changes, a vessel can easily run aground on sandbanks and either local knowledge or marker buoys are necessary. Some waterways are marked with red and green buoys that are positioned as navigational aids. John took over the controls of the boat and positioned the red buoys to the port side. Even with the shallow draft of the *Sargo* boat, he clearly did not want to take any chances of running into a sandbank and having to wait until the tide turned to float off again. Roger swore gently under his breath but John just said, 'Take it easy.'

They chugged down the centre of the river, passing the disused Royal Albert Docks at Liverpool and the docks at Bootle, still very much in use. Unbeknown to them they sailed directly over first the Queensway tunnel then the Kingsway tunnel that connects Liverpool to Birkenhead. Their boat was dwarfed by many of the other vessels in the estuary. Ferry ships, Container ships, Cruiselines and the like were moored at various locations on either side of them. Church could now sense that they were passing into more open water. The wind began to affect the course of the cruiser, making it rock to and fro even more.

In the distance, Church could hear a clanging sound. Muffled at first but then clearer and clearer. The Mersey End Buoy swiftly drifted past them. In reality, it was the boat that sailed past the buoy but movement in the semi-darkness can be an odd thing to judge at sea. The large red-painted cage, similar to a parrot cage with a flashing light on the top and a skirt of rubber at the bottom, receded into the distance behind them. The inside of Church's cabin was briefly illuminated by a red flash and then it was gone just as quickly as it came.

Almost as soon as they had made it past the buoy the wind picked up. It made the boat pitch and roll in the swell of the sea. Church could make out little white-crested waves through one of the little portholes in the cabin. He shifted around once again and looked through the open swing door at his two captors. The one he named Roger was beginning to look a little green. Church was pleased to be out at sea. Perhaps he felt that the odds were not so stacked against him, perhaps he felt that the effects of whatever drug he had been given had almost entirely worn off. Either way, he felt significantly brighter.

The more extreme movement of the boat was easier for his brain to process. The sickness caused by the gentle swaying and the pills that had somehow slipped into him was now replaced with a steely determination. He could see clearly now. Both metaphorically because his head was now clear, and physically because the sun was just about to rise. In the wheelhouse, Roger was looking pale he gulped, turned, took two steps to the side, slid the door open and was sick over the side of the boat.

'Better out than in,' said the one called John.

But Church was not paying any notice now. His attention was caught by the sight of another boat just to the starboard side, perhaps fifty or a hundred metres away. He had no idea what sort of vessel it was, perhaps a fishing boat on its way to Fleetwood a few miles up the coast? Perhaps it was a pleasure boat taking some early morning fishermen out to sea? He looked around the cabin for something light in colour. The plywood shelves were too heavy for his bound hands to lift but he decided that the cushions were more manageable. Church lifted up the beige padded cushion and held it against the starboard porthole as best he could, covering the aperture. Then slowly and meticulously he moved it to one side to uncover it.

He continued to cover and uncover the porthole, sometimes leaving the cushion in place for a short time and sometimes for a little longer. Four short, pause, one short, pause, one short, one long and two short, pause, one short, two long, one short then a long pause. He repeated this twice then added a final two long, pause and one short display of the seat cushion. Church knew that it was a forlorn hope. Hardly anyone knows morse code these days and his makeshift signalling in the gloom with a seat cushion at a tiny porthole would more than likely have been invisible to anyone watching from the other boat. Church watched as the other boat got smaller and smaller, the diminishing size of the other vessel seemed to match the hopes he had of being rescued until eventually both the ship and his hopes faded away.

For another hour or two Church saw nothing out of the port or starboard aperture. Certainly no other ships and, he realised gloomily, not even a seagull. They had been circling around the other boat squawking and screeching, and probably meant that it was associated with fish or fishing of some sort. Now there was nothing but silence. The slap of water against the fibreglass hull of the motor cruiser, the gentle throb of the diesel engine as it chugged were constant white noise. Nothing else interrupted the hum.

Church looked despondently out of the porthole onto the grey water that surrounded them. He noticed that the white tops of the waves were bigger than before. He could only see sky and sea, not a strip of land anywhere in sight. Waves came rolling towards them from the port side, tossing them up and then dropping them down as they passed by. Church wondered if any of them would crash over the raised side deck on the little craft. Wave after wave swept by and each time the *Sargo 25* was swept up and then down. Occasionally it would roll quite violently and Church was pleased to think how Roger was suffering.

At some point in the course of the morning, it began to rain. Dark clouds rolled in and a fine drizzly rain was followed by large droplets that slapped down onto the deck above his head. The portholes began to be obscured by the drops of water blowing against them. Up in the wheelhouse, John seemed to know what he was doing but the apprehension could be clearly seen on the face of Roger. He obviously did not want to go to sea.

Chapter Twenty-Two

Man overboard

Dark clouds heavy with rain filled the sky above the *Sargo* motor cruiser as it sailed farther into the Irish Sea. The appearance of the sea was now dark grey and the only way to differentiate between sky and sea were the white tops to the waves. Waves that crashed around the hull of the small vessel. From the relative comfort and confinement of his small cabin, he could not tell how high the winds were but Church suspected that it was blustery and squally out on deck.

The horizon shifted as their boat rode up and down each wave. Sometimes it was way above the level of the little porthole that was Church's view out onto the world. At other times it dropped so that Church could not see the horizon through the round Perspex aperture even if he stood up as best he could. He did hear a new, unfamiliar sound and wondered if another boat was nearby. But it was the automatic bilge pump starting up to pump out water that had flowed over the gunwale as the cruiser had dipped and seawater had crashed over the top edge of the boat's side.

At the topmost point of a wave, just before the motor cruiser lurched downwards, Church thought that he saw an unfamiliar shape. A black rectangle that broke up the usual grey on grey combination of sea and sky. The boat slid down from the crest of a wave and the shape had gone. But another large swell picked the boat up again and the shape was there again just at the topmost point. This time it was ever so slightly larger.

Waves are produced as a result of winds moving over the surface of a sea. They are formed in sets and travel vast distances until they reach land, or merge with another set of waves formed elsewhere. The time between each crest of a wave is, quite literally, the wavelength. Some wavelengths can be a long time apart, others come and go quickly. Some can coincide and become larger as they merge with another set. One of his older brothers had told him that the seventh wave being largest was a myth. Even so, Church found himself counting aloud. Each seventh wave brought them closer to the black shape and, as the smaller waves dropped out of sight, allowed an uninterrupted view.

The shape on the horizon got closer and closer, it was not black as first appeared but a pale grey. The silhouette of the other ship seen against the sky on the horizon had made it appear dark. Now, as it neared, Church could make out some details. The wheelhouse of the other vessel was sited on top of a tall tower at the aft. The bow at the front of the ship was in fact a ramp that could be raised and lowered when in port. Cargo could be quickly loaded and unloaded from this ramp and also via a huge crane located amidships.

Because he was no expert, Church did not know that this was a multipurpose mixed cargo vessel. Too small to take hundreds of the ribbed metal containers like the giant ships that transport goods around the globe, this vessel had just eight on its main deck. These smaller ships ply their trade between European ports, continuously picking up and dropping off mixed goods. The small cargo vessels rely on complex logistics to pick up and deliver goods to and from any one of a hundred different ports. Church also did not know that the ship had accommodation for a crew of up to sixteen, including the captain, first officer and a mix of engineers, deckhands, navigator or cook, who may well be called on to do other tasks on such a small ship.

Church estimated that the length of the motor cruiser they were on was about twenty-five feet. The length of the cargo vessel was harder to guess, perhaps one hundred and fifty feet, perhaps two hundred feet? It was hard to tell at sea with nothing to gauge it against. It was also hard to tell if they were approaching the other vessel or the other vessel was approaching them. Church could not make out the name on the ship but could see a large painted letter 'T' and the numbers '95'. The weather had not improved and heavy rain now hammered against the porthole obscuring the view before it was washed clean by a wave.

Up in the wheelhouse, John throttled back and let the little boat drift near to the larger cargo ship. Instructions were barked at Roger and it took Church a moment to understand what they were talking about.

'Go and get the policeman. It's time.'

'Okay.'

Footsteps approached and a hand grabbed the second swing door that separated the cabin where Church was sitting from the wheelhouse. The figure of Roger stood in the doorway. Still looking green in the face, still suffering from seasickness. He grasped Church by the shoulder and dragged him up the few steps onto the covered deck. The other ship now loomed even larger, dwarfing the little pleasure craft. Church had a growing sense that he was about to be thrown overboard and crushed against the side of the other vessel. His unease was not reduced when the ties that bound his wrists were cut, freeing up the use of his hands and arms.

The cargo ship was now only a few feet away. Church was surprised at how low the other boat sat in the water. He had no way of knowing what the ship's draft was but it was clearly displacing a lot of water. Suddenly, John throttled forward and the motor cruiser picked up speed.

He swung the wheel hard around and the two vessels inched closer together, port side to port side.

Church was aware that at any moment he would be pitched over the side of the motor cruiser and in all likelihood be dragged underneath the other ship. A lurch of the little motor cruiser made Roger turn and lean over the starboard side. He really was an unlikely sailor. The sound of him being sick generated no sympathy from Church. As the other man's head bent forward and his shoulders lifted, Church seized the opportunity and kicked at the prone figure with all of his weight. Roger yelled as he flipped over the gunwale on the side of the Cruiser and splashed into the sea. Executing, in Church's opinion, a quite passable swallow dive.

Two arms grabbed his shoulders and he fought against the weight now forcing him to the port side. Suddenly he was lifted off of his feet. Church fought against the urge to shout out as he was lifted twenty feet into the air. His belt dug into his stomach and he was temporarily winded. He spun around in the wind and was momentarily disorientated. Rain splashed into his eyes but he could make out the deck of the other vessel getting closer and closer. He glanced back at the motor cruiser and could just make out Roger splashing around to the swim platform at the stern. Church allowed himself a wry smile when he saw that the name of the smaller boat was *'Unsinkable IV'*.

More hands grabbed hold of Church as he hit the deck of the cargo ship. The clasp from a steel cable that ran up to the giant crane was unhooked from the belt of his trousers. Church rolled over and scrambled to his feet. He was baffled by the sight of an outstretched hand held out to welcome him aboard.

'Permission to board your vessel?' said Church who thought that it was rather a good quip under the circumstances.

'Captain Mathias Agurk grants you permission.' Came the reply from the smiling, slim-faced, middle-aged, dark-haired, clean-shaven captain of the cargo ship. 'Come into one of the spare cabins. It is warm and we have some spare dry clothes waiting.'

Church was not sure if it was from the feelings of elation at not having been thrown overboard, or something else but he returned the smile and offered his hand for the other man to shake. This strange tradition, which is customarily done with your right hand, became a friendly greeting allegedly because it proved that you came in peace and were not holding a weapon. It is also a sign of trust and that you believe the other person is not going to draw their weapon to fight with you. Church usually went with his feelings and his feelings were telling him that he could trust this man.

The cabin which was also to be his prison for the next few days was small, clean, tidy and cleverly laid out. No space had been wasted in its design and although it had been designed as a two-man berth, Church was the only inhabitant. As promised, new clothes had been left out on his bed including sensible footwear that Church was surprised to find fitted perfectly. Clearly, he had been expected aboard.

A routine developed as the days passed. The cargo ship docked at Amlwch on the island of Anglesey unloaded a small number of wooden crates and continued to sail around the coast. Church was locked in his cabin each time the ship made port but was allowed to roam the decks freely while at sea. More cargo was unloaded at Milford Haven and additional crates winched aboard. They docked at the Cornish ports of Falmouth and Penryn and took on extra food supplied as well as landing a large crate. Church estimated that they were averaging a speed of ten knots and began to contemplate where this journey would end. A long journey up the English channel to Shoreham allowed Church to have a good look around the ship. The metal containers were out of bounds to him, secured with padlocks and fastened with tamper-proof seals. However, the remaining cartons, crates and plastic-wrapped boxes were open to being examined.

The bills of lading prominently displayed on the outside of each package denoted the details of who was shipping the items, the consignee details, the port of loading and the port of discharge as well as the final delivery destination. The mixed cargo included, as far as he could tell, precision engineering parts for machines that could only be guessed at, dried food that originated in Taiwan but had had a circuitous journey so far and car parts for 'just in time' delivery into the manufacturing supply chain. Church ascertained that most of the cargo originated from Rotterdam and, as they appeared to be returning, that was their final destination.

It was the crate of dried food that interested him. The contents had been vacuum-sealed in thick plastic bags but during the wet weather at the start of the journey, the crate had an aroma of sodium hypochlorite. Commonly used as a disinfectant, it can also be used as an antisceptic in diluted form. However, its main purpose is as a bleaching agent and as such it is very effective at masking and killing smells. Church suspected that the actual contents of these plastic pouches were not nutritional edible treats, but recreational illegal drugs.

The cargo ship bypassed the port of Dover and continued to head North-East out of the Channel. The weather changed as soon as they left the English Channel and began to travel into the North Sea. Calm seas and weak sunshine accompanied their journey. The captain of the mixed cargo vessel was Dutch, the crew mainly Philipino but English was still the language spoken aboard. Church busied himself by tidying up the deck of the cargo ship which earned him the respect of the

Philipino crew. A vast amount of rope was still being used to secure and fasten the cargo. The crew would try and coil the double-braided rope in the same way as the triple-braided lengths. It would kink and twist awkwardly, ending up as an untidy pile. Church worked his way around the ship, looping the triple-braided rope and coiling the double-braided in a figure of eight. He also showed the crew how to soak the rope in a diluted mix of fabric conditioner to make coiling easier.

For most of the journey, the captain kept himself to himself but on the fourth day at sea, his mood changed for the better. Perhaps it was the fact that they were nearing his home port, perhaps he had received some good news? Church did not find out because on the last leg of their voyage he was locked in his cabin for most of the day. At noon, a large meal was brought to his cabin on a tray. Towards late afternoon there was a knock on the door, unnecessary because it was locked, but a courteous gesture.

'I have your clothes. Your suit has been steam pressed and your shirt laundered and ironed.' The captain explained, his outstretched arms holding out a package. 'We will be making port soon. Thank you for causing me no trouble. Goodbye, policeman.'

'I expected to be thrown overboard during this voyage,' replied Church.

'It is difficult to dispose of a body, Mr Church.'

'Even at sea?'

'Especially at sea. Parts of a body may be eaten by crabs and other sea creatures but eventually, most of the body will wash up ashore somewhere.'

Church realised that it was the second time that someone had mistaken him for a policeman but he did not bother to try and correct the ship's captain. He was being kept alive, for now.

Chapter Twenty-Three

Meal for the condemned man

At 17:00 local time, the mixed cargo ship T-95 *Kertmis-ijs* entered the port of Rotterdam. The two hundred feet long vessel carefully navigated its way around the Hook of Holland and into the entrance to the port itself. The ship steered past much larger container vessels that dwarfed it in size. Enormous thirteen hundred feet long container ships that were piled high with steel containers loomed above the *Kertmis-ijs*, just as that ship had loomed above the little motor cruiser *Unsinkable IV* in the Irish Sea.

Church could not see from his side of the cargo ship, but several vessels were docking at the World Gateway Deepwater container terminal. Unloading hundreds of containers filled with goods transported halfway around the world. COSCO Shipping Lines from China, Evergreen Marine Corporation from Taiwan, Maersk Line Group from Denmark and the charmingly named Orient Overseas Container Line, OOCL, registered out of Hong Kong.

The captain on the small mixed cargo ship *Kertmis-ijs* radioed the officer on duty at the Harbour Coordination Centre, confirmed the details of their ship and began to cruise down the *Calandkanaal*. They travelled past the huge oil refineries located on the outskirts. Huge drums storing crude oil to be refined at *Donauhaven* and *Petroleumhaven*. Chemical refineries at *Vopak* created oil-based derivatives. Farther upstream, they passed by *Eemhaven* and *Waalhaven*. More radio contact was made, this time with the Traffic Centre and the Officer in change exchanged pleasantries before signing off with an affirmative. A small pilot boat appeared and guided them to where the cargo ship docked.

Church had been looking out of the porthole at the side of his cabin watching all of this slip by. He was struck by just how flat the countryside was. Little land could be seen from his vantage point and the landscape appeared to be made up primarily of sky. And that sky was dark and heavy with thick clouds. The sun had set a short time before, it would soon be dark. But for some reason, this time Church did not sense that this was an ominous premonition.

Sounds outside the cabin roused Edward Church from his thoughts. A member of the crew walked him very carefully to the starboard side of the ship where he was accompanied onto what he assumed was a pilot vessel. At the last moment, the crew member jumped back onto the cargo ship and the pilot vessel with Church now on board took off at speed. But just a few minutes later their speed reduced and the pilot boat slowed to a more sedate pace. The pilot steered his way under a road suspension bridge and into a quay. Church saw the sign *City Marina* drift by the side of the boat just before a line was tossed over the bow and they moored in a berth alongside numerous other boats.

Church could feel his legs wobble slightly as he stepped onto the gangway and walked up to the quayside. It took a few moments for him to regain his 'land legs' after four days at sea. 'Mal de Debarquement' syndrome, literally translated as *sickness of disembarkment* occurs because the brain has got used to the constant swaying on board a ship. Church made a real effort to walk in a straight line as he walked along the dock. It did not help that he was sandwiched between two heavily built men and that the dock itself was not overly wide.

One of his minders peeled off as they approached a little port authority kiosk. It was illuminated from within by a harsh strip light and the lights glowed from within, spilling out into the early evening dusk. The man stepped inside the portacabin and Church could see but not hear an animated conversation between the man and an official wearing a blue shirt with navy epaulettes on the shoulders. The officer had an identification badge clipped to his shirt pocket and he reached up to the plastic card and retrieved a pen from the breast pocket. Forms were signed, hands were shaken and a moment later the minder reappeared outside. Whatever had just occurred passed without incident.

The little group of newcomers stepped away from the quay, up a short flight of steps and out onto mainland Rotterdam. Church was guided across the street and towards a pair of *Mercedes-Benz* 4x4 vehicles. Church could not recognise the model in the darkness but could see the distinctive three-pointed star in the middle of the large front grille. Cool blue headlights glowed on either side. Almost immediately one of the doors in the first vehicle opened and a figure emerged. He stepped around to the front of the car and Church got a good view of the other man.

He was dressed in a dark suit, similar to Church. The bodyguards who still hovered either side of Church also wore suits. But the other man's clothing was obviously much more expensive. The material shimmered in the electric car headlamps. The shirt was clearly silk, as was the pale pink tie tied with a thick Windsor knot. A chunky watch was just visible from underneath the double cuffs at the man's wrist. His hair was black and cut fashionably short, he was not clean-shaven but had well-groomed heavily-styled stubble. A hand was outstretched towards Church and he noticed that almost every finger on the other man's hand had a ring on it.

'Welkom, politieagent,' the other man said. 'I am Manus, Manus Klimop. You must be hungry after your long journey. Come, we will travel to Amsterdam for dinner and party.'

'Nice vehicle, Manus,' said Church. 'This car must have twenty-two-inch or even twenty-four-inch alloy wheels. They must cost a bit to replace. Nice paintwork too. Is that solid black or midnight blue?' Church continued to walk carefully around the car pretending to admire it. 'These headlights must cut through the fog. Very nice.' He paused for a long time near the front bumper.

Eventually, Church was guided into the back of the second *Mercedes-Benz* and the cars took off in a little convoy before he had a chance to speak. Low-rise apartment blocks drifted by either side of the vehicles and the two cars indicated and turned onto a wide two-lane avenue. The space between the two lanes was occupied by a twin tram line. Taller tower blocks passed them by and the landscape cleared. Eventually, the two vehicles drove onto a suspension bridge and across a large open expanse of water. More tower blocks and low-rise apartments with ground-floor shops filtered by either side of them as they drove through Rotterdam centre. The two-car convoy cruised onto the A13 main road and then onto the A4 motorway which, according to the signposts that flashed by, would take them directly to central Amsterdam.

Church turned to one of his companions, a burly figure with a shaven head that seemed to grow straight from his shoulders. 'Good evening,' Church said but got no reply. 'Your car is okay too,' he said again, but his attempt at small talk was met by silence.

At one point on their journey, Church had the sensation that they were being followed. But he dismissed it as wishful thinking on his part. No one knew he was in Holland. His companions clearly thought that he was a policeman but for some reason, he did not feel threatened by them. The bodyguards were better dressed than

Godfrey Timson's and the man named Manus was definitely better dressed than Godfrey. But because he had not been blindfolded, Church assumed that it did not matter if he saw the route that he was being taken on. There was no need to hide what was being seen, probably because Church would not get the opportunity to use any of the information he might gather en route. It was likely to be a one-way journey.

The journey from the marina in Rotterdam to central Amsterdam took a little over an hour, just as Elsa DeWinter had explained back in Manchester. The roads were wide, quiet and smooth, and the landscape was flat. Very flat. Perhaps during the daytime, you could see for some distance on either side of the road, but at night-time, there was nothing. Just darkness.

Traffic on the motorway was sparse at this time of night. They cruised in the outside lane, passing the few Heavy Goods Lorries that trundled across Europe at night and even fewer cars driven by other late-night road users. As the motorway nears Amsterdam it drops down and underneath the Schiphol airport in exactly the same way that the Wilmslow Road runs underneath Manchester Airport in the UK.

The driver of the black *Mercedes-Benz* cruised along the complicated six-lane road system to the North of the Airport and in no time at all, they were approaching the southern part of Amsterdam. Up until now, Church had been impressed by the clean modern appearance of the country. However, as they exited the motorway and entered Amsterdam Nieuw-West his impressions changed. Social housing that had been poorly maintained, shops that were closed down and businesses that had been boarded up lined the streets. It all looked depressingly familiar to Church.

The car made a series of turns, left and right, right and left. At one point they drove underneath the motorway that they had just exited. It crossed the street above them in a brutal, blunt, concrete overpass that had no style, thought or planning. It simply cut right across the street, forcing housebuilders to stop building low and high rise accommodation for one hundred metres. Each of the concrete pillars that supported the motorway had been covered in garish graffiti.

Eventually, the car in front slowed down, indicated and pulled into the right-hand side of the street. The second car, containing Church and his silent abductor copied suit and pulled in behind.

'Thanks for the guided tour,' Church quipped as they came to a halt, 'It's been most informative.'

The car door was opened by someone from outside, Church stepped out of the vehicle and surveyed his surroundings. They were outside a small arcade of shops. Three high-rise tower blocks loomed behind the shops. A Newsagent cum tobacconist was closed for the night but the next shop a general food, fruit and vegetable purveyor was still open. Two restaurants named *The GrillRoom* and *Pizzarelli* were next in line. Alongside them was a barber's shop and next to that a café, both dark and closed for business. On the opposite side of the street was an open space of grassland with a few trees and some bushes. The last unit in this little arcade of shops was larger, much larger. It was most definitely open and Church could both see and feel what sort of commercial unit it was.

A large electric sign outside announced the *Poesje Nightclub* in yellow neon. Two giant cats' eyes had been painted on the ground floor shutters, yellow elongated circles with black vertical slits. As Church stood outside he could feel the music throbbing through the pavement. It seemed to pulse, beat and pound the pathway from within the building.

'Welcome to *Poesje*,' Manus Klimop said with an expansive sweep of his arm. 'No need for ID, I know security. VIP access for you and me.'
'What is this place?' asked Church.
'I like to think that it is a little like the *KitKat* club in Berlin. But much wilder. Have you heard of it?'
'Oh, I see. Never heard of it, but it sounds lovely.'
'Welcome to the party,' said Manus.
'The last party I went to, I was drugged, kidnapped, tied-up and trafficked to Holland.'
'This will be much wilder.' Manus laughed and showed a set of perfect white teeth. Europeans are blessed with good dental genetics. He guided Church down a covered walkway, past a queue of hopeful clubgoers and into the nightspot.

Some of the past predicaments that Edward Church had found himself in were so crazily extravagant that his spirits were raised simply by the situations he experienced. Church's spirits soared as he walked into the *Poesje* club. They bypassed the door security, the entrance desk and the cloakroom, before entering the main room of the club itself. The girl in the cloakroom was a sight to behold. Very overweight but also very glamorous, the girl wore few items of clothing and had the most enormous amount of hair. It cascaded a long way down past her shoulders and down to her waistline in curls of jet black tresses. She flicked it to one side with an exaggerated swish as Church and Manus walked past her. The beat of the music throbbed through Church's body, making his heart race in time with the song. A stage filled one side of the large room and a booth filled most of the space on the opposite side with a DJ hard at work inside. The space in the middle heaved with nightclubbers. Lights flashed and pulsed, changing time with the music and changing colour on a never-ending kaleidoscopic loop. All-female dancers were hard at work on the stage. They appeared to be professional and well-rehearsed. Illuminated hula-hoops swung in wild patterns around their bodies, adding to the discord of light.

Church stepped around an enormous laughing Buddha statue that appeared to jeer at him with the secret knowledge of something that was about to happen. He followed Manus up a flight of stairs that had been constructed out of scaffold poles and decorated with flashing rope lights. Eventually, they entered a dining room. The upstairs space was equally as large as the ground floor but it had been divided up into select areas by drapes and thick wooden bamboo poles. The music was not quite so loud here, but at the far side of the room, another raised stage area featured more female dancers. Two of them were juggling oversized clubs, which looked like giant ten-pin bowling pins. Flashing lights built into the batons created more patterns of light as the women juggled the illuminated shillelaghs. Church scanned the groups of diners who were sitting at the tables. They were mostly a young crowd, immaculately dressed and clearly wealthy. Someone sitting at one of the tables looked vaguely familiar to Church, a person who reminds you of somebody else. Church was in a foreign country and could not have possibly known the man, but he could not recall who the other person reminded him of. The lighting was subdued as was the sound of the music, he dismissed the thought. A cry from one of the dining table areas made Church jump.

'Oh my God, fancy seeing you here!' a male voice shouted.

'Godfrey? Godfrey Timson?' said Church not able to hide the surprise in his voice.

'The one and only, dear boy. I think that we got off on the wrong foot in Manchester. Nice to see you, Edward Church.'

'Well, what a coincidence,' smiled Manus, but Church suspected that it was nothing of the sort.

The meal that they ate, Church had to admit, was amazing. He was not quite so sure about the after-party.

Chapter Twenty-Four

Pills and Booze

Church had the feeling that he had clearly been brought to the *Poesje* nightclub in downtown Amsterdam for a reason, he also felt that he would soon find out exactly why. He had the impression that Godfrey Timson and Manus Klimop knew each other. The actual reason why the three of them, and the two ever-present bodyguards, were having dinner together in a nightclub eluded him. The spirit of elation that he had felt earlier had well and truly dwindled as the evening progressed. He felt subdued, on edge and alert to everything around him. Godfrey Timson, on the other hand, looked as if he was really enjoying himself. At the dinner table, Church had noticed that Godfrey's pupils were dilated. His behaviour had become more extroverted and loud. Now, as he danced wildly beside the table Manus appeared to be more and more irritated.

'My family are from middle Europe, Mr Church, an area that used to be called Bohemia. But we are quite reserved and quiet, not bohemian at all. I was taught the importance of hard work by my German Grandmother. She emigrated from Prague in what was then the newly created Czechoslovakia just after the Great War. Ironically, she was a victim of discrimination by the Czech authorities.'

'She would get her revenge a few years later,' replied Church cooly.

'She travelled to Holland, but the majority of my family stayed behind. My cousin Ondra runs a club in the city and he inspired me to create something similar here.

That was just four years ago and now the *Poesje* is the best club in Amsterdam. Strict door policy, no large groups of men who just come to view. It has the best DJs, the best light shows, the best entertainers. My younger brother looks after security. My sister is in charge of entertainment.'

'It's a real family affair.'

'Family are the most important,' said Manus earnestly.

'And if you haven't got family, then friends are the most important,' replied Church.

He could not hear above the sound of the music but a young woman at the adjoining table who had been eavesdropping on their conversation said, 'But what if you have no family or friends...'

Manus was clearly passionate about his nightclub and Church was genuinely impressed at his commitment. The man obviously had charisma and Manus Klimop was possibly the least hypocritical character he had encountered along this drug-related search for Amber Garland.

'I despise drug-taking,' Manus eventually said. 'It makes fools of anyone who takes them and they will end up as smackheads and stoners.'

'But you don't mind supplying them if people want to buy from you,' replied Church.

He had to admit that it was the most honest statement about drug-taking that he had heard from someone for a long time. Church had stopped drinking after the meal had been cleared away. He had also tried to pour away most of the drinks he had been given while other guests at the table had been distracted. And there were certainly lots of distractions in the *Poesje* nightclub. The outfits that many of the clubgoers wore were flamboyant. The remixed, vintage-disco music was loud and throbbing. A nightclub photographer pestered their table taking lots of photographs of Church and Godfrey Timson.

'I would like to get a nightclub for Maureen,' said Godfrey as he took another mouthful of drink from his glass.

'Seems like a fair exchange to me,' said Church.

'Have another drink with me, Edward,' he slurred as he stood and swayed by the side of their table. 'The vodka is excellent, although I can't feel my lips now.'

'I've had enough of the wine, thanks. Don't want to mix grape and grain.'

'They also say don't mix pills and booze, but I've had more than my fair share of both this evening,' Godfrey slurred.

A particularly exotic clubgoer walked past and Godfrey was distracted for a moment. She sashayed past them and headed towards a room with a sign outside that read *'Clothes are optional beyond this point.'*

'That meal was delicious but I wish that she was on the menu,' Godfrey garbled and promptly fell across the table.

The woman looked over at them. She was beautiful. Dark hair cascaded down past her shoulders, full lips and a heart-shaped face were heavily made up. She was dressed in a figure-hugging red and black backless dress. Two large wing-shaped tattoos were clearly visible on her back.

'Elsa says get out of here,' she whispered to Church as she walked past.

Church reached across to try and help Godfrey, trying to understand what the woman was warning him about. A movement to one side alerted Church's senses. Instinctively, he stepped back. Making space between himself and the detected movement. Church saw one of Manus's bodyguards, the silent abductor, clumsily reaching in his direction. The mood in the room shifted dramatically. People in the nightclub sensed trouble and began to move away from them. Church took advantage of the space and stepped smartly over towards the raised stage. He grabbed one of the glittering clubs from the dancer as it hovered in mid-air. Immediately Church realised his mistake. The baton was hollow plastic with no weight or substance to it at all. Nevertheless, he swung it towards the henchman and clubbed him around the head. A brightly coloured arc of light curved through the air and suddenly stopped as the baton made contact with the other man's skull. The silent abductor looked shocked, expecting to be knocked out.

As he went through the options, Church made up his mind about what to do. But as he made his next move the room went dark, then stars exploded across his vision. He had the sensation of falling and the last thought that went through his mind was, 'not again'.

* * *

The sound of the music was throbbing. Pounding through his head, making the temples in Church's head hammer in pain. Except that he could not hear anything, there was no music playing anymore. Church opened his eyes, he could see that the nightclub was empty. Bright security lights appeared to have been switched on, replacing the coloured flashing lights that had shone before.

As he came to his senses Church realised that all of the tables and chairs in the nightclub had been cleared away. In fact, now that his vision was clear he could see that everything had gone, the space was completely vacant. It gradually dawned on Edward Church that he was not in the nightclub anymore, he was alone in a vast empty warehouse.

Church slowly got to his feet, checking himself for any injuries. Apart from a large bump on the back of his skull that throbbed wickedly every time he moved his head, he looked to be largely uninjured. It was bitterly cold inside the empty storage building. Condensed breath streamed from his mouth and nose. His legs ached, as did his arm sockets and Church assumed that he had been carried or dragged to wherever he now found himself. Cautiously and methodically he worked his way around the inside perimeter of the warehouse. He warmed up gradually as he walked around. A large steel roller door that was big enough to allow an articulated truck through was securely bolted shut. Windows were non-existent, lighting came from overhead strip lights that make Church's head throb when he looked up at them. Skylights that were dirty with moss or mould let in little daylight. At either end of the space were solid doors marked with warning signs in Dutch and English, *Nooduitgang,* Fire Exit. He tried to push the horizontal metal bar across each door but unsurprisingly they were locked.

A collection of rags in the far corner caught his eye. Church strode over and picked up the corner of a grubby grey tarpaulin. He froze at the sight underneath. At first, it was difficult to make out what had been uncovered. The face was barely recognizable, the clothing was covered in blood and mixed with dirty rags. A hand stuck out at a jaunty angle. It was large, fat and had stubby fingers, a male hand. Church gently wiped the face with a rag and a white face stared back at him with long-dead eyes.

Godfrey Timson had been shot. Underneath the blood that had smeared across a little of his face, Church could see the familiar blue-grey hue of the skin. The colour of death. Church sat back and took a deep breath, taking in his surroundings and thinking through what had happened. He knew that eventually, the police would come for him. Church went through his own pockets with a sense of already knowing what he would find. Sure enough, tucked into the back of his trouser pocket was a small revolver. He knew that it would be covered in the blood splatter of Godfrey and that his own fingerprints would be pressed onto the handle of the weapon. Church leaned forward and with a sigh, gently closed the staring eyes of Godfrey Timson with one hand and with the other laid the revolver down next to the body.

Giving himself a few seconds to assess the situation, Church sat and looked around. He picked up the gun, checked that it was still loaded and shot through one of the warehouse skylight windows. The sound of the bullet echoed through the empty building. Using a rag folded in half, he carefully picked up some of the broken glass, making sure that he had some of the edges with gunshot residue on them, and slid the shards of glass underneath the body of Godfrey Timson. He carefully and thoroughly wiped the handle, trigger, barrel and other parts of the weapon. Then he looked around for a stick or a thin metal tube of some sort. Finding something that fitted the criteria, he poked it down the end of the gun barrel and tried to fling the weapon through the broken skylight. It took a few attempts, but on the third effort, the revolver sailed through the air and flew through the smashed windowpane. Feeling that the crime scene had been suitably disorganised Church looked around once again.

He dragged the tarpaulin to one end of the warehouse and folded it roughly in half then half again. Making himself as comfortable as possible he settled himself in for the wait which he suspected would not be too long. In the quiet, he became used to the sounds coming from outside. A distant rumble of road traffic and the sound of an occasional jet engine overhead suggested that he was close to urbanization. Perhaps on the outskirts of Amsterdam or Rotterdam? Perhaps another major Dutch city?

A rat appeared from nowhere and began to scuttle across the concrete floor. It sniffed the air and ran in random directions. As if drawn by the smell of death, it edged closer to Godfrey Timson's body. Church looked around him and picked up a discarded beer bottle. Taking aim, he threw it in the direction of the rat and it landed with a smash just a few inches away from the rodent.

In the lull between vehicles, he could hear birds singing. Different sounds now made him pay attention. Vehicles nearby but travelling slowly and quietly. Several minutes passed by agonisingly slowly. Church's back was beginning to ache as he rested against the wall a few feet from one of the Fire Doors. Suddenly the lights went out.

Both of the Fire Doors crashed open. Dutch *Politie* dressed in full riot gear burst through the door and into the warehouse. The empty space echoed with shouts and commands from the policemen, their faces covered by riot helmets. Church sat with his hands above his head and waited. Bright torches shone in his face and eventually, he was hauled to his feet to be thoroughly searched, arrested and handcuffed.

A plain-clothed Police officer appeared in front of Church. He stood aggressively, hands on hips, legs wide apart, a cigarette dangling between his lips. In his mind. Church named him *The Commissaris*.

'We have caught ourselves a big fish,' the man said in broken English.

Church attempted to speak but the other man interrupted him before he could say anything.

'Trying to tie up your loose ends before attempting to flee the country. Your plan did not work. We have caught you. Your drug supply line is broken,' he blew cigarette smoke in Church's face and turned away.

One of the police officers dressed in full riot gear stepped directly in front of him and removed their helmet. Church found himself standing face to face with Elsa DeWinter. She could not hide the disappointment in her eyes.

'You took your time,' Church said in as friendly a tone as he could manage under the circumstances.

'I am sorry, Edward. There is little I can do to help you now.'

'I don't much like your Commissaris. How did you know where to find me? An anonymous tip-off? I hate those anonymous tip-offs.'

'My Chief of Police thinks that you are involved in the supply of drugs. He thinks that you are a big-shot in organised drug distribution.'

'Well, it makes a change from being mistaken for a policeman.'

'We have been tracking you since you arrived in the *City Marina*. One of our unmarked vehicles followed you to Amsterdam and we have been watching you ever since.'

'Even in the *Poesje* nightclub?'

'Well, perhaps not all of the time,' she said sheepishly.

'Thanks for the tip-off in there by the way. Nice looking girlfriend.'

'Wife.'

'Sorry. I've had a bump to the head.'

'And you did not realise who was sitting at the next table? We have seized CCTV from the club. We have had a team of people work through the night to view the tapes.'

'Very efficient.'

'Thank you, Edward.'

'So who was sitting at the next table?'

'It was Amber Garland.'

Church quietly swore to himself under his breath. How could he have missed her? And more importantly in what way was she mixed up with this?

'Who was the Arab on the next table?' continued Elsa, but Church's head was beginning to throb.

By some miracle of European efficiency, an ice-pack appeared for Church to use on his head. He appreciatively applied it to the back of his head as he furiously thought through the options. It became clear to Church that the only reason he had been brought to Holland was so that he could be set up for the murder of Godfrey Timson. It is difficult, but not impossible, to dispose of a body at sea. Much easier to frame him for murder which is why someone went to the trouble of transporting him several hundred kilometres from Manchester to Amsterdam. Church was not entirely sure why this had happened but he knew for sure how it had happened. The images that were taken by that annoying photographer at the club would be an added link between Church and Godfrey Timson.

'You didn't tell me how you found me?' questioned Church.

'We lost you at the club but received a tip-off about gunshots being fired in this warehouse.'

'I'm sure that you will be seeing some photographs of Godfrey and me anonymously sent by someone very soon. It will make a link between the two of us.'

'It is worse than that, Edward. The British police have also issued an arrest warrant in your name. It appears that you are wanted for the murder of Neville Smallbone alternatively known as Hookman. You are also wanted for questioning in connection with the death of Tomas Kar.'

'I don't know anything about Mr Hookman's death. But Tomas Kar was assaulted by a road barrier that he ran into while I was chasing him and his death is nothing to do with me.'

'A Champagne glass with your fingerprints on it was identified at the property owned by Hookman. The UK authorities contacted Interpol and your name was added to the list of names and photographs on its Red Notices.'

'I don't think that Champagne was ever Hookman's style. I wasn't even offered a drink when I visited him there. How come it has taken so long to find the glass and link it to me?'

'It seems that the Champagne flute was missed on the first search of the property. However, it was discovered during a second sweep of the flat.'

'Convenient,' said Church.

'And now this,' she said as she swept her hand in an arc that ended at the prone figure of Godfrey Timson. 'I did not particularly like the man, he was too loosey-goosey by far.'

'But he did not deserve this,' added Church morosely.

'I have to take you in for questioning, Edward, and then you will be charged.' Elsa sounded just as depressed as Church.

Chapter Twenty-Five

Amsterdam

'So who is the Arab?' Church asked as Elsa drove.
'What?'
'Back in the warehouse, you asked me if I knew who was the Arab sitting at the next table in the *Poesje* nightclub.'
'We do not know.'
'Do you know where Manus Klimop is?'
'No, he seems to have disappeared too.'
'Did you pick up any of the hoodlums who work for Manus? You could enquire at the *Silent Henchmen* shop or *Quiet Bodyguards*?'
'I am not sure I know what you mean,' replied Elsa sounding confused.
'I don't suppose that you can put out a search for Manus Klimop and question him about Amber Garland either?'
'Mr Klimop has done nothing wrong. Unlike you, Edward.'

Elsa DeWinter had managed to persuade her Chief of Police to let her take Church in for questioning. They had driven in silence for some time. Just the two of them in a brightly marked police car, within a convoy of similar liveried vehicles. After they had driven for a few kilometres she had tried to explain to Church that everything would eventually get sorted out. But Church was not convinced. He glanced out of the passenger side window as they approached Amsterdam city centre.

As they drove through a wide tunnel underneath the raised railway lines and emerged the other side, Church took in the beauty of his surroundings. Tall, narrow buildings stretched for as far as the eye could see on either side of a wide boulevard. The central canal was a dark inky black ribbon that separated two lanes of traffic. Not that there were many cars around at this time of the morning. The only other vehicles that Church could see were parked at a diagonal angle facing the waterway. Everything was flat, very flat.

A flock of pigeons alighted as the cars turned a corner, startled into flight by the unexpected movement of people in cars. A bridge crossed over the canal every few hundred yards or so. At each crossing, a collection of bicycles was neatly stacked ready for use by early morning workers. Church counted at least two cafes for each bridge that they passed. Some were still in darkness, a few had lights on perhaps getting ready to open up in an hour or so's time. Tall towers of chairs leaned precariously outside each of the coffee shops. Church turned to Elsa. Her short blonde hair had been ruffled by the riot gear helmet, but still looked good. She had ditched her glasses, not practical for the raid and her face had the slightly odd, wide-eyed, staring appearance of someone used to wearing glasses but not having them on their face.

'Sorry to do this to you, Elsa,' said Church as they drove past another bridge.

'What do you mean?' she replied, sounding confused.

Church grabbed the steering wheel of the car and yanked it to the left. The police car swerved towards the canal. Church had spotted a gap in the row of parked cars and judged the distance and speed to make his move. Elsa screamed and wrenched the wheel to the right, straightening the car back onto the road. It was then that Church grabbed the wheel again, this time he also hauled it hard to the right. It was too late for her to try and counteract the swerve. The police vehicle crashed through a tower of café chairs, scattering them across the street.

Church heard other police cars braking hard behind them. A sharp-eyed detective in front of them must have spotted the commotion in his rearview mirror because the car in front suddenly braked hard and switched on its siren. Red and blue lights cut through the early morning dawn. The sound of sirens echoed off of the buildings on either side of them.

Church seized the door handle and was relieved when he felt the catch give way. He popped his seatbelt release catch as the door swung open and a second later he was running down a side street. He did not look over his shoulder behind him but ran as fast as he could. The pain in Church's head was immense. He wished that he still had the ice pack in his hand. His feet pounded along the pavement in time with his elevated heartbeat. His head throbbed to the same rhythm.

The doors to the shops, the bars and the cafes were still firmly closed and Church knew that there was no point in trying to hide inside. He had a vague memory of the city centre layout. *De Wallen* district was the medieval centre of Amsterdam. It is surrounded by concentric circles of canals that also criss-cross under streets and pedestrian pavements. He could not remember the name of the old Church that pretty much defined the town centre but if he had bothered to look at the sign as he ran past he would have seen that it read *Oude Kerk*, Old Church. He continued to run down narrow streets past closed and barred commercial outlets. Cafes that smelt of sweet coffee, bars that had the smell of yesterdays beer and offices that appeared to have several doorways and full-length windows with draped curtains covering them. Even as he raced through the streets, the beauty of the city was not wasted on Edward Church.

He ran to the end of an alleyway and suddenly he was out in the open again. A large uncluttered, exposed space. Wide roads ran in four directions. Tree-lined boulevards that bordered shops and hotels. Another street was home to residential properties with cafes, restaurants and food shops on the ground floor. Each direction he looked seemed to be almost entirely deserted. He paused for breath and listened for the sound of footsteps or sirens behind him. Straining his ears, he detected that the sirens were some distance to the North. Looking around he could see a bar with shuttered windows on one corner with an illuminated sign above which read *Rembrandt Corner*. On the opposite side of the square was a large modern building that Church recognised as the Academy for Theatre and Dance. Church knew where he was. The small Rembrandt museum was to one side of the bar, a small modern extension next to it. He ran down the deserted *Jodenbreestraat* with its central one-way road flanked by cycle lanes. His head was pounding once again as he traversed the crossroads a few hundred yards farther down.

Church did not stop at the sets of traffic lights to look for cars or other early morning vehicles. He could hear a set of police sirens in the distance and they were getting closer. Sprinting over the empty crossroads he continued to head South. Church had a vague recollection of where he was heading. It was a long shot but it was his best hope of evading the police chase.

His heart was already pumping inside his chest but it leapt even more at the sight in front of him. Church did not look for traffic as he ran across the road bridge, he remembered that it was for trams only and they did not run this early in the morning. Ahead of him to the left was a huge glass structure, an enormous greenhouse that accommodated the *Hortus Botanicus* Amsterdam. Botanical gardens stretched beyond the wide glasshouse frontage, he remembered that there was a small lake with a footbridge traversing it where tourists liked to pose and have their photograph taken. He also remembered that next to the Botanic gardens was a vast expanse of parkland. Ideal to lose himself in.

As he raced across the tram tracks Church headed right. Almost immediately he plunged into the park. Trees, lawns and bushes surrounded him. He sped down a winding path, heading for what he imagined was the centre of the woodland. Tempted as he was to climb a tree to try and conceal himself, Church decided to head into the deepest undergrowth he could find and wait. Sirens were sounding some distance away. He could not place which direction they were coming from or even if they were getting louder or quieter. The sounds from police vehicles seemed to be coming from several directions and as he twisted his head to try and listen carefully the noise seemed to shift as well. Eventually, he stopped attempting to guess. The throbbing in his head was intensely painful, his heart was still beating loudly and his legs were feeling like jelly after the long sprint through the city centre.

* * *

Church sat and waited, crouched in the bushes amongst the undergrowth in the chilly early morning air. The sounds of the sirens had eventually faded after a few hours. Church had waited, listening to the police vehicles drive close-by then drift farther away. Once or twice he thought that he heard people walking a few feet away. They might have been law enforcement officers, they might have been early morning dog walkers. Church did not emerge from his hiding place to enquire. The slow step sounds of dog walkers gave way to the sounds of joggers, fast footsteps on the gravel paths in the park. Heavy breathing from the morning runners indicated to Church how his own breathing had slowed down.

Voices drifted across the atmosphere in the woods. Church had never learnt much Dutch but he did make out the odd word that had a shared meaning with its German equivalent. The voices were definitely friendly. Perhaps students making their way to college and other people on their way to the office. Church made out several *goedemorgens* and one or two *hallos,* the almost universal greeting of 'good morning' and 'hello' used all over the world.

At around ten o'clock in the morning, Church judged that it was relatively safe to emerge from his hiding place. He waited until he could hear no voices and judged that it would be an opportune moment to materialise from the shrubbery. Unfortunately, his timing was less than ideal and Church found himself face to face with a young woman, startled by his sudden appearance.

'Goedemorgen, Mej,' he said as brightly as he could, hoping to sound friendly.

'Good morning to you,' she replied curtly.

So much for my accent thought Church to himself as he strolled away from her as casually as he could manage.

Church had the notion to head back into the city centre, wander through the narrow streets and alleyways of De Wallen and pick up some food and liquid refreshments. As he exited the park, Church headed West walking slowly and carefully until he came across the wide canal named *Amstel.* He was alert to the sounds of the city. The sound of vehicles, trams, people and bicycles. Everywhere bicycles. You really could not escape from them. Church was rather pleased because it reminded him that he was not alone, there was a whole city surrounding him. People going about their daily lives, rushing to get from one place to some other place. Normal life and he felt himself to be a part of it.

As well as being the name of a popular European lager, the Amstel is also the name of a river that flows through most of northern Holland. The impressive frontage of the Amstel InterContinental hotel loomed before him. Church ascended the short flight of steps and patted his jacket pocket as he entered the hotel. A natural reaction when one is about to part with a significant amount of money. He felt securely covered by the first canopy, supported by eight cast-iron pillars and then shrouded in comfort by the sixteen pillars supporting the inner canopy. For no particular reason, he chose the right-hand doorway to enter the hotel and, out of the choice of three swing doors, it proved to be the closest to the dining rooms.

After a brief exchange with the restaurant attendant who did not seem to understand the concept of a 'walk-in' customer for breakfast, Church settled for a long and luxurious morning meal at his table by the window. As he waited for his food to arrive, he considered why Manus Klimop had not taken his wallet, keys, phone or passport. In fact, the other man had been rather pleased to see the passport when Church had his pockets emptied by his silent abductor. It was, concluded Church gloomily because the nightclub owner wanted the police authorities to easily and quickly identify him.

As his scrambled eggs, warm buttered toast and strong black coffee arrived, Church planned his revenge on the nightclub owner from the Czech Republic who thought so little of drugs and so much of family. He also considered why so many people in the chain of characters associated with his search for Amber Garland had ended up dead. His first port of call would be the exotic *Poesje* nightclub a few miles South but a lifetime away from his current location. His breakfast was delicious. The most important meal of the day and Church made it last as long as he could. Two hours later and feeling much refreshed, he had another brief exchange of conversation with another member of the InterContinental Hotel. This time the middle-aged man on the reception desk could not quite understand why Edward Church was asking for the cheapest taxi service in Amsterdam.

'There are many good reliable taxi services in the city, sir.'

'I'm sure there are. However, I want the one that will charge the least amount of money,' replied Church patiently.

'But there are many good services, sir?'

The conversation went on for some time until the receptionist gave up trying to persuade Church otherwise, lost patience and dialled a number on the hotel switchboard telephone system. The man waved an arm to indicate that Church should wait in a nearby armchair. He picked up an English language newspaper and worked his way through the headlines. For Church, reading a broadsheet was always a pleasant way to spend a few minutes.

A news story on the inside pages caught his eye. The cargo vessel *Kertmis-ijs* had been stopped by a Royal Navy patrol vessel and searched by United Kingdom customs officials. They found nothing untoward onboard but a further search uncovered an empty submersible vessel being towed by the cargo ship. The chamber being towed underwater was the size of a shipping container and used gyroscopic controls to keep it below the waterline. The Captain of the ship, Mathias Agurk, has been charged with drug smuggling offences but denied any knowledge of the empty container beneath his ship. He was granted police bail in The Netherlands but is suspected to have fled the country.

'Poor old Captain Mathias, I rather liked him!' Church said to himself, then, thinking about his own flight from custody he added, 'And to lose one suspect from custody is bad luck, to lose two in the space of two days is distinctly careless.'

Church sat and waited for nearly an hour watching the receptionist shrug his shoulders and roll his eyes as he looked at his watch. Edward Church did not mind waiting.

Every minute he spent sitting in this hotel was another minute that the police would waste looking for him. Eventually, the search would be wound down thus improving his chances of evading capture even more.

He had to admit to himself that right now, right here, there were worse places to be.

Chapter Twenty-Six

Prague by way of Poesje

Church left the warmth, comfort and security of the Amstel InterContinental hotel and the chill of a Dutch winter morning instantly drained the heat from his body. As he paced smartly down the few steps from the hotel, Church wondered how long it would take the authorities to track the use of his credit card. In an hour or so there might be a rush of uniformed officers running back up these very steps.

With that thought in mind, Church opened the door of a battered, ancient, Peugeot estate car that had a handwritten sign reading *Taxicab* stuck to the window. The heat from within the car hit him as if an oven door had been opened during cooking. Unfortunately, the smells from inside the car were not the same. The driver, who it turned out was Albanian, had the odour of hard work about him. An odour that permeated the whole interior of the vehicle. The heaters in the car were wedged full-on and fully open. The whole of the journey was spent listening to the man complain about his life.

'I miss my homeland but my wife says we must export to get a better life. Back home I had a good car, now I have to drive this piece of dirt. The traffic is always bad, always busy. Cars and vans everywhere, take a long time to get everywhere. And cyclists! Everywhere cyclists. They come up behind you, they come out in front of you. They come from everywhere. Trams are trouble too. Rails are everywhere. Bump, bump, bump.'

Church gazed out of the steamed-up window and looked at the near-empty streets. The driver continued his ranting.

'My wife says that I must work hard. But she sits at home and eats. I work all of the hours. I get home and have a beer, watch the football I have recorded. Do not say to me the results, I tell her, 'no point' she says, 'no-one scores', then she eats some more food.' The driver paused for breath then continued, 'I like warm. Is it too warm in the car for you? Europe is cold in winter. Albania is warm. My home was *Sarandë*, very warm, very nice. I will go back one day to live.'

Church could not think of anything to say to the man and so he sat, breathing as shallowly as he could until they pulled up outside the *Poesje* nightclub. In contrast to his first visit late at night, the two restaurants were open for lunchtime business and the nightspot was in darkness. The security shutters had been taken down from the windows of the tobacconist and a display of newspapers had been placed neatly outside. However, the nightclub itself was evidently closed for business. The two cats eyes painted on roller shutters were still clearly visible but the neon sign had been extinguished for the day. A heavy steel door barred the entrance to the club.

Church pressed a button on an intercom panel set into the wall to the left of the steel door. He stepped away from the intercom and out of sight of the security camera built into it. Unsurprisingly, no one came to the door.

'Do you fancy a coffee while you wait?' Church shouted over to the driver. 'Leave the meter running and I'll pay.'

'Very kind, sir. Thank you.'

The café was entered and the coffees were purchased. While the driver drank his, Church asked around inside the coffee shop to find out if anyone had seen Manus the nightclub owner. He went next door and asked in the newsagent cum tobacconist. Unsurprisingly no one had seen or heard of Manus Klimop.

Church left the glum Albanian taxi driver drinking his coffee and explored the rear of the business units. A smelly, dark, damp alleyway awaited his exploration. It seemed to yawn and sneer at him to dare to enter. A row of heavily barred windows and equally uninviting doors stretched out for about fifty yards, coming to an end at a brick wall where one of the tall residential tower blocks extended backwards. A cursory check of the doors told Church all that he needed to know. The rear of the nightclub property was just as securely shut as the front. As he retraced his steps, Church picked up a small empty cardboard box that had not succumbed to the dampness in the alley. He filled it with some rubbish and detritus that had accumulated nearby and emerged from the rear of the row of commercial units, looking rather more pleased with himself than he should be under the disappointing circumstances.

'Would you like to earn a tip on top of your taxi fare?' Church asked the driver who was still sitting nursing his coffee outside the café.

'What is a tip? I do not understand.'

'More money. Would you like to earn some more money?' Church explained.

'Yes, of course. What do I need to do?'

'Take this cardboard box, ring on the security buzzer outside the nightclub and wait for someone to come to the door.'

'That is it?' he replied hesitantly.

Slowly, the taxi driver lumbered over to the *Poesje* club, leaned against the doorway and pressed the intercom buzzer. A voice that sounded tinny and detached sounded through a small loudspeaker. 'Yes?' The driver looked over to Church unsure what to do next.

'Say that you have a delivery for *Poesje*,' Church said helpfully but feeling exasperated by the other man's lack of acumen.

'I have delivery for you please,' the driver shouted through the intercom panel.

The driver grinned at Church who rolled his eyes and smiled. A metallic click of the door heightened his senses. His heart leapt ever so slightly as the steel security door swung open. The confused face of the cloakroom girl with the long black hair poked its way through the entrance. The woman had looked so glamourous the night before but in the cool, harsh, winter daylight, she looked frowzy. The woman tried to take the package from the taxi driver who, unsure what to do, attempted to keep hold of it. Then her eyes alighted on Church.

'You,' she said.

'Me,' replied Church. 'And him,' he added nodding towards the driver.

'Me?' said the driver blankly.

The woman made an attempt to shut the door but Church was too quick. He put his full weight against the outside edge and the girl toppled backwards. She fell in an awkward heap of arms legs and very long hair on the floor just inside the nightclub. As she struggled to her feet, Church and the driver stepped smartly inside and closed the steel door behind them.

She made an attempt to run but the driver reached out a hand. He grabbed a huge handful of hair but looked dumbfounded when the girl carried on running. He looked down at a clump of jet black hair extensions.

She turned and screamed at him. '*Varken!* They cost me a lot of money.'

'Sorry,' he mumbled by way of an apology.

'Enough of this,' said Church authoritatively. 'Where is Manus Klimop.'

'He is not here,' she pouted sulkily. 'He has gone.'

'Gone? Gone where?' asked Church.

'I do not know. All of his stuff has gone. He left the club last night when he was here with you and has not been back today. He has gone, I do not know where but his stuff has gone.' She repeated, 'All of his stuff has gone.'

Her mood seemed to change and the cloakroom girl became more conciliatory, even perhaps more helpful. She led Church through the empty nightclub and into a small office space.

There is something quite odd about walking through a nightclub during the daytime. A place of entertainment that was so busy, bright, cheerful and alive at night. The *Poesje* club appeared to be far more shabby, worn and tatty in the harsh reality of the daylight. Glossy black tabletops that looked so shiny now looked dull. Glittery surfaces seemed to be damaged and patchy. The floor, which Church had barely noticed when he was walking through the club last night, was sticky underfoot. It also felt much smaller than he remembered. Even the laughing Buddha statue seemed to be less confident in the daylight. He sat at the bottom of the staircase looking overweight and tacky. Brushstrokes of gold paint were clearly visible over his chubby body. His paint peeled fingertips were supporting a half-empty beer bottle.

The office space of Manus Klimop was a tiny temple of bad taste. A cacophony of purple and gilt clashed everywhere. The wallpaper had a pattern of a vintage damask flock in a deep purple colour. Art prints had been framed in thick, gold, antique swept, frames. The ceiling had been painted with glitter paint. His desk was heavy mahogany. Even the wastepaper basket by the side of a filing cabinet was ornately decorated. Church suspected that Manus was something of a parvenue, recent celebrity status but humble origins.

'Money cannot buy you taste,' he said as he looked around the room.

'I like it,' said the taxi driver gazing around the room.

'I designed it,' said the cloakroom girl.

Church ignored her and set about rummaging through the wastepaper basket. He tossed the contents of the bin onto the office floor. Junk mail, flyers, leaflets and assorted wrappers for food and sweets. Two plastic tags caught his eye. Church examined the labels carefully and after a few seconds, he put them into his jacket pocket.

The ornate desk looked slightly at odds with the state-of-the-art computer perched on one corner. However, it was an odd-looking black box connected to the computer that caught Church's eye. It appeared to be an ordinary black box, with multiple slots on the top. Each slot held a mobile telephone SIM card. Church did not know, because he had been kidnapped at the time, but it was exactly the same item that the Police retrieved after raiding the home of Godfrey and Maureen Timson in Manchester. One hundred Subscriber Identity Module cards connected to a computer enabled Short Messaging Service texts to be sent from the computer and appear to have been sent from any one of a hundred mobile phones.

'Do either of you know where I could buy a reliable car?' Church asked.

The cloakroom girl did not speak, she simply stood in the corner of the gaudy office looking crestfallen. The taxi driver scratched his head and looked like he was really concentrating, after a great deal of thought, he suggested his brother-in-law. The man explained that his wife's brother had a small lock-up garage that did auto repairs and sometimes sold on cars that were beyond economical repair.

'It is very close by. I can take you there if you like,' he added helpfully, 'but you have the use of my taxi why do you want to buy a car?'

'I don't think that your car would survive the journey. I'm going to the Czech Republic.'

'Why Czech Republic?' the man replied.

'Because that is where Manus Klimop has gone. Gone to hide in the safety of his family and of his brother. Somebody once said to me that when you feel you are in trouble, you yearn to be at home.'

'That is quite a hunch,' said the cloakroom girl.

'Well, the old airline luggage tags that I found in the bin were another clue. People often leave the old labels on their suitcases when they get back from a trip, only taking them off when they want to use their suitcase again.'

'I do that,' added the taxi driver.

The cloakroom girl did not speak, but Church knew from her downcast eyes and dejected body language that he was correct.

Fourteen hours later, it was Church's turn to feel his eyes dropping down and his body beginning to feel dejected.

* * *

His body ached, his neck felt stiff and his shoulders had set into a spasm of rigidness. Fourteen hours ago he had been standing in the office of Manus Klimop. Church suspected that the nightclub manager had fled the country and gone back to his family in the Czech Republic. He remembered the other man talking fondly of his brother, another nightclub owner. Back in Amsterdam, it seemed perfectly plausible that Manus would abscond to Prague. Now, after more than ten hours of driving, he was not quite so certain.

The taxi driver had been good to his word and his brother-in-law did indeed run a small car repair garage. It was situated in one of a series of run-down railway arches and most of his trade seemed to be patching up ancient minicab vehicles and mail-order delivery vans. An assortment of engine parts, tyres, oil cans and rags littered the area in front of the garage. Old dented panels from the vehicles of previous customers were stacked up along an outside wall.

Ten hours ago Church negotiated a price on a fifteen-year-old *Range Rover*. He was assured that the car would make the journey by the mechanic and Church had been very sceptical at the time. Now, as he approached the outskirts of Prague city Centre, he was happy to be proved wrong.

The car had performed magnificently. The heated seats had long since stopped functioning but the air conditioning and heater blowers still worked pretty well. Its four and a half litre engine drunk fuel at an alarming rate, however, it meant that Church had to make several stops to refill the petrol tank. The stops at the motorway service station also permitted time to eat and drink.

Church had started driving late the very same evening that he purchased the vehicle. His first stop had been at the *Bentheimer* Service station on the border of Holland and Germany. The A1 Dutch motorway changes into the A30 Autobahn at the border. At *Rehme*, in northern Germany, he navigated the beautiful cloverleaf intersection and merged onto the A2 Autobahn. It was here that Church managed to master the cruise control settings on the *Range Rover* and at around midnight, he edged the city of Hanover on its northern outskirts.

At around three o'clock in the morning, he was beginning to fade. The concentration was taking its toll and his eyes were beginning to smart each time a set of headlights approached him on the opposite lane of the motorway. When he switched from heading West on the A2 to heading South on the A14 Church wound down the window to change the air inside the car. A blast of freezing cold night air instantly freshened the atmosphere inside the vehicle.

Leipzig and Dresden would both have warranted a stopover under different circumstances. However, once the border with the Czech Republic was within sight, nothing would have enticed Church to make a detour. His only lengthy stopover was at a huge *Rastplatz* motorway service station where he spent nearly an hour eating and wandering around the shops. He purchased a small suitcase and spent another pleasant hour buying items to fill it. As the *Range Rover* emerged from a short section of a tunnel, corrugated metal panels on either side of the motorway signalled that he was crossing the border out of Germany. When three lanes of German Autobahn changed into two lanes of Czech Dual carriageway Church knew he was getting close to Prague.

Chapter Twenty-Seven

Nightclubbing

It had just started to snow as Church entered the outskirts of Prague. The digital display in the dashboard flashed 3am, or was that 5am? Church was too bleary-eyed to stare at the read-out for too long, concerned that the break in concentration would cause him to have an accident. Bleak-looking high-density housing loomed on either side of the main road. A haphazard collection of precast, reinforced, concrete that was already showing signs of age and decay. He drove past a small green open space, a rarity in the northern approach to the city. At some point in history, just after the Velvet Revolution, a half-buried tank had been installed in the small lawn as a protest against a previous military conflict.

He checked in to the first hotel he came across that he recognised from previous visits. An old traditional building which had been converted into five-star accommodation. He awoke the sleepy night manager, tried to explain his unannounced arrival and paid extra for early check-in. Parking his battered *Range Rover* in the courtyard car park, Church wearily made his way to his hotel room. He made a quick telephone call, leaving a message for Alexander Drake back at the Cabinet Office and climbed into a luxurious king-sized bed and slept the sleep of the exhausted traveller.

There was a buzzing noise in his ears. A residue from the road noise and of having spent ten hours driving at speed on the motorway. It was still dark outside. Church realised that he had forgotten to close the curtains in his hotel room. He tried to turn over in bed but the effort on his sore limbs woke him up. He was aware that the buzzing noise was now louder. It was nothing to do with driving and everything to do with the telephone in his room ringing. Dreamily, and achingly, he reached for the handset while thinking 'do people use hotel telephones anymore?'.

'Yes?' he mumbled.

'Where on earth are you, Edward?' The unmistakable voice of his superior at the Cabinet Office, Sir Bernard Trueman, resonated out of the phone. 'Have you found Amber Garland?'

'I have been following Manus Klimop, sir,' answered Church, now fully awake.

'Have you found the girl?'

'She was in a nightclub with this Klimop character.'

'So were two hundred other young people but I don't' suppose that you have followed any of them. What are you doing in Prague?'

'How do you know where I am, sir?' replied Church now fully awake.

'We do have a very good security service, Edward,' Bernard Trueman sighed. 'It was not too difficult to keep tabs on you.'

'I can't help but feel that Amber Garland is mixed up in this drugs-related business, sir. I felt that it was worth following a hunch.'

'Tomas Kar dead in Manchester. Neville Smallbone AKA Hookman is also dead in Manchester. They have both crossed your path in the search for this girl and both of them are dead.'

'And Godfrey Timson dead in Amsterdam.'

'You were in Amsterdam, Edward?'

'Two days ago, sir. I wish that you had known I was there, sir. It would have saved a great deal of trouble.'

'Godfrey Timson,' repeated Trueman.

'He was the next link in the chain of this drugs business.'

'And you mentioned a nightclub owner, Manus something-or-other. Who exactly is he?'

'He would be the next link in the chain, sir.'

'Might I remind you,' Sir Bernard Trueman sighed, 'that you are supposed to be finding a missing girl. Not investigating an international drug chain.'

'The two are related, sir. I follow the links in the chain, I find the girl. It's only a matter of time.'

'Well, I will give you two more weeks on this, Edward. Which is rather serendipitous as by then it will be Christmas Eve.'

When the call ended, Church held the telephone receiver in his hand and listened to the silence. Trueman had not even bothered to say goodbye. He got up and walked over to a small suitcase propped in the corner of the room deciding that there was no time to waste.

The case and all of its contents were purchased at the *Rastplatz* motorway service station. Church had been astonished at the range of goods for sale there. As well as two restaurants, a supermarket, an impressive range of food and drink stalls, there were shops selling clothing and footwear, holiday essentials and technology of all sorts. There was even a shop selling hardware equipment such as power tools and paint. Who needs paint on a motorway trip thought Church to himself. It was in one of these stores that Church purchased a small suitcase, some items of food and other travel essentials.

In the clothes shop, he browsed the rails looking for something that would blend-in in a nightclub. After scanning the shelves for some time he gave up and purchased a reasonable quality charcoal grey suit, a white standard collar shirt and a burgundy silk tie.

As he ate a late evening supper in the near-empty hotel restaurant Church realised that he had slept for nearly fourteen hours. The remaining diners had long since finished their meals and either retired for the evening or had headed out to sample some evening entertainment. Church caught the eye of one of the waiting staff.

'Can you tell me what is the best nightclub in Prague?'

'We have many good nightclubs, sir.'

'If you had to pick one and the best in town, which one would it be?' Church asked again. Church had not banked on there being a vast choice of nightspots in the capital city.

The waiter thought for a moment, asked Church to wait and returned a minute later with a leaflet about Prague nightlife and a map from the reception desk. Church was once again pleasantly surprised by the efficiency and helpfulness of hotel staff. The leaflet, written in English, was examined. The map was marked with a pen. Church had a list of discos to visit that night. His last task before he left the hotel was to ask if there was a computer and printer available for him to use. Ever-obliging, the receptionist directed him to a small table in a private lounge. It was there that Church printed off twenty copies of a photograph of Manus Klimop that Alexander Drake, the computer technical wizard back in England, had found on a file somewhere and prepared for him. The image was clear enough and the large *Interpol* logo in the corner of the image that Drake had added gave it exactly the air of authority that Church had needed.

Interpol provides investigative support, expertise, and training to law enforcement worldwide, focusing on three major areas of crime that traverse national borders. Terrorism, Cybercrime, and Organised crime. Each member country has a Bureau offering investigative support, forensic support and analysis. It coordinates and shares Police databases from around the world. The Interpol logo itself is somewhat complicated and incorporates several elements. The globe illustrates its worldwide activities. A sword that penetrates the world is supposed to show police action. Two olive branches wrap around the edges of the earth representing peace and a set of the scales of justice prop up the whole graphic insignia. In a typically complicated addition, the letters OIPC and ICPO balance on either side of the hilt of the sword. Most countries have adopted the acronym *International Criminal Police Organisation* the French, of course, insist on *Organisation Internationale de Police Criminelle.* Thankfully, all member countries agreed on *Interpol* as the address for Telegraph messages in 1946 and the name has stuck ever since.

Church gathered together the sheaf of printed photographs with their fake authenticity and headed out of the hotel. He was surprised at how dark it was and how quiet the streets were. A glance at his wristwatch told Church that the time was fast approaching midnight. It had also started to snow once again. As he walked along the pavement, past solid-looking buildings on either side of the road, his shoes made a crunching sound. The snow was not exactly deep and crisp and even but it did feel rather festive.

Church had walked a little way down Wenceslas Square, a traditional meeting place of student demonstrators and location of several overpriced restaurants. The square is really a boulevard with one way traffic running either side of a long pedestrianised area. It has the beautiful National Museum building and a statue of Saint Wenceslas, Wenceslaus Duke of Bohemia, better known as Good King Wenceslas in the Boxing Day carol at one end of the thoroughfare. It has absolutely nothing at the other end. Church continued along another pedestrianised plaza and headed through the Old Town square. The snow was coming down a little heavier now. The yuletide sensation was enhanced even more by the sight, sound and smells coming from a Christmas market.

If there is one thing that the Czech people know how to do better than a revolution, it is a Christmas market. The Old Town square was still full of people wandering around a collection of fifty or so wooden huts. The huts were brightly painted and festooned with fairy lights. Music seemed to compete from one side of the stalls to the other. And the smells from a vast array of food and drink outlets mingled together into one overpowering sweet, spicy, cooked meaty aroma. It made Church hungry even though he had just eaten. He briefly stopped at a hut selling sweet treats and bought a *perničky*, spicy gingerbread, biscuit. As Church devoured the chewy, spicey, bar he made his way out of the festive market. The last stalls, selling wooden toys, scented candles, Christmas tree ornaments, hats and gloves, faded away and the streets got quieter.

Church continued to walk without stopping and without looking around. He had memorised the important parts of the map and trusted his sense of direction to get him to his first destination. The buildings that he walked past were bathed in the glow from streetlights. Modern blocks competed with more old fashioned Baroque and Rococo styles. From a previous visit, Church remembered that modern buildings had been constructed in a traditional style called Historicism to blend in with their surroundings. He particularly liked the Art Nouveau style which seemed to pop up unexpectedly throughout the city.

As Church passed by a late-night Pizza shop that still had a rowdy clientele, he heard the familiar beat of the music that thumped through the ground and spread outside of *Chapeau Rouge*. Prague's finest nightclub according to the leaflet from the hotel. After a quick word with the door security Church was allowed entry to the club. He toured all three floors of the nightspot walking through several bars in the same building, showing the photograph of Manus Klimop to anyone who would pause long enough to engage in conversation. Most of the bars were brightly coloured red or purple neon, loud music played through speakers dotted around everywhere but he did stop for a drink in a quieter cool blue-grey bar. As he sipped his drink Church retrieved the map from his pocket and plotted his route to the next venue.

The *Roxy* is a vibrant nightclub located a little farther North of his previous stop-off. Once inside the vast open space, he was confronted by a sea of bodies jumping up and down roughly in time with the music being played by a DJ. The light show was bright, brash and blindingly fast. At some point in its history, the venue was a theatre or cinema. The stage now housed the DJ booth and mixing decks, the seats in the auditorium have been cleared away to form a vast dancefloor. The original Dress Circle seats from its time as a cinema have also been cleared away to provide more space to dance. Church quickly retreated to a bar away from the heat and perspiration of the huge noisy auditorium. He showed the photograph to a few people but blank looks were universally returned.

It was then that he saw her.

Standing in the distance with a group of other young women, she glanced sideways and her blond hair flicked to one side. It was Amber. Church wasted no time and put down his half-finished drink, making his way over to the small crowd of women. She was dressed in tight jeans and a plain black t-shirt. Church touched her gently on the shoulder.

'Amber? Amber Garland? I can't believe you're here.'

'Kdo jsi? Ja ti nevim.' The woman looked confused.

'What?' replied Church, slightly unsure of himself.

'She said, 'I do not know you',' explained her friend.

'I'm sorry I thought that she was someone else,' Church stumbled his apology.

'Nice try. Not a very good chat-up line I'm afraid, mister,' replied her friend as the group of girls walked away.

An hour later and undeterred, Church set about plotting his route to the next club. It seemed as though the third most popular nightspot in Prague was also a super-club. Spread over five floors of a converted classical building, the *Karlovy Lazne* club was described as the largest nightclub in Europe. Several dancefloors catered for every type of music and it even advertised elevators to take club goers between floors. Church was vaguely aware of someone moving into the seat next to him but he was still surprised when a woman's voice spoke to him in English.

'Would you like to go somewhere quieter?' she asked, leaning close to his ear and resting a hand on his shoulder.

'What I would really like,' replied Church showing her one of the printed photographs, 'is to find this man.'

'You will not find him here!' she laughed. 'He would not be seen dead anywhere near the competition.'

'Is he at *Karlovy Lazne*?' asked Church.

'Hah! He would not be seen in that place either. *Karlovy Lazne* is far too mainstream a nightclub for him.'

'You seem to know a lot about Czech nightlife.'

'It is my business to know,' she replied. 'If you want to find Ondra Klimop he will be at his nightclub, *Mužný Muž*. It is in *Letná* province just over the river.'

'Thanks,' said Church. 'You might just have saved my ears from a long night. But this isn't a photograph of Ondra, it's of his cousin Manus Klimop.'

'What?' she asked.

But Church had already left his seat and was making his way outside.

Chapter Twenty-Eight

Over the River and Through the Woods

Edward Church had walked over the iconic *Charles Bridge* in Prague many times before tonight. On each of his previous trips, the historic Fourteenth Century pedestrian river crossing had been packed with tourists, hawkers and street vendors. However, on this occasion, at approximately 2am on a Tuesday morning just over two weeks before Christmas, it was empty. Church had the whole bridge to himself.

Despite the need to rush, he paused and took in the beauty of the surroundings. Prague new town was behind him, Prague old town was ahead. Beneath his feet, the stone cobbles had been worn smooth with endless shoes. A fine dusting of snow collected at the edge of the walkway. A parapet of waist-high sandstone blocks hemmed him in on each side of the bridge and every few yards was a stone sculpture of a religious figure. The feet of the Virgin Mary had been worn smooth by the touch of countless visitors hoping for a miracle, large or small. A small collection of candles in little glass jars had been placed around the base of the statue. Church wondered if he too should pause. In the middle of the bridge, Church glanced at Christ on the cross. A little farther on were statues of three Saints. *Norbert*, *Sigismund* and the far more famous *Wenceslaus* looked down on him from their stone pedestal. *Wenceslaus* had far more candles collected around his plinth than the Virgin Mary. Candles, oil burners and ornamental flickering electric lamps glowed around these three saints on the bridge.

Church remembered that both *Wenceslaus* and *Sigismund* were patron saints of the Czech Republic. He was not sure who or what *Norbert* was the patron saint of. But it did not matter because by now, he had reached the end of the bridge. He descended down a gentle incline and passed under the entrance arch to the old town. The buildings here were all traditionally styled. Left unpainted in stone or decorated in colours of cream, brown, pastel green and the occasional mustard yellow.

He cut down a narrow side street and doubled back on himself. Before long he reached the last arch of the bridge, which was now high above his head. To one side was not the *Vltava* River but a small narrow canal, signposted *Certovka*. He was not sure why Prague had one solitary canal but it was this waterway, edged by a wide walkway, that he was looking for. The inky black water slapped against the man-made canal wall. It made a rhythmic slap, slap, slap sound. The broad cobbled footpath that he now walked along was lined with Bars, Cafes and Restaurants. All were closed for the night except for one or two where the staff were sleepily stacking tables and chairs at the end of a long evening. The door to a bar opened and a small group of drinkers staggered out onto the pavement.

'*Dobrou noc,*' they shouted their goodnight's loudly as the door swung behind them.

'*Sbohem,*' came the weary goodbye from the cafe staff.

According to his list of the best nightclubs in Prague that Church had obtained from the hotel, the *Mužný Muž* nightclub was not in fact number one but way down on the list. The building was unassuming from the outside. A large detached building that was once perhaps a private dwelling built in the traditional Czech *Historic* style. There was no obvious sign that the venue was a nightclub. No door security outside, no loud music reverberating through the walls and no people milling about outside. A purple canvas awning sign-posted the entrance door and Church cautiously stepped inside.

A long passageway stretched out emptily before him. His footsteps echoed on the tiled floor and a series of lights set in the architrave and skirting board pulsed down the corridor. It drew him further inside. Church could hear faint music coming from a distant room. He passed six or seven doorways that were firmly closed and locked shut. Beyond, he could see that other doors at the end of the passageway were open. Bright lights spilt out into the corridor, music and voices could be heard drifting out from within the rooms.

Church paused as he reached the first open door. Not quite sure what to expect from within the room, he pressed himself against the wall and took a deep breath. Despite himself, Church could feel his heart pounding inside his chest. Slowly, carefully, he peered around the doorframe.

The room was full of people. It was difficult to see just how big the space inside was. A blend of lighting, smoke and partitions of curtains divided up the area, making it impossible to see the far wall of the room. One or two faces turned to examine the newcomer peering round the door frame. They soon lost interest in Church and turned back to their friends. Feeling a little foolish, Edward Church stepped inside. The sound of music enveloped him but faded just as quickly as he walked a little more. He glanced up and saw some acoustic directional loudspeakers set into the ceiling. He walked a few more paces towards a bar area and his arm brushed by a heavy curtain, draped from floor to ceiling. Almost immediately the sound of the music faded away. An acoustic curtain muffled any noise meaning that drinks could be ordered in a hushed tone of voice.

Church liked this club. The lighting was subdued, soft and diffused. The dancefloor was packed with eager nightclubbers. Directional stroboscopic lights pointed away from the main area of the room and across the floor that was full of figures dancing in time with the music.

'Halo, Hello?' a voice behind him said. 'Would you like to order a drink? What can I get you?'

Church spun round. Judging from the deep tone of voice, he had been expecting to see a man behind the bar but he was confronted by a young woman. He ordered a beer but, along with the other drinks he had ordered that night, had little intention of drinking it.

'I'm looking for Ondra and Manus Klimop,' he said to the waitress.

'Over there,' she replied sonorously, pointing towards the far corner of the nightclub.

Church paused, allowed himself a mouthful of his drink and watched the group of people in the far corner of the room.

Disappointingly there were only men gathered around a large table that was piled high with drinks. Church thought that he recognised Manus and his cousin Ondra Klimop but it was difficult to tell exactly with the smoke from a dry-ice machine that pumped out every few minutes. There were three other men gathered near the table but not close to the central group. Church assumed that they would be bodyguards or minders of some sort. The smoke cleared a little and he thought that one of the central cluster of men looked familiar. Was it the Middle-Eastern man from the evening in Manchester at the St Charles Partners dinner? It seemed so long ago and so much had happened since that night a week before. The man was wearing a western-style suit rather than the black thobe and blue and white check keffiyeh from before. And what a suit. Expensively cut, clearly tailored to the man's physique and manufactured out of a dark silk mix fabric. It stood out from the cheap suits that the bodyguards wore. Trousers too tight, jackets too loose, probably to accommodate a holstered weapon. Manus and Ondra

Klimop were dressed in similar-looking dark shirts and dark trousers. They might have been cousins but they looked more like twin brothers.

Church scarcely noticed the other people in the club. He had the general impression of young men in tight-fitting clothes that were meant to show off a body shape toned over many hours at the gym. Young women in loose-fitting clothes that were meant to show off their underwear. Older men seemed to be sitting around watching the young people, but scarcely any middle-aged women.

As Church observed the little assemblage in the distance, he saw two ladies walk over to join the group. Both had dark hair, had their make-up applied heavily and were very tall. Lamentably neither of them was Amber Garland. A movement at his side caught Church's attention. A young man was lingering at the bar.

'Would you like a drink?' he asked Church.

'Thank you, but I'm fine,' Church replied lifting his glass.

'Would you like a cigarette,' the young man continued. 'Or some grass, weed, cannabis or salvia?'

Eventually, the young man walked off but a few moments later the same thing happened again. Church politely declined for a second time. On the third occasion, the barmaid clearly thought that this was amusing. Church was slightly annoyed.

'A friendly crowd in this nightclub,' he said to the woman behind the bar.

She just smiled at him and carried on rearranging glasses and bottles. Church was somewhat exasperated and turned his attention back towards the table in the distance and Manus and Ondra Klimop. It was at that exact moment that Church realised his hunch to drive all of the way to Prague had been correct.

The smoke cleared a little on the dancefloor. One woman in a tight-fitting silver sheath dress stood out amongst the other clubbers Bizarrely, she was wearing sunglasses. Inside a nightclub, in the middle of the night. She stepped away from the crowds who were still engrossed in the music, heading towards the bar and towards Church. He thought, for a moment, that she might offer to buy him a drink like the previous customers but the idea faded in a second. As the woman approached he could see that the sunglasses were Aviator style with reflective lenses. Church's heart lept. He had seen those glasses before, in a photograph on a table inside Claverton Hall. Anthony Fairfax's second wife had been wearing them in the photograph. Now it was her daughter, Fairfax's step-daughter, Amber Garland who was wearing them and she was standing right in front of him.

'Would you like a drink,' he asked her.

'Don't mind if I do,' she replied.

'It's Amber isn't it?' Church asked casually, sure of the answer but asking anyway having been caught out once before with a mistaken identity tonight.

'Do I know you?'

She stood there for a moment. An angel standing next to a mortal man. For some reason, Church decided against telling her that she had been reported missing and that her step-father had sent him looking for her. Instead, he said, 'You knew Tomas Kar in Manchester? I think that you knew Hookman too.'

'Yes, I like Tomas. He's a friend of mine. I thought that Hookman was a friend too, but it turned out that he was just a sleaze.'

Anymore conversation was cut short by the arrival of one of the bodyguards. He bent down and mumbled something close to the ear of Amber so that Church could not hear what was being said. Her mood changed.

'Goodbye,' she said dismissively and began to walk off in the direction of the table closely followed by the minder.

'Is that Manus Klimop,' Church said brightly, following the pair of them, 'I really must come over and say hello. I've not seen him since Amsterdam.'

'You were in Amsterdam?' Amber paused halfway between the bar and the table. 'I remember, you were with Godfrey Timson.'

The bodyguard took her arm and guided Amber forcefully towards Manus and Ondra Klimop. Church followed, his senses heightened, his wits finely tuned to any changes around him.

'Godfrey is dead, as is Hookman and Tomas Kar,' Church whispered to Amber as he walked past and approached the table. He heard her gasp but the bodyguard carried on guiding her towards the group in the far corner of the club.

'Manus Klimop!' Church said loudly as he approached the cluster of men. 'What a surprise to see you here. Although you are probably more surprised than I am, as you left me unconscious in a warehouse on the outskirts of Rotterdam.'

Manus did not speak. He simply stood there with his mouth open. Eventually, he looked around at his cousin. The two heavily made-up women who had been at the table sensed that their presence was no longer needed and quickly faded away.

'Would you like me to make a call?' Ondra asked the Arabian man in the expensive suit.

'Don't' make the call,' said Church firmly. 'I just need to speak to Amber about Tomas Kar, Neville Smallbone, AKA Hookman and Godfrey Timson. Actually, I already know about Godfrey so let's not bother about him.'

'Are you a policeman?' asked the Arabian man calmly.

'Interpol,' lied Church.

'At 3am in the morning?' he asked again.

'His name is Edward Church and he works for the police,' interrupted Manus Klimop.

'Crime does not stop at night-time and neither do I,' replied Church. 'Is Amber being held against her will?'

'No, no. Of course not. She is free to answer your questions,' the Arabian answered smoothly, sweeping his hand expressively around the table.

'Shall I make the call?' Ondra Klimop asked the Arabian once again.

'Don't make the call,' hissed Church as he grasped hold of Amber and led her to one side.

He led her towards the bar but kept one eye on the group of men around the table. Church sensed that Amber was confused, she hesitated a little.

'Why did you lie? You're not police,' she said.

'How would you know that?' asked Church in response.

'Edward Church, I've met enough policemen to know that you are not one.'

'I'm working for your step-father. He's concerned about your welfare.'

'You're not a politician or a civil servant or an advisor either. I've met enough of them to recognise one.'

'I do work for the British Government. Think of me as a sort of envoy. A special envoy.'

'For some reason I trust you,' she spoke quietly.

'Because I work for the Government?' asked Church.

'Because you lied about being a policeman.'

'Trust me when I say that when we make a move to leave the club, those bodyguards will come after us. And they are not here to keep you safe but to keep you with these men.'

'I liked Tomas Kar,' she said again but this time using the past tense. 'I did not like Hookman, he was creepy and Godfrey Timson was annoying. He had lingering eyes but

I did not wish ill of him. I met his youngest son at a party and we sort of became friends. Manus Klimop said that you killed Godfrey.'

'We need to get out of here, Amber. It was a long shot to look for you in Prague but I'm really glad to have found you here.'

'Why did you think that I was in Germany?' Amber asked solemnly.

'Prague isn't in Germany.'

'I know, I know,' she replied quickly. 'Prague is in Austria right?'

Church was annoyed. He was usually a patient man but in the past few days, he had been assaulted, arrested, then kidnapped in Manchester, been taken on a boat along the English channel, assaulted once again this time in Amsterdam. He had escaped and embarked on a wild goose chase across Europe and all to find this young woman who did not even know what country she was in.

'Come on, Amber. We need to get out of here and fast,' he said abruptly.

'Okay, okay I'm coming.'

'What hotel are you staying in? We need to get a bag packed for you.'

'To be honest, I don't know. It rhymes with Chemist or something.'

Church sighed and cursed his bad luck. Then he racked his brains for the name of the hotel that she might be holed up in.

'Is it the *Alchymist*?' he asked eventually.

'Yes, that's the one.'

A few moments later they were inside her hotel room and Church was imploring her to pack as many essential items as she could into a small suitcase.

He looked around her suite. Heavy mahogany furniture was dotted around the spacious bedroom. A huge, ornate four-poster bed with odd-looking metalwork inlay did not even fill the space. The painted, vaulted ceiling, as well as the Biedermeier style, striped Jacquard bedding and curtains, added to the Baroque style. It was impressive, he had to admit.

A modern looking laptop on a side table caught his eye. Next to the hinged screen was a small black box. Church had seen one just like it before. It had been in Manus Klimop's office in Amsterdam. Church picked it up to examine it closer and several mobile phone SIM cards fell out of the slots located on the top. He pocketed them and carefully set the box back next to the computer.

The suitcase that she eventually packed was far too heavy to carry. Church woke up a startled receptionist and asked her to send the case on to his hotel, the 'Four Seasons'. As he hurried Amber down the steps and out of the hotel, Church looked around and listened for any approaching vehicles.

'Is that where you are staying, the Four Seasons hotel?' Amber asked as they set off back towards *Charles Bridge.*

'No. But they will send it on to my hotel and will be discrete about it,' replied Church. 'Now hurry up, we really need to get a move on.'

'I'm going as fast as I can. These shoes are not made for running in.'

'If you can dance in them, you can run in them,' said Church.

'I can't run, my dress is too tight.'

'Then roll it up or something.'

'Slow down, Edward. I'm getting out of breath.'

'How can someone who parties all night, not even be able to run across a bridge.'

'I've got a blister. I can't run anymore!'

With that last complaint, Church lost his temper. He spun around and picked Amber up, hoisting her across his shoulder. She gave out a little scream, but Church ignored her. He held onto her legs tightly as her arms flailed around behind him and strode along the cobbled path. She weighed so little. The bridge was still deserted and a fine mist had settled in the air. It formed a halo around the glow from the street lights. As Church strode past the *Wenceslaus* statue it looked as if the stone figure was floating in mid-air on a cloud of vapour. As he passed the figure of the Virgin Mary, Church could not resist but to touch her foot and say a quick prayer to himself.

'Where are we going?' she eventually asked.

'To the city centre,' said Church.

'But Prague must be back there, where we've come from?'

'Give me strength,' sighed Church. 'Prague Old town is back there. The new town is on this side of the river. How long have you actually been here?'

'Only a few days. To be honest, I've not been out of my hotel.'

Chapter Twenty-Nine

Escape

Church was in a foul mood. The almost constant whining of Amber Garland had got on his nerves and now he was tired as well as annoyed. He was also worried. They had eventually made it to his hotel, Church had thrown his belongings into his case and they made their way quickly down to his car.

Amber had looked at Church's tiny suitcase and asked, 'What did you pack?'

'Everything,' replied Church.

She raised her eyebrows and then, looking at the ancient dirty worn-out *Range Rover*, she laughed.

'What sort of a car do you call that!' she had exclaimed.

'I call it a very reliable car,' Church replied tetchily.

She had reluctantly climbed in after making a show of brushing down the front passenger seat. Church angrily started the engine and quickly manoeuvred the car out of the hotel courtyard. The labyrinth of side streets around his hotel was paved with an assortment of surfaces. Patches of concrete, tarmac, block paving and cobbles merged into one roadway. Potholes appeared at random positions, sometimes in the middle of the street, sometimes at the very edge but most often at the exact position of the wheels of a vehicle. Church did his best to miss the faults in the road but misjudged a pothole full of water for a patch of tarmac. The wheels of the *Range Rover* on the passenger side dropped.

'Not a very smooth ride in this car,' Amber remarked.

'It's not a very smooth road,' answered Church.

He would have said more but his attention was caught by the sight of two police vehicles. They were parked and waiting just a few streets away from his hotel. Too much of a coincidence for Church. He checked the rearview mirror a few seconds later and sure enough, both police cars appeared to be following them. Two silver coloured Skodas with blue and yellow high visibility stickers and the word *Policie* emblazoned on the bonnet.

Church tried a couple of manoeuvres to make sure that his suspicions were correct but the sinking sensation in his heart told him all that he needed to know. Trust your intuition and your instincts, if something feels wrong then it probably is wrong.

He stamped his foot on the accelerator and the *Range Rover* picked up speed. He was not worried about potholes now. The main purpose of his driving was to try and lose the two police cars. The *Range Rover* sped down one of the main streets in Prague. Church was not entirely sure where he was or where he was heading. A series of tall, cream coloured, residential buildings lined the street. Every now and then was a café, a bar or some other commercial shopfront. Their car bumped over a set of tram lines and the tyres made a fast thump, thump, over the steel rails.

Church made a quick right-hand turn but immediately regretted it. The street had looked safe enough with a corner shop and a café just beyond it but unfortunately, the end of the road was sealed off by another building. A cul-de-sac is not the best route for escape. Church knew that it was too late to make a u-turn and desperately looked around for a means of escape. The road began with the corner shop, then a short run of residential apartments, a café, a bar and more residential units that stretched down the remainder of the street and curved round to seal it off. On the opposite side of the road was a solid-looking brick wall, then some garages in various states of repair.

Church's eye settled on the small shabby lock-up opposite the café. It had a dented up-and-over steel door that was heavily rusting at the corners. From what Church could see in the darkness, the walls and the roof were made of corrugated tin sheets in an equally poor state of repair.

'Do not try to escape, Mr Church,' a policeman shouted. 'We need to ask you some questions.'

One of the police vehicles had pulled up at the entrance of the cul-de-sac. The officer had his weapon aimed at the back of Church's car.

Church wound down the driver's side window a little. 'Ask whatever you like,' he replied. 'It doesn't look like we are going anywhere.'

But Church was scanning the street, weighing up his options. He kept the engine running in the *Range Rover* and told Amber Garland to sit a little lower in her seat.

'Your fingerprints have been found on a weapon that was used to kill Godfrey Timson,' the policeman shouted. 'We need to take you in for questioning. Do not harm the woman who is your passenger.'

Fingerprints thought Church to himself. His mind went back to the warehouse and discovering the body of Godfrey under the dirty tarpaulin. The sickening knowledge that he would find the murder weapon concealed in his pocket. Fingerprints discovered on the weapon after he had cleaned it so carefully. A trace of deoxyribonucleic acid, better known as DNA, he could believe. A closed-circuit television, CCTV, recording he could believe. But Church was absolutely sure that his fingerprints could not have been discovered on that pistol.

His mind made up, Church checked that Amber was wearing her seatbelt and reversed the car slowly back up the side street. After a short distance, he dipped the clutch, let the car coast a little and put the gearstick into first. Just as the car came to a halt, he stamped his foot onto the accelerator and the car jerked forward. Amber was thrown back into her seat by the momentum, she let out a gasp. Then, as Church drew level with the café on one side of the road and the dilapidated garage on the other, she screamed.

Church threw the steering wheel over, aiming the car towards the shabby lock-up. Amber continued to scream as the *Range Rover* headed straight towards the up-and-over door. Her sustained cry carried on as the car ploughed through the contents of the lock-up. Here screams eventually subsided as they emerged out of the other side of the garage. A trail of broken plastic furniture scattered behind them.

'How did you know that there wasn't a car in that garage?' she asked Church breathlessly.

'I didn't.'

'Oh my God. You're mad, we could have been killed.'

'We almost certainly would have been if we'd stayed to listen to those supposed policemen. And it was a calculated guess that the lock-up would be full of tables and chairs used by the café opposite. I certainly wouldn't use it to store my car in.'

'Not sure if this car is worth it, Edward. I certainly....'

But her voice trailed off as flashing lights illuminated the back of their car and the sound of sirens broke the silence around them. Church pressed his foot down hard and gunned the engine. He looked around to see if he could get his bearings and suddenly spied a building that he recognised. They were driving down the main road that skirted the River *Vltava* and just ahead, Church could make out the famous *Dancing House* building.

Church remembered having lunch in the rooftop restaurant of the iconic building, designed to look like two figures intertwined as they dance. It had spectacular views across the waterway, a bridge that was opposite and towards parkland on the opposite bank of the river. He continued to drive straight ahead avoiding the slip road on his right-hand side. Then, at the last minute, he swung the steering wheel hard around, and headed round a traffic island and over the bridge.

A squeal of tyres and a nasty sounding metallic crunch told him that at least one of the police cars in pursuit had crashed. His feelings of elation were short-lived as the illumination from blue flashing lights filled the interior of the *Range Rover* once again. He sped to the end of the bridge and followed the lane of the road as it veered to the right-hand side. Church pressed his foot hard on the accelerator pedal as they crossed the first road intersection. Then, at the next crossroad, he took a left turn down a narrow street. Buildings whizzed by either side of them. The noise of the *Range Rover* echoed off of the walls of the apartment buildings. Almost immediately the road opened up onto a wide, complicated junction. But Church was not interested in which road to choose. His attention was focused on the narrow entrance to a park directly ahead of them.

Their vehicle easily squeezed through the wide concrete pillars and tall iron gates at the entrance to the park. The cobbled path sent tiny vibrations through the car as they accelerated along the walkway. Church did not even bother to look at the speedometer as they approached the turn at the end of the path. His mind was focused on the hairpin turn that would take them back in the direction that had just come, but a little higher up the side of the hill that made up *Kinsky Gardens*. A series of long sloping footpaths wound their way up the side of a hill that was one hundred and fifty metres high. At the end of each stretch of path was a tight hairpin bend. Church navigated it as quickly as he could. But, as they made their way higher and higher, the drop below made him more cautious. At some points on their route, the drop was steep. Church heard Amber gasp when she looked out of the passenger window as they navigated one particularly tight turn. From then on she either had her eyes fixed firmly ahead or screwed tightly shut.

Eventually, they made it to the top of the hill. Church's attention was caught for a second as they passed an Observatory complete with three viewing telescope domes, a pink-painted church and what looked like a replica Eiffel Tower.

Although Church could not see as he sped around the base of the Petrin Tower, it differed from its more famous Parisian cousin by size and shape. It has an octagonal, rather than square, cross-section design. Architectural details were wasted on Edward Church because his attention was focused on the flashing blue lights of the police car that was still in pursuit some distance behind them.

Church glanced over at Amber. She looked tiny, a petite figure in a silver sheath dress. The large, generously sized, passenger seat in the car swamped her tiny frame. Another sound of a metallic crunch behind them made her jump. She shifted round in her seat and Church looked in the rearview mirror.

'That police car has been taken out by another car,' said Amber. ' That was lucky.'

'Not really,' replied Church looking at a black *Mercedes-Benz* 4x4. 'The replacement is much worse. I recognise that numberplate from Rotterdam.'

The *Mercedes-Benz* had shunted the police vehicle off of the path and it now careered down the slope of the hill with its blue lights flashing wildly. Just as the police car dropped out of sight, Church was sure that it had flipped on its side and began to roll over. But his attention was now on the new automobile.

'Do you have a plan?' asked Amber nervously.

'Do you mean a kill all of the bad guys sort of a plan?' replied Church.

'Any sort of plan that will get us out of here.'

'I had the idea to drive to Germany and find the British Consulate in Nuremberg, or if we can't get out perhaps the British Embassy here in Prague.'

'It doesn't sound like much of a plan,' she said despondently.

Church accelerated back down the path they had just taken. The wheels skidded on the smooth cobbled surface and loose stones kicked up underneath the tyres. The black *Mercedes-Benz* 4x4 had recovered from shunting the police car and was now bearing down on them. Church turned the steering wheel hard as they drove around a tight turn at the end of the path. The car behind cornered as if it were on rails.

'Why do you think that they are chasing you?' asked Amber.

'Me?' replied Church. 'It's you they are chasing, not me.'

Church swerved down a small flight of steps to take a shortcut down the side of the hill. The silencer on the exhaust, or the air conditioning or something, scraped angrily on the steps. He straightened up as they reached the foot of the flight of stairs and accelerated along a straight section of path. The tyres shuddered against the cobbled surface sending vibrations through the interior of the *Range Rover*. Church could see the police car tumbling down the side of the hill. Its flashing blue lights had been extinguished and they now flapped about loosely as the vehicle plummeted.

The *Mercedes-Benz* was right behind them now. Bright headlights from the black 4x4 reflected off of the rearview mirror in the *Range Rover*. Church could see the fear in Amber's face. She looked very, very pale. He wanted to say something to reassure her but no placating thoughts came to mind. The headlights dropped back for a yard or two, then came up close behind.

'Grab hold of your seatbelt and brace yourself,' said Church.

The *Mercedes* rammed into the back of the *Range Rover* and Amber screamed. Church heard a clatter behind and felt the change in the engine of their car. The exhaust pipe dropped off and the *Mercedes-Benz* swerved to avoid it. Church spun the steering wheel as they reached the end of another stretch of footpath. The *Range Rover* began to lose power as it skidded around a hairpin bend. The engine stuttered.

'What sort of car did you call this?' Amber asked again, nervously laughing.

'Well, it was a reliable car!' replied Church in good humour.

Their car came to a halt. The gearbox had been damaged and the engine revved pointlessly. Church was expecting another shunt from behind at any moment. Then, just a few metres ahead of them, the police car came crashing down. It came to rest just a few metres in front of them. The boot flew open and a car wheel lazily rolled off into the distance.

By some miracle, one of the police officers climbed out of the vehicle, radio in one hand and gun in the other. He began to run around the side of the vehicle to check on his colleague. Church was out of their car in a second. He kept his hands in the air as he ran towards the police car.

Church looked at the second police officer in the vehicle. His leg appeared to have been crushed by part of the engine block. The first policeman appeared next to Church. He was out of breath, gasping for air due to the rush of adrenaline. He pointed his gun at Church, then lowered it and looked at his colleague. For a moment the first policeman seemed unsure what to do, he had the choice of arresting Church or saving his colleague.

After a few seconds, he seemed to make up his mind. The first officer grabbed hold of the door on the police car and yanked it open. He reached inside for his colleague but Church took a step forward and the man paused. He reached for his gun once again.

'Don't move him,' said Church calmly. 'Keep the pressure on his leg. If you free it, the blood loss might kill him. Make him stable and call it in. Your friend needs to get to a hospital quickly.'

The first policeman pointed his gun at Church, unsure as to what to do. He swiftly decided to save his colleague, holstered his weapon and lifted his radio to call in the accident. But the *Mercedes-Benz* 4x4 pulled up behind them. One of the occupants stepped out from the black car and shot the officer. The policeman flung his arm up in an instinctive gesture of self-defence, but his body was twisted sideways by the impact of the bullet. The uniformed officer slumped to the ground by the side of his colleague.

Church heard Amber Garland scream, then his legs were kicked from beneath him. A cloth bag was pulled roughly over his head. Amber screamed again and then Church felt everything close in.

Chapter Thirty

All at sea, again

As a young man, Church had loved to sail. He had grown up near to the seaside and had spent several summers learning to navigate small, one-person sailboats, dingies and yachts. Summers seemed to last forever as a child. Getting sunburnt, tasting salt on your lips, arms or legs aching from sailing all day, forgetting lunchtimes because you were having so much fun. As a young man, Church had laid awake at night, his back sore from the sun, his head still turning with the motion of the waves and his ears full of the cry of seagulls. Learning to sail had been one of his most enjoyable memories. Church had been looking forward to competing in his first regatta but the weather was against him. It was a beautiful sunny clear day, with not a breath of wind. The beach where the competition was to be held was packed with holidaymakers enjoying an English summer but Church had been bitterly disappointed.

The next day had been stormy as is often the way in this country. Heavy rain and high winds made the waves crash on the beach and out at sea, the swell was equally strong. The regatta had been postponed once again. Church had not been tempted to sail. Respect for the weather and the elements had been drilled into him during every lesson. His instructor was very clear about that. But the elderly sailor who had been teaching them had told the class a funny story about how seasick he had been as a merchant seaman. Rough seas were not a problem, the swell from a calm sea had made him more seasick than any storm that he had encountered in the *North Sea*, *English Channel* or the *Bay of Biscay*.

The only time Church had felt seasick was during a mission to babysit a minor Royal on a cruise ship around the *Caribbean* and the *Gulf of Mexico*. The member of the Royal family was so minor so as not to have a title and had behaved impeccably. Her friends, however, had been an absolute nightmare on the whole trip. They had been drunk most of the time and very, very loud. There had been complaints from other passengers about the behaviour of the group, bad language, late-night revelry and general obnoxiousness. Church had received several telephone calls and messages from Sir Bernard Trueman asking him to do something but Church had politely reminded his superior that his task was to protect the Royal, not control her friends.

The Princess, who was in her early twenties, had spent most of the time in her cabin being seasick. Church had held her head and supported her body as she suffered the most awful nauseous episodes. He had to be honest that watching her be sick, he himself did not feel too bright. But Church hid it well.

He felt rather nauseous at this very moment. And he was sure that he could hear the cry of seagulls as well. Church moved his head slightly.

'Are you okay, Mr Church?'

'I must be honest, I've felt better before now,' replied Church, opening one eye and seeing Amber sitting on the end of the bed he was now laying on.

'I thought that you were dead,' Amber said.

'Well, in that case, I'm feeling better than that. Where are we?'

'We are on a cruise ship. We have been for the last two days. You've been out cold.'

'That explains why I'm so hungry. Absolutely starving.'

'There's plenty to eat,' she said brightly. 'In fact, dinner has just arrived. Perhaps the aroma brought you round?'

Church sat up and looked around him. They appeared to be in a large room. He could see another bedroom through an open door. Yet another doorway led to an even bigger room that had two sofas facing each other with a small low coffee table in between them. Large windows in each room showed panoramic views outside. It was not, in fact, a single room but a complete, well-appointed, luxury suite. The décor in the cabin looked slightly dated but nevertheless luxurious and expensive. The deep-pile cream carpet looked a little grubby, the teak woodwork looked a little faded by bright sunlight streaming in through outsized picture windows. Heavy drapes framed the window and fine net curtains showed a view of a balcony beyond. The view outside reaffirmed the sensations that Church was experiencing. They were indeed at sea. An area of water a deep blue-grey colour stretched from the balcony doors out to the horizon. The sea was perfectly calm, a solid body of water with no white tips of waves anywhere to be seen. The sky was a clear pale blue with fluffy strands of white cirrostratus clouds, like white candy floss unravelling in the atmosphere.

Church looked into the sky for some time, observing the sun, he also looked at the shadow being cast by it. Then he looked at his watch. It read twelve noon exactly. Church retrieved a pencil from a writing desk in the suite and started drawing rough calculations on the wall of the cabin. It was the most rudimentary of calculations, estimating angles to the horizon by eye rather than an accurate measurement. However, it suggested a value for a latitude of around twenty-five degrees North. Unfortunately, he could not work out longitude so could only guess at their exact location. But he estimated they were somewhere near the West coast of Africa, or perhaps even somewhere North of the *Arabian Sea*. *The Gulf of Aden* was too far South. For no apparent reason, Church settled on *The Gulf of Oman*.

Church glanced around the room once again. His eyes settled on the tray of food and he realised once again how hungry he was. The food was basic but delicious. Some sort of slow-cooked stew with North Africa or West Asian flavourings. They talked as they ate.

'What are we doing here?' Church asked.

'I've no idea. I was hoping that you would know,' Amber replied. 'Why were we being chased by the police and that other car? You said that they were looking for me and not you.'

'The police were after me. But the others were trying to capture you.'

'But why? I haven't done anything!'

'You clearly know something, otherwise, they would not have gone to so much trouble. And they are going to a lot of trouble to discourage me. Which only makes me suspect that there is something to find.'

'Did you murder Godfrey Timson like they said you did?'

'No.'

'I believe you,' Amber whispered quietly.

They had finished their food and Church felt replete but also rather queasy. To take his mind off the feelings of nausea he asked Amber about herself.

'How did you end up hanging around with Tomas Kar and his drug dealer friends Hookman and his bodyguard Malcolm?'

'Tomas was fun. He knew everybody. The first year at university was good, I really enjoyed it. But the second year was tough. Hanging out with Tomas made me feel better.'

'Did taking drugs make you feel any better?'

'Well, they didn't make me feel any worse.'

'But you knew he was a dealer.'

'Like I said, the second year at university was tough. Brutal, really brutal. The first time I took drugs in a nightclub, it was like an endless summer holiday. The holiday that had just ended. It was like being bathed in warmth and comfort. The music sounds better, people are better company. Their jokes are funnier, your own jokes are funnier. I never wanted it to end. But like any holiday it has to stop at some point and it hurts. During the week I missed the people, their company, the feelings. I wanted to do it all again. Do you know what I mean? I couldn't wait for the next weekend so that I could go on holiday again. Then again and again.'

Amber Garland had a faraway look about her. Church suspected that she was craving some narcotic stimulant and wondered if she was a regular user of ketamine, methamphetamine, ecstasy, or something stronger.

'You have a pill,' she continued, 'and it's the best feeling you've ever had, you know? All of your senses are heightened. Not that I was eating much, but food tasted better. Touch is more intense, you think that you can hear the music better, clearer than you've ever heard it before. You have another pill a few days later but it's not quite as good as before. I yearned for those initial feelings. Every time I take something, I'm trying to recapture those first feelings. But it doesn't work. Drugs don't work. I never recaptured that summer holiday feeling. It never happened.'

'Why did you want to go back to the summer holidays? What was so bad about that year?'

'It was the first time that it hit me that I was alone. I mean really alone,' Amber looked into the distance. 'Do you ever feel that you have lost everything, Mr Church?'

'Because of the laws of primogeniture, I lost quite a lot.'

'I don't understand what you're saying. But sometimes I feel that I have nothing at all in my life. Nothing to hold on to, nothing to call my own.'

'What about your step-father?' asked Church.

'Oh, he means well I'm sure. But he's not family. Not real family. My father died when I was young. My mother died just a few years ago. They were both only children which might have drawn them to each other, I don't know. It occurred to me that I was the only child of only children and it struck me that I was completely alone. Have you got sisters or brothers, Mr Church?'

'Yes, a sister and two brothers. But at times I'm sure that I would have preferred to be by myself.'

'As a child, you think that your parents will go on forever,' she continued, not really listening to Church. 'You think that your parents will always be around to look after you. That they will somehow live forever. You know that they won't but you want so much for it to be true. When my mother died I thought that I was okay, I thought that I handled it as well as anyone could have. All of my friends were sympathetic at first. Then they didn't want to talk to me. I think that they found it awkward or embarrassing. My school offered grief counselling but I felt that it didn't do any good.'

'I thought that you had left school by then? Anthony Fairfax said that you decided to enrol at university the summer that your mother died.'

'He drinks quite a lot.'

'I gathered that.'

'And he gets things wrong. Like dates and names.'

'I gathered that too.'

'Why are you doing this?' she asked, suddenly more serious.

'I fell into this almost by accident. Being in the right place at the right time. But I love what I do and I get to meet interesting people and travel the world in style.'

Church swept an arm around the luxurious surroundings of the cabin. 'To be honest, there are worse things I could be doing.'

'I had a gap year between finishing school and starting university. Anthony did not even know that I was working. He was too wrapped up in his political career. It was a succession of rubbish jobs for low wages and it made me think about what I am going to do for the rest of my life. The first job was in a café serving teas and coffees to groups of old ladies and single lonely men. Then I worked in a call centre making cold calls about advertising. That got closed down and I ended up in another call centre sending thousands of spam text messages.'

'It sounds monotonous. How do you do that?'

'We used one of those black-box SIM farms, you know? It's a small cube with slots on the top that hold dozens of mobile telephone SIM cards. I sat at a computer typing in messages that would be sent to hundreds of random mobile telephones.'

'Is that what was in your hotel room in Prague?'

'That's the sort of thing. Hookman explained that someone he knew wanted to keep in touch with a lot of people via secure text message and I happened to mention that I used one of those black boxes when I worked in a call centre. He seemed very excited by them, I don't think that he had heard of them before. Hookman got one, and Godfrey Timson got one. They can talk to hundreds of people at the same time.'

'They used to talk to thousands of people,' Church corrected her.

'Manus Klimop got one too, but he gave it to me to look after.'

'So what about the drugs?' asked Church.

'What about them?'

'Do you still take?'

'No. I stopped a while ago. I realised one day what I was actually doing to myself. While I was using I was lying to myself. I gave drug taking a name which made it less personal. So it was *The Wolf* that made me take cocaine. *The Wolf* attacked my arms with needles full of heroin, not me. *The Wolf* also stopped me from eating. But it was all lies. It dawned on me that the very thing that led me into drug-taking was the very thing that I had stopped doing. I stopped going out. I had no real friends. And I was failing in my studies. Back to the tea shop or the call centre for me unless I did something about it!'

'Not many people are that self-aware.'

'Thank you for listening,' said Amber, she suddenly leant over and kissed Church on the cheek. 'Nobody has taken the time to listen before.'

Chapter Thirty-One

All ashore

Church and Amber sat together on the cabin floor, empty dishes between them. He was aware that the ship was moving by the dull rumble of engines. They sounded far away in the bowels of the ship but the gentle vibration could be sensed up in their cabin. After digesting the hearty meal and having a long luxurious shower Church was feeling much brighter. He was disappointed to find that his mobile telephone had been taken. The insult was more keenly felt by the fact that a handful of mobile phone SIM cards were still clustered together in his inside jacket pocket. At least he still had his watch and could tell the time.

He paced around the suite that was their cabin and at one point slid open the huge patio doors that led onto a private balcony. The heat hit him immediately. It blasted into the berth like a hot fan. The heat was accompanied by a cacophony of shrill cries from flocks of black-headed gulls flocking above the ship. But Church did not take any notice of the sounds. His attention had been caught by a sight on the horizon.

The horizontal blue line of the sea and the sky was now broken by a line of irregularly shaped objects. They were too far away to make out what they were but the cruise ship was approaching something. Church stood, transfixed by the sight unfolding before him. The irregularly shaped objects were, of course, mountains. A long row of white-tipped peaks and highlands that blended into one another so that it was impossible to tell how far back they went. A finger of land began to form to one side of the horizon far away to his right-hand side. Church assumed that it would form a huge bay of some sort and that another arm of land would appear to the left. But what kept Church's attention was not the mountains or the bay but something closer to the shoreline.

At first, they looked like buildings but some were at a slight angle as if the structure had been caught in an earthquake. Some of the buildings seemed to lean or list to one side, others were upright. Some had structures on top that looked just like chimneys. They also had row upon row of windows, balconies and railings.

Their ship got closer to land and the sight began to get clearer. To one side were huge oil refinery containers, to the other side was a wall of a cliff that extended far out into the sea. In the middle were a collection of supertankers, giant cruise ships and other assorted cargo ferries. There were perhaps twenty or so vessels. They had been run aground in the bay and the bows were several metres onto dry land. Their sterns were still in the water, some perfectly upright and others listing to one side. Looking slightly drunk and higgledy-piggledy, the massive ships clustered and clung together as if trying to gain strength in numbers. What they were attempting to protect themselves from became clearer as the ship that Edward Church and Amber Garland sailed on approached the coast.

'What on earth is it?' asked Amber.

'It's a shipyard. But not like any shipyard I've seen before,' replied Church.

'What are those things?' she asked pointing through the window of their cabin. 'I don't like the look of them. They look frightening.'

She pointed towards a large mechanical crane that was busy at work to one side of a ship. Instead of a bucket or scoop on the front of the articulated arm, there was what looked like a pair of giant tin snippers. The massive mechanical pincers cut through the steel sides of a beached supertanker as if it were made of cardboard. The hinged cutters sliced through the two-inch-thick steel plate with ease. Opening wide, the cutters moved down the side of the ship's hull then clamped into another section. Pausing while the pressure built up, the pliers gripped tight then slit through the sheet metal as it incised its way down the side of the ship's keel.

There are less than a dozen ship breaking yards in the world. The three largest are located at *Gandi* in Pakistan, *Alang* in India and *Chittagong* in Bangladesh and China also has a large ship recycling yard. Shipbreakers in the United States, Belgium and the United Kingdom cannot compete with the low wages and even lower safety standards of less regulated yards around the world.

Supertankers, car ferries, cruise ships, container vessels and other large cargo ships are usually run aground or beached in these ports at low tide. An army of casual labourers boards the stricken vessel, stripping it of anything that can be unbolted or unscrewed. Fixtures, fittings, furniture, lockers, carpets, window glazing, wood, metal or plastic and any other decorative item that may have some value. More navvys arrive and remove cables, wiring, electrical components and any other equipment. Once it has been stripped bare, the boat is broken down into small sections by mechanical cutters or cut by oxyacetylene. The health and environmental risks are high but the rewards from recycling scrap metals are higher. Stripping out toxic materials such as lead, asbestos, residual fuel oil and other noxious resources comes at a high human cost. But the economies of India and Bangladesh make good use of recycled steel that covers a significant amount of the countries needs. Precious metals are often smelted on-site in small-scale refineries. Scraps of precious metal melted together into ingots. Reclaimed gold and silver are too precious and too valuable to risk being pilfered while transported to another site. A ship can take up to a year to dismantle and yield around thirty thousand tons of steel. Church realised that this shipbreaker was a huge and valuable site.

He had spent some time helping out in a shipbuilders yard in *Hakan Yatcilik*, repairing and repainting tourist boats that sailed around the Mediterranean coast to the yard in winter. The constant sound of power tools was deafening. Sanding hulls, striping decking, welding sections of steel, drilling wood or bolting in new sections of a ship, all used power tools of some sort. Church loved it, but he was equally happy to go home at the end of the day and sit peacefully on his veranda watching the sunset in silence. This shipyard was something else entirely.

Beyond the row of stricken boats was a collection of shacks and cabins the size of a small town. As their own cruise ship approached, Church and Amber could make out one or two figures clambering over the beached ships. As they looked closer they could make out more and more workmen swarming across decks or hanging off of ropes. Safety equipment appeared to be in short supply.

'What's happening?' asked Amber. 'We seem to be going faster.'

'I think that we might need to brace ourselves for an uncomfortable berth, Amber.'

'What?'

'They are going to run this ship aground.'

'Oh my god. Are they trying to kill us?'

Despite Church's assurances Amber did not seem to be convinced. The truth was Church did not feel too confident about their future prospects either. The noise of the engines had been steadily growing and the vibrations aboard their cruise ship were more noticeable. As they approached the coastline and the seawater became more shallow, the noise inside their cabin became deafening. Suddenly the floor of their cabin lurched upwards.

An ear-splitting grating sound boomed around them. Amber grabbed hold of Church's arm and held on tightly as the ship keeled over to one side then, just as he thought that they would capsize, the ship brushed up against another and with the sound of screeching metal against metal reverberating through their cabin, the cruiser came to a halt. The engines stopped and the metallic echoes died away leaving them sitting on the floor in silence. Church glanced over to Amber. She looked worried.

'Tell me about the Arab,' he said, attempting to take her mind off of their current predicament.

'Okay, what do you want to know?'

'Everything,' replied Church patiently.

'Okay. I met him first in Manchester, at a party organised by Godfrey Timson. I had gone there with Hookman but for some reason, Hookman and Malcolm had been asked to leave. I wasn't really bothered because Godfrey's son was there and I rather liked him. The party was decent. People were in a good mood, the vibe was positive, you know? It felt like being in the right place at the right time. By the way, how come you were at Godfrey Timson's house?'

'Wrong place at the wrong time,' replied Church.

'Anyway, the Arab turns up and everything seemed to change. Music turned down so low that you could hardly hear it. Other people seemed to have drifted away and there were just a select few left. I felt good to still be around, you know? There must have only been about ten or twelve of us in the room. People I knew and Manus Klimop and two of his friends. The Arab and four of his friends were there as well. Actually, they were more like bodyguards come to think of it. Anyway, he's not really Arabian. He told me that he is from Persia, but he's not actually Persian either.'

'I am Parthian,' a voice behind them said.

Amber jumped and let out a little shriek. Church hid his surprise well. Two well-built bodyguards followed the Arab into the cabin. Suddenly the room seemed crowded.

'It is a tribe, or clan, or family originally from an area that is now in central Iran,' the Arab continued. 'But we moved around throughout history. Afghanistan, Pakistan and for some time, in Iraq and Saudi Arabia as well. Not nomadic, but displaced by others.'

'And now we are here,' said Church calmly.

'Indeed we are, Mr Church. And I am very pleased to see you both.'

'I thought that you were keen to see the back of me.'

'On the contrary. It has been useful to keep you alive to find out how much you know about my business operation.'

'Drug trafficking is not really business is it?'

'And that, Mr Church, confirms my suspicions that you know very little about me.'

Church had to admit that the Arab was speaking the truth. He had been trying to find a missing person. Trying to track down Amber. But it was clear that there was much more going on than a simple missing person, she was mixed up in something altogether larger and more complicated. Tomas Kar was dead, dead from a drugs overdose. Hookman was dead, murdered in his flat. Godfrey Timson was murdered in an Amsterdam warehouse. Two of those murders had been pinned on Church in an attempt to put him off what he thought was the search for Amber Garland. In reality, implicating him in the murders of Hookman and Timson was to stop him from investigating the Arab's narcotics business. He had very little knowledge about the links in this supposed drugs chain. But his mind was working fast. He was temporarily wrongfooted when the Arab spoke.

'Would I be permitted to show you around my shipyard facility? I believe it is customary under these circumstances.'

Church was not entirely sure what circumstances the other man was referring to but he got to his feet and held out a hand to help Amber to her feet. She staggered slightly as she stood. Church could feel the floor swaying gently even though the ship had berthed. The pitch and roll of the cruise liner had stopped. The sway, surge, yaw and heave that they had experienced out at sea was no more. Just as it takes time to adjust to the rocking sensation of being on a ship, gaining your 'sea legs', it also takes time to adjust to being back on dry land and to gain your 'land legs'. It can last a few hours or a few days, it can even last longer. In rare cases, *Mal de Debarquement* may last for years.

The Arab led them out of the cabin and Church carefully followed. Amber walked beside him, holding his hand for emotional and physical support. As they walked along a narrow corridor, Church could feel her lurch to one side every now and then. It gave him the chance to examine the Arab as they walked the length of the ship. The man was in his late forties or perhaps early fifties, exceptionally well dressed. He wore a mid-length, dark navy *thobe* with pure white loose-fitting *serwal* trousers beneath. The man wore nothing on his head, unlike in Manchester, and his hair was neatly trimmed. It was the man's skin that really set him apart. It was perfectly smooth, freshly shaved and free of any blemish whatsoever. It was the sort of close-shave that you would only get from an expertly wielded cut-throat razor.

Eventually, they were led down a narrow gangplank and off of the ship. The Arab, Church and Amber and the two bodyguards departed the cruise liner. The little group of figures was dwarfed by the size and scale of the enormous ships that surrounded them. A gang of scruffily dressed workmen formed a welcome party on the shoreline as they patiently waited to climb aboard to start dismantling and stripping down the old cruise ship. Beyond them was a smaller shipping vessel. A sleek superyacht sat low in the water at the end of a long straight pier. It seemed to be being prepared to sail and a thick black electric cable ran along the length of the jetty before dipping into the water underneath the luxurious sailing vessel. Church glanced over his shoulder but the boat was lost behind the bulky figures of the two minders.

Chapter Thirty-Two

A Tour of the Facilities

'And these are the smelting facilities, where we have a furnace running twenty-four hours a day to melt silver, which is poured into ingot moulds,' said the Arab. 'We have a series of these lines doing first, second and third pours to purify and refine the silver to ninety-two point five per cent purity.'

He had been talking for quite some time as he proudly showed Church and Amber around his shipyard. She had not spoken since they left the cruise liner and Church was now well and truly bored by the infinite detail of every part of the reclamation process that was being explained to them at great length. He had regained his land legs and no longer had the sensation of movement underfoot. Church was not so sure about Amber Garland, she still looked pale and worried.

'And here,' continued the Arab, 'we have the last part of the reclamation process. Anything that is of unknown origin and that may be combustible is fed into this blast furnace for incineration at ultra-high temperature. It is powered by Marine diesel and we have a plentiful free supply. All that is left after this process is a pile of fine ash. It is the place to tie up loose ends.'

'Or to dispose of loose ends,' added Church gloomily.

He regretted speaking his mind as soon as he said these words. He sensed Amber's anxiousness beside him. She gripped his hand tightly.

'Did you see what that foreman was wearing inside the warehouse?' she whispered as they left the last facility.

'I wasn't paying that much attention to his clothes, Amber.'

'That was the same shirt that Manus was wearing in his cousin's club in Prague. Black silk, slim fit, cut-away collar with mother of pearl buttons. I'd recognise it anywhere.'

'Your geography knowledge is a bit sketchy but your fashion knowledge is right up-to-date,' said Church.

'What?'

'Never mind,' replied Church. 'Mercifully, I think that we are at the end of our tour.'

They had been walking around for several hours. The Arab had been pointing this way and that, gesticulating towards buildings in the distance and walking them past lines of recycled equipment, parts and fittings. An area the size of a large car park was full of fluorescent orange lifeboats destined for other ships. Another smaller area was piled high with lifejackets. To Church, they looked rather sad. Like the brightly coloured leftover flotsam and jetsam from a disaster at sea. They had been led through a warehouse that was full of furniture. Cupboards, lockers, writing desks, cabinets, beds, tables and chairs filled the store. Now they were walking towards a large prefabricated hanger that had an ornate but oddly out of place portico built at the entrance.

As they stepped inside, they left the noise of the shipyard behind them. It was cool, air-conditioned and quiet inside the large hanger. The floor had been covered in cream marble, the walls were painted white. The space was vast, perhaps the size of a football pitch, and full of armchairs laid out in row upon row. A long table with office style chairs had been set up at the end of the room. Church was suddenly aware of a ringing inside his ears. Probably due to several days of travelling in a ship with the engines running or waves crashing against the side of the boat. He was also tired after walking around after the

Arab, his legs had started to ache. It was like listening to a dictator making a speech to the party faithful for several hours. One of the bodyguards had disappeared at some point, leaving just one minder with the Arab. Wherever they were, the Arab obviously felt safe. The bodyguard had been sweating profusely in the heat outside, he was still covered in perspiration now. Church concluded that the well-built thug was good for show but would be utterly useless for protection purposes.

'Please, sit,' said the Arab pointing to a row of empty chairs behind the long table.

Amber slumped into the nearest seat and Church gratefully sat down next to her but hid his relief at the opportunity to rest. The Arab and his bodyguard sat some distance away. Almost immediately a meal appeared and was placed with great deference in front of the Arab. The aroma of freshly cooked steak filled the air. Church and Amber were not served.

'We thought perhaps at first,' the Arab said while still eating, 'that you were a policeman, Mr Church. It was inconvenient to run into you in Manchester. You caused an upset to part of our operations there. Then we thought that you were a rival drug dealer. In Amsterdam, I thought that you were a policeman once again. Then, once again, a rival. Now I know that you are neither. You are just a Government busybody trying to take back someone who belongs to me.'

Amber tensed and started to speak, but Church gripped her leg and almost imperceptibly shook his head at her.

'By coincidence, the Police thought that I was a drug dealer when you thought that I was a policeman. And I was working with the Dutch police when you thought that I was a drug dealer,' replied Church. 'It just goes to show how wrong you got things. And now both the British and Dutch Governments know where I am. And I suspect that the Police are on their way here as we speak.'

It was a wild statement and Church knew it. In reality, he had absolutely no idea where he was. And nobody else did either.

'Hah!' the Arab exclaimed. 'I doubt very much if anyone could have traced you to our little Islamic Emirate state.'

Probably not, thought Church to himself, but it confirmed his assumption that they were somewhere in the *Gulf of Oman*.

'And now,' the Arab continued, pushing his empty plate to the far edge of the table, 'it is time to tie up loose ends. After I have met with various village leaders, local warlords and militia leaders, you will be dealt with. Actually, you might be treated as some entertainment during the meeting.'

The bodyguard rose from his seat and walked over to Church, lifting him from his own chair by his arm. Church shook himself free and walked placidly alongside the thug. Amber got up from her seat and followed unsteadily alongside them. As they walked the length of the table, Church carefully judged the distances.

As they drew level with where the Arab was still sitting, Church extended his leg and tripped up Amber. She crashed into the side of the table and let out a high pitched yelp as she fell to the ground. The Arab pushed his seat back and stood quickly out of harm's way. The bodyguard knelt to pick her up from the marble floor and Church took the opportunity to grab the steak knife from the empty plate. He smoothy palmed the weapon up the sleeve of his jacket.

'Take them to the workshop,' the Arab snarled, 'and tie them securely.'

Two strong hands gripped Church's arms and he was led out of the large open room and down a long corridor with doors leading off each side. A door was open at the end of the passageway and he was roughly pushed inside.

It was some kind of small maintenance repair room. A bench ran along one side of the room, with various tools and equipment stored on the walls. Plastic cable ties were fastened securely around his wrists and ankles and then the same restraints were applied to Amber. She protested a little but saved her worst glares for Church.

'What did you do that for?' she asked when they were alone.

'Sorry, Amber, but I did it for this,' said Church, shuffling out the knife from his sleeve.

'Oh, you genius!' she exclaimed. 'You are forgiven. Just get me untied and let's get out of here fast.'

'All in good time,' said Church as he cut away his restraints, 'I want to have a little look around before we make a run for it.'

They were both free of their restraints in a few minutes. Church listened carefully at the door and eventually tried the handle. It was, of course, locked firmly shut. He looked around the room for something to pick the lock with but nothing seemed to lend itself to the task. Eventually, Church's gaze fell on a piece of equipment.

'Can you break the lock or something?' asked Amber desperately.

'Better than that, Amber,' said Church grabbing hold of a small pneumatic jack, 'we can break the frame.'

'What?'

'Grab a hold of this while I look for something to pack out the gap.'

She looked confused but did as she was told and held the pneumatic jack level with the lock on the door. Church returned with a thick chunk of metal and wedged it against the frame where the door hinges were. He settled the other end of the metal bar into the shoe of the jack and started to pump the hydraulic handle. The head of the jack extended from its housing and gradually pressed against the door frame that housed the lock. He continued to pump, extending the head of the jack until the frame began to buckle. The plaster on the walls on either side of the door began to crumble as the pressure built. Eventually, the frame gave way and the door swung open with hardly a sound.

The corridor yawned emptily ahead. Church ducked underneath the mechanism he had constructed to prise open the door and started down the hallway.

'Follow me,' he whispered.

'What are you looking for?' Amber asked.

'An exit, of course. But a little look around on the way out wouldn't hurt.'

Church glanced inside the offices and rooms as they walked down the corridor. As tempted as he was to look inside, his priority was to get out of here with Amber. One room, in particular, looked worth exploring. At the end of the long hallway was a fire escape door complete with a push bar to exit. Church leaned gently on the horizontal bar and eased the door open.

Almost immediately the corridor was filled with the sound of a siren going off. Rubbish had piled up against the outside of the door. Tissues, plastic wrapping and bottles scraped against the ground as the door swung open. He grabbed hold of Amber's hand and was vaguely aware of flashing lights filling the narrow space behind them. Church did not hear the footsteps on the marble floor of one of the bodyguards running down the passageway. He was busy packing a piece of rubbish into the recess of the fire escape bar. However, he did hear the bullet that crashed into the wall just beside his head.

He flung open the fire escape and ran outside into the afternoon sun. The heat struck them immediately. Church tried to guide Amber to run in a zigzag but she stumbled almost immediately. More bullets flew around them and in the confusion, she let go of his hand and she was gone.

Church took cover behind the closest pile of detritus. The bodyguard was lumbering out of the fire escape and squinting around, holding his gun level with his face. Church frantically looked around for Amber and his heart sank when he saw her being led away by another of the guards.

A bullet hit the side of a discarded lifeboat way to the left of where Church was crouched. Another bullet was fired but they were random shots, fired in an attempt to draw him out. The familiar empty click of an empty gun magazine made Church's heart soar. He set off running. Jogging in this heat was painful but not as painful as being shot or captured. He sprinted past the remaining rows of lifeboats and continued alongside the pile of lifejackets. No more bullets came his way and he suspected that the muscle-bound thug could not reload because he only had one magazine for the revolver. A rookie error, thought Church to himself.

Church continued to run. A pile of fine ash had been dumped alongside the path he now took. The contents of the incinerator. Church glanced across and saw part of a human skull perched on top of a mound of grey powder. Difficult to dispose of a body at sea but easy to incinerate a corpse and turn it to ash.

'Manus or Ondra Klimop I presume?' said Church to himself.

He was now out of the central compound and could see a rusty chain link fence ahead. Church jumped and grabbed the top of the interlinked galvanized wire, lifting himself up with the momentum of his leap. With the grace and agility of a high-jump athlete, he cleared the fence and dropped gently down on the opposite side of the barrier.

The terrain ahead was composed of dusty soil and the occasional small stone or rock dotted about here and there. No place for cover and no place to lose the bodyguard now running in close pursuit. Church had eased up his pace on purpose. He now jogged quite slowly and steadily, keeping just enough distance between him and the thug to make sure that he was not caught. At the same time, he wanted the bodyguard close enough so that the other man thought he might be in with a chance of catching him up.

After twenty minutes he could hear the other man gasping for breath. The over-developed legs of the thug stumbled and he paused for a moment. Church eased up his pace even more and began running in an exaggerated zigzag once again. the minder was encouraged to continue his pursuit. Another five hundred yards and the guard stopped again. This time Church was ready. He spun around and sprinted back. The muscle-bound thug was doubled over gasping for breath. Sweat was dripping off of the other man and he was puffing, wheezing and holding his chest.

As Church approached the muscle-bound figure he swung his leg back and delivered a firm swift kick to the sweat-drenched head of the thug. He went down with a grunt. The bodyguard dropped to the ground with a solid sounding thud and lay still in amongst the dust and stones. A muscular figure with his head in the sand. Church bent over the prone figure of the guard and retrieved the pistol from the man's inside jacket pocket. He tucked it down the belt loop at the front of his trousers.

'These things are very dangerous,' he said but got no reply.

Church slowly made his way back to the compound.

Chapter Thirty-Three

Escape and evade

Edward Church retraced his steps back to the shipyard compound. He was surprised at how far he had run to wear down the guard. Each time he walked over a small hill or mound of dust and stones he thought that he would see the compound. He imagined the bodyguard regaining consciousness after a few hours and trying to make his way back. The other man was muscular but unfit. After what seemed like hours he walked up yet another steep incline, sending showers of gravel back down the slope as he ascended. The buildings of the recycling complex were some distance away. The sun was getting low in the sky over his right shoulder and the shadows cast by the small stones were now getting longer. It was, however, still swelteringly hot.

    He eventually found a path of some sort that had been cleared of stones and rocks. It seemed to lead down to the coast and Church happily trudged along the dusty track. A battered and rusty signpost announced the name of a nearby town, *'Pasabandar'*. For some reason, the excursion had cleared his mind and a plan of sorts was forming somewhere in his mind. With thoughts of organised drug operations, finding Amber and a means to escape running through his head, Church did not notice the sound of bells getting nearer and nearer until they were nearly upon him.

    The sight of a small boy walking in front of a small group of goats seemed incongruous but entirely expected. Church had not learnt to read Arabic, he found the letters too difficult to master. But as he approached the young man Church nodded and spoke.

'Hello,' he said.

'*'Ahlan*,' the boy replied and then added in English, 'Drink? Water?'

The youngster held out a plastic bottle of water. Church gratefully clutched it and took a deep swig from the bottle. It crunched a little and the label folded in on itself. He looked at the lettering on the side and smiled as he read *Highland Spring Water, Bottled in Scotland.*

'*Shukran*,' said Church. The only Arabic word he had learnt and probably the most helpful or useful was the word for '*thank you'*.

Church rested a little as he approached the shipyard compound. He found a seat next to a collection of plastic storage containers and watched the sun setting over a low mountain range some distance in the West. Wherever he was in the world right now he had to admit that it was a beautiful sight.

Darkness descended quickly as the sun finally dipped below the mountains. Eventually, Church decided that it was time to make a move and roused himself from his seat. His legs ached and he was hungry but his mind was focused on the task ahead.

An assortment of cars had been parked close to the portico in front of the prefabricated hangar. *Isuzu*, *Mitsubishi* and *Toyota* pick-up trucks seemed to be the most popular vehicle of choice but there were other oversized SUVs parked in amongst the utility vehicles. Drivers stood outside the vehicles either smoking or wiping down the bodywork of the trucks. Some had gathered together to chat and share some tea served in little glass tulip-shaped cups.

Church crouched low to the ground, silently made his way back to the fire escape door and gently prised it open. He prayed that the bar had not clicked back into place and that the little piece of rubbish that he had packed into the recess had stayed in place. Thankfully it had, and mercifully the alarm was not reactivated when he opened the door. Church thanked his luck but took nothing for granted.

Cautiously, slowly and methodically he made his way back down the corridor inside the hangar. At the far end of the hallway, he could see that some sort of conference was going on. Church cursed himself for his lack of Arabic and he had no idea what was being discussed by the delegates sitting inside the vast hangar. The Arab sat at the end of the room behind the long table, like an immaculate spider in the middle of his web. A screen behind him was covered in Arabian script. It meant little to Church. He had unwittingly stepped on one of the threads of the spider's web and it had led to this.

Undeterred, he made his way silently back down the corridor. He carefully listened at each door before trying it to see if it opened. The room inside the first door contained little more than stationery and office supplies. Shelves were neatly stacked with everything a place of work would need. The next door led to a large storage space, now empty apart from two or three of the armchairs that had been laid out in the large space of the air-conditioned hangar.

'A few people are not going to make it here today then,' quipped Church as he shut the door.

The third door led to an office space. The room that had looked tempting on his first reconnoitre with Amber a few hours before. It too was air-conditioned and decorated with the same cool marble floor and white walls. Large television screens lined one wall and an enormous desk sat in the opposite corner. Church opened the desk drawers and rifled through the contents. His hand rested on the cold metal barrel of a semi-automatic pistol. Church checked the chamber and noted that it contained a full eighteen 9mm bullets. He carefully tucked the weapon down the back of his trousers. Church retrieved the empty weapon that he had taken from the bodyguard and placed it at the end of the desk.

The remainder of the wall space in the office was decorated with either fine art or shelving containing sculptures, carvings, trinkets and other objects. Every item was neatly arranged in an organised and orderly fashion. As beautiful as these items were, they did not hold Church's attention. It was the small black box that was sat on the edge of the desk that he now considered with great detail.

He had seen one of these before. And Amber had explained, when she had a part-time job, how she used one to send thousands of spam messages. Church strongly suspected that this was how the Arab contacted other associates in his drug cartel. It was how Manus Klimop contacted his distributers and probably how Godfrey Timson communicated with his dealers. Encrypted messages that were sent to dozens or hundreds of mobile telephones. And as Alexander Drake had explained to Church, those messages would be hidden from prying eyes in a phone within a phone.

'Hopefully no password,' said Church to himself as he switched on the desk computer.

The screen burst into life and illuminated the room in a digital glow. He was relieved that the computer booted up without needing a code. Church quickly scrolled through the list of programmes until his eyes rested on the application named *Enkryptation*. He double-clicked and hit the return key but the pop-up window on the screen just shook from side to side.

'How does this bloody thing work?' said Church to himself aware that his recent run of luck had just ended.

The small pop-up window in the middle of the computer screen needed a four-figure password. Church tried the usual sequences of 1,2,3,4 and combinations of 1,1,1,1 or 2,2,2,2 but after working his way through the numerals he sat back on the leather office chair and pondered.

'Roughly how old are you Mr Arab?' he said out loud, then started typing in combinations of reversed birth years.

Eventually, he guessed the password combination and the *Enkryptation* programme began to run. Church frantically typed at the keyboard, desperately trying to send a message. He had the vague idea to send a message to all of the Arab's contacts saying that the drugs operation was to be shut down. He would warn that their identities were known to the authorities and that they should get rid of any drugs in their possession. He then had the notion to send a message to any mobile telephone number he could remember sending his approximate location, that of a shipbreakers yard in *Pasabandar*. Someone somewhere would get an unsolicited message and hopefully, somebody would pass it to the authorities. Unfortunately, he did not know how the programme worked and could not understand the onscreen prompts that appeared in Arabic.

A sound close by made his heart quicken. He looked desperately from the black box to the computer and back again. The noise was getting closer and he suddenly realised that the little slots in the top of the box were empty. Those slots in Manus' office were full of little SIM cards. The same cards that were now in his pocket.

Desperately he fumbled to retrieve them and pushed as many as he could inside the black contraption connected to the computer. He was just about to attempt sending another message but a cool metal touch on his neck made him freeze. The slow metallic double click of a pistol cocking made him lift his hands gently from the keyboard. The Arab stood close by with a pistol in his hand. One of the bodyguards hovered nearby with his hand gripping one of Amber's thin arms.

'How careless of you to leave this at the end of my desk, Mr Church,' the Arab said calmly.

'Far too many weapons,' said Church as he slowly raised his hands from the keyboard and rested them on the top of his head.

'And far too many interruptions for one day, Mr Church,' replied the Arab.

He punched the side of Church's head but there was little force behind the blow. However, another punch from the bodyguard sent him flying across the room and Church stayed down while his head cleared and lights flashed before his eyes. He was dragged to his feet and another punch landed in his stomach. Church was ready for this one, he made a great act of doubling up and coughing loudly. He feigned a step to the left then exaggerated a stagger to the right towards the doorway. The bodyguard was lining up to land another blow on Church's body but the Arab interrupted.

'Enough of this. Take Mr Church to the yacht.'

The bodyguard marched Church towards the doorway and it appeared that Amber would be temporarily left behind.

'Do not forget the girl,' the Arab barked at the minder.

The other powerful arm of the bodyguard seized Amber by the arm and the two of them were funnelled through the narrow doorway by the muscular minder.

As they walked back down the corridor, Amber was smiling broadly. It seemed odd to Church given their predicament but he was not about to spoil her apparent buoyant mood. They walked back through the vast warehouse space but detoured away from the conference area. The cool night air enveloped them as they stepped outside. The heat of the sun had dissipated and a cloudless sky above showed a canopy twinkling stars. The air was crisp and clean. Unlike the dry dusty atmosphere during the day when the machinery was operating and the workmen were toiling. As they walked along a dusty path towards the shoreline, the only sound apart from their own footsteps was of night-time bugs chirping or the occasional nocturnal animal scuttling away to safety. Church wished that he could join them.

The four of them approached the superyacht moored at the end of the narrow jetty. The Arab led the way, Amber followed behind. The bodyguard had let go of her arm and she placidly kept her place in line. Church's arm was still held in a vice-like grip but he did not struggle. He did not want to give the minder any reason to search him.

The yacht looked beautiful. Long, low in the water, painted white but finished with the addition of a dark stripe that swept along the length of its hull and then curved upwards at the stern. Lights from the boat glittered in the reflection of the sea. The thick black cable that Church had spotted earlier had been disconnected at some point in the afternoon. A slightly thinner cable now ran from the lower deck of the ship, down over the transom and stern at the rear, where it disappeared into the inky black water.

The Arab jumped aboard the ship. Amber was helped over the gunwale by a Filipino deckhand. Church was pushed aboard by the bodyguard. Another figure appeared, temporarily silhouetted in the doorway of the wheelhouse cabin. The Arab spoke to him briefly and the man who Church assumed to be the ship's captain answered in Russian. Lights appeared and the whole ship was illuminated. The captain was a nasty looking individual and Church took an instant dislike to him. The man had a thick neck and a shaved head that appeared to grow straight out of his shoulders. He was short, barrel-chested, most of his body and a fair amount of his face was covered in tattoos. Church nicknamed him 'no-neck'.

No-neck grinned when he saw Amber. The Eyes of the tattooed Russian Captain swept up and down Amber's body, lingering over her every detail. Church's low opinion of the man was endorsed.

No-neck disappeared back into the cockpit and the engines were started immediately. Another deckhand appeared and the two Filipinos danced across the superyacht, clearing ropes and lifting the plastic fenders that had protected the hull of the ship while it was berthed. In all of the action of disembarking, Church did not see another figure sitting just inside the cockpit doorway. As they slowly manoeuvred out into open water he became aware of a third captive amongst them apart from himself and Amber.

The bruised and battered face of Mathias Agurk, the Dutch Captain of the cargo vessel that had taken Church to Rotterdam, looked at Church with the appearance of a condemned man. Another loose end to clear away considered Church.

'You. To the back of the boat,' the Arab said, pointing a gun at Church. 'And you too,' he added, waving the weapon at Mathias.

'Good to see you again, Captain,' said Church as they stood together at the stern of the yacht.

'I wish that it was under different circumstances,' Mathias replied gloomily.

'Face the sea and stop your talking,' interrupted the Arab levelling his gun at the Dutch seaman.

'If you're going to shoot someone,' said Church, 'you'd better make sure it's with a loaded gun.'

The Arab paused for a second then squeezed the trigger.

Chapter Thirty-Four

Call my bluff

Church was sure that the Arab had picked up the empty pistol he had put on the edge of the desk in the office back in the shipbreakers yard. But now that it was pointed at Mathias, he was not so confident. Church flinched as the trigger was pulled on the gun. His heart skipped a beat and it soared as he heard the sound of an empty single click. Without waiting, Church reached behind his back and pulled the second weapon from the waistband of his trousers. In normal circumstances, he disliked the Glock semi-automatic pistol. But now he blessed its trigger mounted safety catch which meant a smooth transition from safety to live in the squeezing of the firing mechanism.

He raised his own weapon and swept round to point it at the bodyguard in one fluid movement. Still in a state of shock, the guard was slow to reach for his own pistol. Church fired and the bodyguard toppled backwards. He heard rather than saw the body splash into the sea.

The weapon was trained onto the Arab a split-second later.

'You would not shoot me,' the Arab said hastily. 'You are a Government man, you are not permitted to undertake such an action.'

Church lowered the weapon.

The Arab smirked triumphantly.

And then Church shot the Arab in the foot.

The Arab fell to the deck, holding his leg and screaming in agony. He swore at Church. The shot and the screams of agony from the Arab brought the rest of the crew and the no-neck Russian captain onto the deck. Church swiftly moved away from the aft of the yacht and pointed his gun at the thick head of the Russian.

'Do you speak English?' he asked.

'*Der'mo,*' the Russian swore back at Church.

He pulled the trigger and the evil faced, bald-headed no-neck fell to the floor with a sickening thud. Church barely glanced down at the body. It was clear that the shot had been fatal. The hatred in the other man's face, which had been there a second ago, was now gone. Replaced with the nothingness of death. Church considered that it was in fact surprisingly easy to dispose of a body at sea; if you did not care whether it was found or not.

Church moved to the nearest Filipino deckhand. 'Do you speak English?'

'Yes, sir,' he replied instantly.

'Meet your new captain,' said Church.

The other Filipino deckhand bowed his head slightly in Church's direction.

'Not me,' said Church calmly and nodded his own head towards Mathias Agurk. 'Him. He's the new captain.'

Mathias seemed to snap out of the daze that he had been in since they left the shore. He staggered slightly as he walked away from the gunwale and made his way unsteadily across the deck to the wheelhouse.

The Arab had stopped screaming and sat, slumped on the floor holding his leg and moaning softly. Church looked around for a length of rope and gave the free end to Amber.

'Tie this around his calf. Make it tight or he will bleed to death.'

'What shall I do with the other end?' she replied. ' It's wrapped around this metal thing.'

'Cleat,' said Church.

'What?'

'That metal thing is called a cleat. And if we're are going to be at sea for a while, you'd better start to learn your aft from your elbow.'

* * *

After three days at sea, Church was beginning to get restless. They had been making good progress on the course he had plotted with Mathias Agurk but were still around one thousand nautical miles from the Mediterranean Sea. For some reason unknown to Mathias, the superyacht was running slow. The two powerful engines that propelled the craft were working perfectly. Contrary to popular opinion yachts are often powered by an engine rather than sail. The two crew were either unwilling or unable to explain the poor speed and Church had resigned himself to a slow, steady journey around the coastline of Oman and Yemen, into the Gulf of Aden and finally up through the Red Sea and Suez Canal to the Mediterranean. Church had tried to retrieve the thick black electric cable then snaked over the starboard side of the ship. One of the Filipino sailors explained that one end was connected to the generator onboard the ship. Church gently pulled at the free end of the cable but after coiling up three or four metres it seemed to snag. As it looked like it was doing no harm, Church dismissed it as a distraction.

Amber had taken to sunbathing in a white bikini she had found in one of the cabins. Her thin body and pale skin looked extraordinarily delicate. She insisted on making drinks for everybody on the boat as part of her role on board. It only added to the distractions of the journey. She had been keen to explore the ship and choose her berth as soon as she felt that the Arab was no longer a threat. She had been even more excited when she found a complete wardrobe for a woman within the cabin.

'I can't think why there would be all of these beautiful clothes on board,' she said archly. 'But I'm going to pack a suitcase full of these exotic clothes for myself.'

Church had rifled through the belongings of the Arab and was now walking around the upper deck wearing dark blue cotton trousers, a white linen shirt and some very comfortable grey suede espadrilles. The two Filipino deckhands had settled into their routines almost immediately. One looked after the engine room the other took on cooking duties. Everything else involved in running the ship was shared between the two of them. Captain Mathias Agurk looked fitter and stronger each day. He soon recovered from his beating and was obviously relieved at being spared being shot and dumped overboard. However, as their journey progressed Church noticed a change in the amiable Dutchman. Then, one morning he was back to his old self. Humming a tune quietly to himself as he checked and re-checked instruments and pilot computers in the wheelhouse. Church wondered why the mood of the Dutch captain had lifted.

'You seem brighter today, Mathias?' Church asked eventually.

'We have company,' he replied. 'Company of a good sort. Not trouble like I worried about. Sailing off the coast of Oman is safe and Yemen is secure. But Somalia has a bad history. There are many pirates and terrorists. Ships are sometimes captured and held for ransom and you must admit this is a good looking vessel.'

'I only got a glance at this superyacht as we left another ship during daylight. We were aboard a cruise liner that was due to be scrapped. It was night-time when we boarded her in *Pasabandar*. You don't appreciate the shape and size of a boat when you are actually on board. It's a bit like driving a good looking car. You don't see the outside when you are driving on the inside. You only get to see the shape of it when you have parked. Anyway, what sort of company do you mean?'

'We have had a Royal Navy patrol ship behind us since daybreak. For the last three hours, it has been keeping a steady distance between us. Usually at a distance of no less than two thousand metres or one nautical mile, sometimes a little farther away. But it is company nevertheless.'

'Well, that's reassuring,' said Church.

Mathias nodded and continued his checks as he hummed a quiet tune to himself. The only person aboard who did not look any better as the days passed was the Arab. His smooth-cheeked, baby faced complexion had changed dramatically. Three-day old dark stubble had appeared and he complained bitterly each time he was within earshot.

'You cannot keep me tied up here like this. I will die from exposure. Look at my foot, it is all swollen and black. I will surely lose the use of this leg.'

'Better to lose a leg than to die of blood loss,' replied Church absently.

In reality, the flesh wound in the leg of the Arab had clotted and Church had asked one of the Filipino's to bandage the wound and re-tie the rope a little looser. The foot had turned black because of bruising and there was very little chance of the man losing his leg but Church was not about to explain any of this to the Arab. Let him suffer, Church reflected, as he has made other people suffer.

Church decided to walk around the ship to break the boredom of the morning. The boat was about thirty or forty metres long and propelled by two powerful engines. They purred smoothly and vibration-free somewhere deep in the hull. Church did not see anything of the engine room and kept out of the wheelhouse too, that area was the domain of the ship's captain. The rest of the ship was his to explore. Starting at the rear of the yacht, the stern, he walked from a wide dive platform then over the transom and onto the midship deck. Staircases led up either side of the ship from the lower deck to the upper. The lower deck was mostly covered by the overhang of the upper and comfortable seating had been built around the edges, ending with a view of the ocean beyond the railings on the gunwale. Doors from this area led into the cabins of the ship with dining, living and sleeping quarters arranged off of a central corridor.

Church walked up the port side steps and onto the upper deck. He passed by the wheelhouse, the enclosed compartment that contained all of the navigational equipment and the computers that monitored the performance and operation of the ship. More areas for entertainment were constructed on the upper deck. It was, after all, a superyacht. Built for luxury and ultimate pleasure at sea.

The bow of the boat, at the very front, had a long pulpit constructed out of teak with chrome rails. Any previous practical use of the pulpit had long since ceased when this yacht was designed. It was purely a recreational space for guests to sit and watch views of the sea uninterrupted by anything else onboard.

Church scanned the horizon, looking for the Royal Navy patrol vessel. He thought that he saw it once or twice, but it could so easily have been another ship in the distance. They are, after all, painted a pale grey colour to blend in perfectly with the sea and sky on the horizon. He watched one ship in the distance that appeared to be getting closer, but it turned out to be an oil supertanker. Another boat was a giant container ship with steel boxes piled so high on the decks that it looked as if it must surely topple over.

He was lost in his own thoughts for a moment and did not notice their own yacht slowing down. Church did observe that the horizon in the distance on the port side was now broken by a strip of land. He assumed that they were slowing because the captain was navigating around something on the seabed. Shallows and sandbanks can stretch out from land for many miles.

Captain Mathias Agurk stuck his head out of the wheelhouse and looked around the side of the ship. Seeing nothing he disappeared back inside for a moment then reappeared, walking down the deck to where Church was standing at the bow.

'We are dragging on the seabed,' he said anxiously looking over the side of the ship once more.

'It looks too deep here,' replied Church. 'There's no keel or centreboard on this yacht. Is there?'

'Not that I know of. But I'm not really the captain of this ship.'

'Let's get a length of rope and rig up a sounding line,' said Church, suddenly interested.

A length of thin rope was found and a heavy weight tied to the free end. Church threw it over the side of the boat. It plopped into the water and sunk. Down and down it dropped. Church fed out more rope from the coil by his feet, but the weight still descended. Eventually, the line went slack. Church tied a knot near the water level and re-coiled the rope. He stretched one arm lengthways holding the free end of the line and formed the coil of rope near his opposite shoulder.

'It's got to be over twenty metres deep here,' said Church. 'I wonder if there is any diving equipment on board?'

Minutes later one of the deckhands had been summoned and returned with a selection of goggles and snorkel equipment. Minutes after that, the engines had been shut down and both Church and Mathias were climbing over the swim platform at the stern. He dipped his goggles into the seawater and fastened them tightly around his head.

Church slid from the low wooden platform into the clear pale blue sea in one graceful fluid movement. He did not wait for Mathias but kicked down underneath the swell of the waves. Church followed the line of a thick black electric cable that he had previously noticed draped over the gunwale of the boat. It merged with another thick steel cable that had been fastened to the hull of the yacht about four or five metres below the surface. Church grabbed hold of the steel cable and pulled himself down.

After ten metres the water was not as clear as it seemed from the surface. After another ten metres, Church began to wonder quite what he would find at the bottom if indeed he could hold his breath that long.

Just as he was beginning to feel the first pangs in his lungs that told him he would have to kick back up to the surface, a shape appeared before him that made his heart leap.

Chapter Thirty-Five

Showdown

Church was in high spirits as he surfaced. Mathias appeared beside him. For some reason, the other man had fitted a snorkel in his mouth and it had delayed the Dutch captain a little.

'Did you see it?' Mathias asked Church as he fiddled with the snorkel mouthpiece.

'I certainly did. Although I'm not entirely sure what it is,' Mathias replied.

'It is the size of a small shipping container but has electrical power supplied to it.'

'And a strange fin-like device fitted to the front,' added Church. 'It looks like it's controlled by gyroscopes or something. I think that it is shaped like that to help keep the container submerged at a fixed depth.'

'There was one of those containers fixed to the hull of my boat *Kerstmis-ijs*. I did not know it at the time but the Dutch authorities showed me images of it before I was released on Police bail. Before the Arab helped me escape only to double-cross me when we made it to *Pasabandar*,' he reflected gloomily.

They clambered back aboard, slightly less gracefully than they had entered the waters. Amber was standing at the stern of the yacht ready to greet them with her arms full of towels. She noticed the smiles on their faces and looked quizzically at Church.

'Is everything okay?' she asked.

'Everything is more than okay, Amber,' replied Church.

'You look like a child who has found a toy that he had lost,' she said brightly, passing a towel to Church. 'Do you know what day it is today?'

'No idea, I'm afraid. Days merge into one another at sea.'

'It's Christmas Eve.'

Church paused. It certainly did not feel like Christmas. They were surrounded by clear blue water and an almost cloudless sky. The sun was high, hot and dry. There was hardly a breeze and the only other living things around them were some gulls floating lazily in the sky. Church did not feel at all festive.

Mathias Agurk limped the yacht into port at *Djibouti*, the capital city of the tiny republic of the same name that sits between *Eritrea* and *Somalia* at the mouth of the Red Sea. Anchoring a kilometre or so out in the bay, he radioed for a tender to take them ashore and to arrange for refuelling the next day. The more time Church spent with the amiable Dutchman, the more he liked him.

Mathias also seemed to know his way around the streets of the city and was a useful guide as they made their way from *Port de Peche* marina. While he and one of the crew sourced supplies, Church and Amber booked lunch for the four of them at the *Djibouti Palace* Hotel and then headed off to the *Riyad* Market. The fifteen-minute taxi ride in an antiquated green and white vehicle took them down the incongruously named *Rue de Venice*, before heading inland and down a myriad of haphazard streets.

Amber seemed in awe of her new surroundings, looking this way and that, craning her neck left and right to take in every sight. Church was just as excited to be here but hid it well. His mind was on other things as they drove steadily through narrow streets and past buildings that looked as if they had been built decades ago and repaired ever since. The previous French colonial influence was still clear in many of the larger buildings but Moorish and African influences were apparent everywhere. Fleets of small minibuses flowed down every road, dropping people off and picking others up at seemingly random places. Low-rise buildings housed cafes, shops and small convenience stores but the street market was a sight to behold. Chaotic, makeshift, hectic and improvised. It thronged with life. The stalls were immaculately clean with wooden poles supporting temporary awnings of frayed canvas to keep the heat of the sun from spoiling the fruit and vegetables on show. Piles of apples, oranges, pomegranates, lemons, grapefruit, peaches and apricots had been arranged in perfect pyramid shapes. Onions, beetroot, potatoes and other root vegetables were being washed and arranged in neat rows by proud stallholders. Church recognised most of the offerings but some of the vegetables left him guessing. Was it a Yam, or Cassava? Church was not sure. Amber insisted on buying a watermelon simply because of its size.

'They are enormous,' she squealed. 'It will take us a week to eat it! They look much nicer than those overripe bananas.'

'Plantaines,' replied Church. 'For cooking rather than eating raw.'

Amber did not listen to Church's answer because she was too interested in trying to buy a bag of carrots. The stallholder had enormous sacks of the orange wonky vegetables piled up on some wooden pallets.

'How do I ask for a small bag?' she implored Church.

'If you can't speak Arabic, you could try *petit sac*,' said Church trying to hide his exasperation.

They took their leave from the street market after an hour. Amber was loaded down with carrier bags and Church had gallantly offered to carry the watermelon. She staggered a little as she walked, loaded down with bags of produce and a little shaky on her legs after being at sea. They hailed a passing taxi and stashed their purchases with an obliging receptionist back at the *Djibouti Palace*. The deckhand declined dining with them explaining that he had more chores to do. Church suspected that the man felt out of place in such opulent surroundings or uneasy about eating with them. As they sat and ate in the hotel dining room, Church regretted not booking a room for the evening. He had had enough of sailing for a while. The luxury of their dining surroundings would no doubt be matched by the luxury of the room service. Church thought of their yacht anchored just off the mainland. It was every bit as luxurious as the hotel.

Satisfied and satiated after a sumptuous meal, Church, Amber and Mathias waited on the quayside late in the afternoon for the Filipino crewman. The sun was getting low in the sky and it silhouetted the enormous container port in the distance just outside Djibouti. The cranes that lifted the large corrugated steel boxes from cargo ships had stopped working for the day. They were frozen against the skyline as if paused partway through a crazy dance. Church was sorry to leave this place, he made a note to himself that he would return for an extended visit when he had the time.

That night he slept deeply and soundly. The gentle plop of water against the side of the ship and the sway of the boat against its anchor only added to the restful state that enveloped Church. He awoke to the sounds of a refuelling tug pulling up next to their vessel. Ropes were passed from ship to ship and the flotilla of two boats joined in a temporary convoy. One exchanging fuel with the other.

Amber insisted on cooking that day. She attempted a full English roast dinner and prepared it with such enthusiasm that Church paid little attention to its quality. Which was just as well because Amber was no cook. The meal was barely edible. Vegetables had been cooked for as long as the meat. The meat itself, which was supposed to be lamb, was definitely on the side of mutton and the gravy was watery and almost clear in colour. Everybody praised her cooking and expressed encouraging comments. Even the two Filipinos ate well, although that might have been out of politeness or hunger, and celebrated the food even though they were excellent cooks themselves.

Church slept badly that night. It was not due to indigestion or any childlike festive excitement. Was it the disappointment that the search for Amber was really over, was it his mind going over the contents of the steel container being dragged twenty metres below them? Perhaps the poor sleep should have been an omen or a sense of foreboding because two days later, as they sailed away from Port Said at the exit of the Suez Canal, he spotted another patrol ship following them.

* * *

The Suez Canal has Egypt, Sudan and Eritrea to the West, Isreal, Jordan, Saudi Arabia and Yemen to the East. A collection of countries that border the Red Sea that are frequently in the news for all of the wrong reasons. Church could sense the tension in the captain and both crew members as they progressed quickly up the narrow sea towards the relative safety of the Suez Canal.

The modern-day, expanded and enlarged, Suez Canal is the most recent and well-known of many waterways constructed across Egypt by Pharaohs and Kings, Emporers and Engineers. Most of the ancient canals snaked across the Nile Delta, one may even have connected the Red Sea to the Mediterranean Sea. Construction in the area foiled Napoleon Bonapart because of a mistaken calculation by one of his engineers that the sea level was lower in the Mediterranean. The

British Government were against the construction of the Suez Canal quite possibly on the simple, political, grounds that it was proposed by a Frenchman and had the support of the then French Emporer, Napoleon III.

Since its opening in 1869, the canal has allowed direct trade to flow between the Indian Ocean and the North Atlantic Ocean via the Red Sea and the Mediterranean Sea. It also permitted Edward Church to sail from the dangers of *Pasbandar* to the safety of the tiny Greek island of *Karpathos*. He did not know the Island but both Captain Mathias Agurk and the two Filipino crew seemed well acquainted with its geography. The tension of the last few days and the concern about being followed by another vessel seemed to dissipate as they made their approach to one of the small bays that are dotted around the island.

'This evening we will celebrate,' Mathias said as he guided the cruiser towards the island.

'Do you know any good restaurants?' asked Church.

'There are plenty,' he smiled. 'And cheap bars if they are open at this time of year. Relax, Edward, you still look concerned but we are nearly there.'

Church was still concerned. He would not be happy until he was back in England. But he had to admit that the village surrounding the bay looked inviting. A narrow road snaked along the coast, a more substantial motorway had been carved into the mountains and hills above. Houses stretched back from the cove, standing to attention like pastel-painted sentries as they stretched up the hillsides. Orange roofs constructed with terracotta tiles swept back down to the inlet. As they berthed in the harbour Church could see a row of commercial shopfronts stretching along the promenade. Several restaurants, one or two bars that looked to be closed for the season, a supermarket selling every essential a person might need, some clothes shops and jewellers. Tourists shops selling souvenirs and trinkets had their shutters pulled down until the spring months brought more holidaymakers to part with their money within the air-conditioned emporiums.

Church stepped gingerly ashore, feeling each step carefully until he regained his land legs. One of the Filipinos made good the ropes after dropping fenders over the side as the superyacht docked. After much discussion, he insisted on treating Church, Mathias and Amber to a drink in a bar he knew nearby.

'My cousin owns the bar, he will give good drinks for us. Nice price. No problem.'

'That is a good enough offer for me,' answered Mathias and Church was in no mood to disagree.

The bar was functional, shabby, worn, dated and immaculately clean. Whitewashed rendered walls inside and out had been ornamented with decorative borders in the traditional Greek key design. The hand-painted blue bands meandered around the room at waist height and were complimented by clusters of *mati*, evil eye motifs manufactured out of glass. The talisman, meant to ward off evil spirits or protect against evil glances, had been hung at irregular intervals. They sat in the early afternoon sun, eating and drinking for an hour or so until the worries that Church had been feeling seemed to fade. He forgot about the patrol vessels that had followed them, forgot about the perils of the journey, forgot about the threats that had been made against him and even forgot about the Arab, tied up after being shot in the leg aboard his own yacht.

The Filipino deckhand spoke to Captain Mathias as Church settled the bill for their food and drinks. It did not seem to Church that the man's cousin had given them much of a deal on the refreshments but he paid and left a small tip. Mathias announced that they needed to stop at a food warehouse located behind the row of seafront shops to stock up on provisions for their onward sail. Mathias explained that the owner was related to the Filipino.

Church did not intend to continue by boat. He had had enough of the sea and was already thinking about booking air travel back to the UK if planes were still flying at this time of year.

As they made their way back down the seafront footpath Church did not see the dark coloured vehicle parked partway up a narrow side street.

Chapter Thirty Six

Rescue

The walkway along the seafront was quiet. No tourists visited the Greek island at this time of year and many of the restaurants and shops were closed for the season. Church's senses were not alerted when they turned off of the promenade and up a narrow, deserted, side street towards a warehouse building. He was still immune to any sense of danger as they stepped up to the doors of the steel fabricated building. However, as soon as they stepped inside Church knew that something was wrong.

The vast warehouse space was completely empty. Mathias paused and scanned the room with a confused look on his face. Church was grabbed by the arms from behind, he tried to wriggle free but ended up feeling like a bug trapped in the spider's web. The scuffle kicked up a cloud of dust from the dirty floor of the warehouse. The Arab stood at the far end of the building. He did not look as immaculate as he did back in the warehouse at the shipbreakers in *Pasabandar*. Blood had congealed down his leg staining the *serwal* trousers. Dark stubble covered the previously smooth cheeks and a lack of sleep had made his face appear gaunt and haunted. But his malevolence remained undimmed.

He was not alone. One of the Filipino deckhands appeared from behind the Arab. It was the man they had left on the yacht. His colleague had clearly delayed Church, Amber and Mathias with food and drink while his accomplice freed his master. One of the bodyguards was there as well. Beside the musclebound figure stood Maureen Timson, she looked both beautiful and angry.

Church was surprised and disappointed in equal measures. The deckhand walked over to Amber and grabbed her by the arm.

'Leave me alone you little shit,' she wailed.

'Bring her here,' said the Arab, spitting out each word slowly. 'I have some associates who would like to get acquainted with you before they toss you into the desert.'

'Let me go,' she sobbed.

The scuffle between Amber and the Filipino kicked up yet more fine powder from the dirty warehouse floor. She was pushed to the ground. Amber spat out some dirt as a foot rested on her head pushed her face into the floor.

'Kidnap was supposed to be so easy, Mr Church,' the Arab said slowly.

'You know that you won't get away with this,' said Church defiantly. 'Other's know that we are here. It's only a matter of time before my friends come to our rescue.'

Church tried to sound convincing but his hollow invention of unknown support did not even reassure himself. He looked at Amber's dust-covered face now streaked with tears. A pinpoint of green light briefly flickered across her head and was gone as soon as it appeared.

'It is important to know who your friends really are, Mr Church,' continued the Arab glaring at Mathias Agurk. 'And I think we know whose side you are on, Agurk.'

The Arab hobbled over and with some effort kicked Mathias in the leg, the Dutch captain went down on one knee. More fine powder clouded around the prone figure of Mathias Agurk. Once again, Church was sure that he saw a pinpoint of green light sweep over his body. As if the Arab could read Church's mind he limped over and stood inches away from his face.

'I am like a spider sitting in the middle of my web, Mr Church. I have been alerted to your every move. Every step that you have taken, blundering around in my organisation, has been alerted to my senses through the threads of my web. But the time has come for your little caper to come to an end. You will watch my treasonable captain die, you will watch Amber suffer and then you will feel the pain I have felt for the last three days.'

'Nothing could compare to the pain of listening to you for the last ten minutes,' Church replied. 'And you want to be careful around her,' he nodded in the direction of Maureen Timson, 'the female of the species is more deadly than the male.'

The bodyguard who had been holding Church's arms behind his back suddenly let go of him. He took two steps back, withdrew a pistol from his shoulder holster and levelled it at Church. He judged that the distance between them was too far to disarm the thug. The bodyguard glared at Church and it was only then that he saw the livid bruise that disfigured the henchman's face.

'I hope that hurts,' said Church.

Slowly, the thug circled around until he was close to the Arab. He handed the weapon over and the Arab pointed it at Mathias. The Arab swept around and pointed the barrel at Church and then continued the sweep to rest the gun pointing at Amber.

'A Parthian shot,' said Church coldly.

The Arab swept the weapon back, past Church and levelled it at Mathias Agurk.

'Not too late to change your mind, Agurk,' the Arab said.

'I know that my time has come,' Mathias Agurk said in a dull empty voice.

'So be it,' said the Arab in such an offhand way that even Church was taken aback. He raised the pistol and Amber screamed.

A shot rang out.

Church knew that it was not a shot from a pistol. The sound was all wrong. Church dropped to one knee as the sound of another shot ricochet through the warehouse. Then another, then another.

Church could see the trails of green laser lights flickering through the dusty atmosphere in the building. The first shot had taken out the Arab. He fell to the ground with a bullet through his leg. Church hoped that it was the same leg as he had been shot at before. And he hoped that it really hurt. As another bullet pierced the Arab's arm, the weapon dropped from his grip. The third and fourth shots had felled the bodyguards. They had whizzed through the air simultaneously from different directions.

Four more shots echoed through the metal warehouse and both of the Filipino crew were taken out. Amber screamed again, or perhaps she had not stopped from her earlier shriek. The sound continued until it eventually faded away. Contrary to popular fiction, there was no smell from the shots that filled the warehouse. Perhaps a slight acrid aroma from the bullet propellant, perhaps a slight warmth. Maybe it was Church's imagination.

The doors of the steel building were flung open and silhouetted figures appeared in the doorway. Light from outside streamed into the warehouse. Voices shouting instructions in Dutch and English filled the huge space. Church stayed very still, controlling the thumping of his heart and not really knowing just what happened. He was pushed forward onto his front and expertly patted down for weapons, then dragged into a kneeling position.

Figures dressed in dark clothing darted backwards and forwards, checking the bodies of the dead, retrieving weapons and stowing them safely, administering first aid to Mathias who appeared to have received a flesh wound. More figures appeared and offered assistance to Amber who appeared to be in a state of shock. In the distance, the tall figure of a man dressed in a dark navy suit stood against one of the far walls of the warehouse. He appeared to be in charge of the situation because the soldiers or policemen spoke to him to receive orders or give updates on the situation.

Maureen Timson was handcuffed to an officer by her left hand. She threw a bunch of keys towards the prone figure of the Arab. The chunky key fob, with a *Mercedes* logo imprinted on it, bounced off of his head and flew across the room landing at Church's feet.

'You had one job to do!' she exclaimed.

Eventually, Church was aware of another figure standing in front of him. The person appeared to be slightly shorter than the others but dressed in similar black military-style fatigues. Goggles were lifted from the face and a matt black Kevlar helmet lifted from their head.

A voice said, 'Nice to see you in one piece, Edward.'

'Elsa? Elsa DeWinter? Is that really you?' said Church barely able to hide his shock as he knelt in the dust.

'I could get used to you being down there,' she smiled. 'Promise not to run away. Again?'

'What exactly just happened,' said Amber finally regaining her voice.

'We have got you to thank, Miss Garland. We had been trailing you for some time but lost you in Prague. It was only by chance that three days later we received your message, Amber.'

'What message?' asked Church.

'The message sent to over three thousand mobile telephones giving your location in a shipbreakers yard in *Pasbandar*.'

'Oh, that message,' Amber grinned. ' It was the best I could think of under the circumstances.'

'Genius,' said Church.

'You're the genius, Edward,' said Amber. 'You tried to pass on the information but didn't know how to send it.'

'Actually,' interrupted Elsa DeWinter,' you are a genius, Edward. A Royal Navy patrol vessel picked up your rather elementary morse code somewhere in the Irish

Sea which is how we tracked you to Rotterdam and then on to Amsterdam. Sir Bernard Trueman tipped us off about your whereabouts in Prague. We had long suspected the Arab of running this International drugs syndicate but had nothing on him.'

'Until now,' added Church.

'We can link him to attempted murder here of course, but it was the drugs operation that we really need to arrest him on. And with the knowledge of their communications systems that Miss Garland has, we can build a strong case.'

The man in the navy suit whom Church judged to be in charge of this operation started to walk towards them. The progress of his passage towards them was interrupted by a figure dressed in black military fatigues but with the word *Politie* in large letters on the back of his jacket and underneath in smaller print the words *Koninklijke Marechaussee*. Even though their voices were hushed, the sound echoed through the empty steel building.

'We have been over the yacht twice, there is nothing there,' said the Politie agent. 'It must be somewhere else.'

'You thought that the servers would be underneath the cargo vessel *Kerstams-ijs*,' the man in the navy suit replied tetchily. 'You were sure that the servers would be at the boatyard. Then you thought that they would be on the yacht. It has been thoroughly searched. The buildings and boats at the shipbreakers yard have been searched as well.'

'I do not know what to say, sir,' the agent answered perplexedly.

'I don't mean to interrupt,' said Church still kneeling on the ground. 'The thing that you are looking for is twenty metres below the hull of the superyacht belonging to the Arab, secured by two steel cables and linked to the generator on the boat.'

'How do you know about that? It is classified.'

'And if you want any assistance cracking the security surrounding that server, I know a young man in London who would be only too happy to help. He gets excited over a mobile phone. I can't imagine how he would feel about a whole computer server.'

* * *

Three hours later the crime scene was finally cleared, taped off and a police cordon placed around the warehouse building. After lengthy questioning, Church was allowed to leave and he was surprised to see Amber and Mathias sitting on a low wall at the end of the alleyway leading to the building. The shape of the large *Mercedes* could be made out behind them.

Church ducked under the blue striped hazard tape and strode down the narrow side street. He approached the car and took a long look around the outside of the *Mercedes*.

'What now?' asked Amber as Church approached them once again.

'Time to take you back home,' said Church firmly.

'I have a boat you can use,' added Mathias brightly.

'Thanks, Mathias, but I think that I've had enough of boats for a while. It's going to be a plane back to the UK for me. Although I know a good boatyard nearby that could do a good job of refurbishing that yacht. I think that a certain Russian Oligarch would not take too kindly to seeing his old superyacht still on the sea when he expected it to be scrapped. They can be a bit funny about other people playing with their toys.'

'Sounds fair to me,' replied Mathias. 'No direct flights from this Greek Island to England at this time of year, Edward. You will have to travel via Instanbul.'

'Is that okay with you, Amber?' Church asked.

'It seems rather apt,' she replied with a smile.

'On the other hand,' replied Church, 'we could always drive.'

He swung the key fob for the 4x4 in front of him.

'You will have to put your bags on the back seat because the boot of that Mercedes is full of cardboard tubes.'

'What?' replied Amber bewilderedly. 'Can't you just throw them away?'

'Not a chance, they are very valuable cardboard tubes. Very valuable indeed.'

Epilogue

February is not the kindest month. Too long after Christmas and too far away from Easter. The weather is often dreary and the days still seem so short. It was raining in Manchester as Church walked along the pavement crowded with commuters heading back home after work. If it had been visible through the rainclouds, the sun would have set about an hour beforehand and it was now a dark early evening.

The newly refurbished building stood proudly on the corner of Deansgate and St Mary's Street. Once a large department store, now the new home of St Mungo's homeless centre. A neon sign glowed warmly above the doors, welcoming all of those who stepped inside. The building welcomed Church as he stepped inside out of the rain. He slipped off his macintosh and shook off most of the rainwater.

The drop-in shelter looked, and smelt, clean and fresh. Tables and chairs matched floors and walls. The food counter looked like something you would see in a budget restaurant chain. There, behind the counter, serving a line of appreciative customers stood Amber Garland. She looked fit, well and healthy. Through a doorway behind her, Church could see Tony Brownstone. The MP for one of the Manchester boroughs had his shirt sleeves rolled up and was unloading a dishwasher. Church joined the queue.

'Edward! Oh my God, Edward. It's you!' Amber squealed.

'Hello, Amber. Nice that you came back to Manchester to finish your studies. You look very well,' replied Church. 'And your cooking has certainly improved.'

'Cheeky,' she replied. 'I'm probably pretty well qualified to help people out on their diet and healthy eating having been through so much myself.'

'I can't argue with that, Amber,' said Church.

'Edward Church!' exclaimed Tony Brownstone as he emerged from the kitchen.

'Hello, Tony. Still in the shadows, I see. But perhaps not for long.'

'Cheeky,' the MP replied with a smile.

'But there was someone else who I expected to see but doesn't seem to be around,' continued Church.

'That would be me, Mr Church,' said a voice from behind.

'Hello, Freddo. Nice to see you again. But I'm sorry, it wasn't you that I was looking for.'

'I know, I know,' said the homeless Freddo. 'I was only joking.'

'That might be me,' said another voice.

'Hello, Malcolm. Good to see you too,' said Church to the giant figure dressed in a brightly coloured tracksuit. 'What sort of a sentence did you get for that late-night drive into a bollard?'

'They let me out on remand then a suspended sentence. Reckon I got away lightly this time,' said Malcolm sheepishly.

'Actually, I've got a present for you,' said Church.

'For me?' Malcolm replied, sounding confused.

'It took me ages to sort out the paperwork, you cannot imagine how many forms I had to fill out and how many questions the DVLA asked me about the transfer of ownership. But if you want it this car is yours. Although, it was someone else I was looking for.'

Church handed him the chunky keyfob to a *Mercedes-Benz* 4x4. The same keyfob that had bounced off of the head of the Arab from the bunch of keys thrown by Maureen Timson.

'In that case, I think that it might be me,' said yet another voice.

Anthony Fairfax stood to one side of the group that had now formed around Church. He looked even older than Church remembered and had lost quite a lot of weight. In one hand he held a mop and in the other a bucket. He appeared to be the most unlikely cleaner you could possibly imagine.

'After expressing my deepest remorse to the PM, the party and most of all to my constituents, I tendered my resignation,' said Fairfax quietly. 'The public deserves more than I was able to offer. St Mungo's was kind enough to offer me some kind of occupation. And after the initial hostility from some of the patrons, I would like to think that they have rather taken to me.'

Anthony Fairfax looked around the large dining room and a few arms were raised in greeting from the homeless customers at some of the tables.

'Well, Anthony, there was another MP who had a similarly spectacular fall from grace in 1963 and things didn't work out too bad for him in the end,' said Church.

'I was down in London the other day, Edward. Had lunch with Sir Bernard Trueman. The old man said that he had a job lined up for you when you are ready. Something about gold smuggling. Sounds right up your alley.'

Acknowledgements

As always very many thanks to you, the reader, for going on this journey through the book with me. Thanks to my proofreaders and to my family for their humour and encouragement. Thank you to Gwen and the team at PublishNation. A final thank you to all of the people who supplied tips and information that has been used in this novel. Any errors or mistakes in detail are entirely my own.

Printed in Great Britain
by Amazon